Vintage Alice

Jessica Adams

ARENA
ALLEN&UNWIN

First published in 2009

Arena, an imprint of
Allen & Unwin
83 Alexander Street
Crows Nest NSW 2065
Australia
Phone: (61 2) 8425 0100
Fax: (61 2) 9906 2218
Email: info@allenandunwin.com
Web: www.allenandunwin.com

Cataloguing-in-Publication details are available
from the National Library of Australia
www.librariesaustralia.nla.gov.au

ISBN 978 1 74175 829 0

Set in 11.75/15 pt Granjon by Bookhouse, Sydney
Printed in Australia by McPherson's Printing Group

10 9 8 7 6 5 4 3 2 1

To Peter Clarke
and his award-winning dog Ollie

one

I am moving to Australia because I want to see some wildlife that isn't a pigeon. This is not the kind of thing I can admit to Australian immigration officials, but it's the way I feel this afternoon. The next time I see a bird in the wild, I'd like it to be something that doesn't strut around like James Brown singing 'Sex Machine'. London's male pigeons are like 1970s medallion men. If they could wear cheap aftershave and leave their shirts undone, they would. I can see one of them in front of me now, stalking a female. Soon she'll be lured back to his loft and, after copulating with him, will be left to bring up the chicks on her own.

There's a dirty teaspoon on the next table and the temptation to throw it at James Brown is strong. Now he's trying to eat a cigarette butt. He also has the pigeon equivalent of man boobs. If my chest looked like that, I wouldn't puff it out.

When Nash and I finally land in Australia there will be emus, not pigeons. There's an emu decorating the national coat of arms on Form 80. I bet emus don't try to eat cigarette butts.

I am sitting in this café studying Form 80 like a woman possessed because today Nash and I have our final meeting with Nice Heidi from Australia's Department of Immigration and Citizenship. Should Heidi throw me any trick questions about recent war crimes, terrorist activity or freedom fighting, I am ready for her. The answers will be no, no and no. Unless you count the woman I shoved out of the way outside the tube just now to get a free shampoo sample.

Nash and I are using shampoo from the £1 shop at the moment. Of course, it may not be shampoo at all. It could be mayonnaise. The label is printed entirely in Arabic. When I had a proper job, I also had proper hair. It was short and blonde, and streaked and conditioned, and blow-dried and moussed. These days, I have one-quid hair. Like a credit crunch Agyness Deyn.

I read through all the letters from Nice Heidi. She has been in charge of our application for months, steering us gently towards a sympathetic doctor when Nash and I had to get our medical checks and coaching us through Form 80, the character assessment form. She even got us over the awkward bits about our relationship. Not the awkward bits *within* the relationship, of course, because that would have made her a counsellor – or possibly a modern miracle-worker. Rather, Nice Heidi's role was to find out if Nash and I really constitute a bona fide couple in the eyes of the Australian government.

She needed to test all this because Nash is the sponsored employee going to Sydney and I am merely the secondary applicant. In other words, I'm just like a WAG, but without the handbag. If all goes well, Nash will be the next head of music at St Joseph's Boys School, North Sydney, and I will be – according to Form 80 – his interdependent partner.

Nice Heidi has been very kind throughout – waving away my embarrassing employment history, and even overlooking the fact that Nash and I don't share a bank account, a mortgage or bills to prove we've been together for longer than six months. Nash and I have never even discussed a joint bank account. I think both he and the bank manager would be too frightened. Even when I was a child, my piggy bank had a crack down the centre. And after two years together, we still don't split the bills. Instead, Nash pays for everything, and I clean all the rooms on the top floor of the Swiss Cottage International Travellers Hostel, where we're currently living rent-free.

The rooms have to be cleaned between check-out time, 10 am, and check-in time, 2 pm. I wear a Walkman that I bought from a charity shop and play old compilation tapes that one of my ex-boyfriends made for me back in the '90s. I used to have a portable CD player but one of the backpackers pinched it. Once we're in Australia, I'll never be able to listen to old Manic Street Preachers songs without thinking of the smell of rubber gloves. I sniff my hands now, to check, and sure enough they smell like the inside of an old hot water bottle.

There is a kind of mad hope in my heart at the moment, and it all hinges on Australia. It's the sort of deranged optimism that defeats everything – being broke, being stuck in this café in the pouring rain, even being surrounded by over-sexed pigeons. I have never been to Sydney (though Nash has) and I have never been married (although Nash has) but in my dreams I see us on Bondi Beach a year or two from now, standing on the sand in our wedding clothes, while he puts a ring on my finger. By then, Vintage Alice will be a shop, not just an imaginary fashion design label. All the ideas I have about recycling old clothes to make new ones will finally become a reality. All the plans I have to single-handedly wipe out size zero skinny jeans and the tyranny of the smock top will have succeeded.

If I keep picturing these dreams perhaps they will become real. Isn't that the theory?

There are practical reasons why Australia might turn things around too. When we move to Sydney, Nash and I will instantly lose all the problems we have here – namely, not having any money and being forced to live in two rooms on the top floor of the Swiss Cottage International Travellers Hostel. All the good bits I love about Nash – the sexy, soulful, sensitive musician bits – are bound to come back once he stops working so hard and worrying so much. And he can get a motorbike again, and ride it on those long Australian highways that go on forever.

I just want to design clothes for Vintage Alice, and make women feel wonderful, and grow my hair and go barefoot. The last time I went barefoot in London, I skidded on a tomato sauce sachet and fell on an old nappy. That just about sums this place up.

Form 80 is terrifying. Nice Heidi says she is very happy with my employment history, but what if some all-powerful Australian official scans the form at the last minute and realises that my last proper job was Woman With Key In Back, which involved me standing on a crate outside Covent Garden station painted silver while small children threw crisps at me? Worse still, what if the Australians find out that I'm not a fashion designer after all (as I printed in such beautiful letters on the form), but a wannabe fashion designer who only made three dresses last year and spends her whole life doing McJobs? The sad thing about Form 80 is there aren't enough boxes to take all the casual and part-time work I've done.

Nash says that's the price you pay for spending your entire university life being terrified by exams, watching daytime television and eating instant noodles. Not to mention your entire fashion college life hiding in the library reading all the *Vogues*.

When Nash was at university, of course, he was in the Chamber Orchestra and the University Funk Group. Yes! The University Funk Group! He was also in the Italian debating society, which was where he learned to speak proper Italian, which is how he seduced me – not in Italy, though; in The Slug and Lettuce in Clapham, when we were both somewhat drunk. We wandered back to his place via Clapham Common, where he kissed me for the first time, before nobly helping me onto the back of his motorbike, then driving me home. I still like kissing him. And I still occasionally have daydreams about all the things we've done on the back of that bike. It just doesn't seem to happen very often these days. Perhaps it's the fact that we have to have sex on a proper bed now. Or maybe it's that it's a bed in the Swiss Cottage International Travellers Hostel with the kind of mattress that you flip over to hide the stains, then realise the stains are worse on the other side.

Nash is fifteen minutes late now, and we're due at Australia House at four. I can't text him because my phone's out of credit, and he probably can't call me because he's stuck on the train.

I think about my conversation with Nash this morning, when we tried to come up with a practical way of breaking the news about Australia to everybody. If you include relatives, friends and all the teachers at Nash's school, we have about a hundred people to tell – not easy.

Nash suggested we send everyone a bulk email, but I told him if we did that, nobody would ever speak to us again.

'Spam is for Viagra, Nash.'

Anyway, half our relatives aren't even online. Or, as one of my uncles so quaintly puts it, 'in the internet'.

My best idea about breaking the news is a Christmas party, though preferably at someone else's house rather than the Swiss Cottage International Travellers Hostel. If we tried to have a going-away party in our two rooms, people would bang into the trouser press and stun themselves on the fold-up ironing board. I expect we'll just end up going to the pub, as usual.

My God. It's quarter to four already. Where is Nash?

When he finally arrives at the café, he has damp, flat curls, a drip running down his neck and a soaked leather jacket. Despite this, of course, women turn their heads to look at him. Nash could be covered in sewage and he'd still be unfairly good-looking.

He picks up part of an old newspaper off an adjacent table and sits down next to me. 'Bloody England,' he says, shaking his head. 'It's all floods and David Beckham's feet.'

I pull the paper away. 'You only read it so you can moan. Anyway, you're so late we're going to have to run.'

He yawns. 'Can you please just stop lecturing me?'

'Can you please just stop moaning?'

Nash looks through his G'day Australia pack, deliberately making me wait. Nice Heidi gave us these packs on our last visit. There's a giant wall map inside, which Nash finds irresistible.

'Woy Woy.' He picks out a town with a teaspoon, playing for time to annoy me. 'Woy Woy and Wagga Wagga. Does everything have two names in Australia? Imagine if they did that here. People would be forced to live in Stoke-on-Trent Stoke-on-Trent. Think about it, Alice. If you'd grown up in Woy Woy instead of England, your favourite band as a child might have been Duran Duran Duran Duran.'

'Hmm.'

According to this library book I've been reading, if I could share jokes with Nash – in other words, actually laugh at them – it would be a good sign. It would mean that after being on separate journeys, we would have ended up on a small bridge together. We need lots of small bridges if we're ever going to get married. Not just the big obvious ones, like the Sydney Harbour Bridge.

I do want to get married. Despite the fact that right now I could strangle Nash with my black opaque tights.

We set off for Australia House, me dragging him along in the rain. Nash suddenly pulls me under his umbrella. 'Put yours away,' he says, grabbing my silly tartan umbrella that never keeps the rain off. Then he pulls me inside his coat and I put my hand in his pocket. It's like this between us all the time at the moment. The day begins with an argument and ends with a kiss. Or starts with a kiss and ends with an argument.

He kisses me now, and he tastes of chewing gum and instant coffee from the machine at his school. But I love the smell of him. No matter how annoyed I get with him, it's that warm, familiar Nash-scent that always pulls me back.

There's a crowd of people pushing against us along the Strand, so Nash and I hop into the gutter and half-walk, half-run along the double yellow lines. It seems to take forever. Australia House is always further away than you think it is. Like Australia, I suppose.

'Why are you so short?' he complains as he pulls me along.

'Why are you so tall?'

'Why are you so blonde?'

'Why are you so curly?'

We've been saying this kind of thing to each other for so long that we hardly notice we're doing it.

When we arrive at Australia House, we wipe our feet on the front doormat (on the national coat of arms as it turns out) so that the people watching the CCTV cameras can see how clean and responsible we are, then we take the lift to Nice Heidi's office.

The receptionist tells us that Heidi won't be a moment in an accent that means it comes out this way: 'Hardy warnt be a marment.'

I read some weird Australian women's magazine with the accusatory headline RUSSELL CROWE – YO-YO DIETER? while Nash looks at his map and quietly laughs at more silly place names.

Still no sign of Nice Heidi. I put down the magazine and inspect Robyn's keys and letter instead. Robyn is my cousin. The last time we saw each other we were six years old. She stuffed a Mars Bar up my recorder and I put a dead hamster in her Barbie bunk bed. Apart from that, we get on brilliantly.

My impression of Australia so far is based on Nice Heidi and Cousin Robyn, both of whom are helping me feel braver about moving. If all Sydney-siders are like Heidi and Robyn, then I think I can cope.

Robyn's letter reads:

> *Dear Alice and Nash, please use the spare bedroom as long as you need to. Call me if you need anything before you get here. See you when I get back from Bali – can't wait! Love Robyn xxxx*

'She's a four-kiss person,' Nash says, reading over my shoulder. 'I didn't see that before. She has four actual kisses on her letter.'

He goes back to reading out place names from the map of Australia. 'How about this one, Alice? Delicate Nobby. Imagine living in Delicate Nobby!'

'You're just making that up.'

I think about my library book. It's called *Should I Stay Or Should I Go?*. Nash refuses to have anything to do with it because of its calculated misuse of a perfectly good Clash song. The book is full of little tests to help you decide if you should stay with your partner or run away screaming. I borrowed it hoping to pass all the tests that suggest you should stay. I'm cheating slightly, but so far it seems the answer to the question Should I Stay Or Should I Go? is yes, alright then, stay.

'Goodness me, Alice, what a relief!' Nash said when I told him. 'Otherwise I would have cancelled our flights to Australia.'

I read the book again this morning, after he'd gone to work. One of the questions asked if my memories of the best-ever times with Nash still make me feel good. I think about this now as he reels off Australian place names. Nash and I were so in love two years ago. The phone calls went for hours. I used to wear his leather jacket when he wasn't there, just to feel closer to him. I even used to draw his nose, over and over again. It's a noble nose. Quite Roman and dignified. Once I found out his real name was Sebastian I doodled it all over the place – even today, I still find old notebooks or bills with Sebastian written on them. And drawings of his noble nose, of course.

Because he'd been married before, Nash seemed sexier, somehow, when I first met him. Older, wiser and altogether more experienced. You know that old film *The Horse Whisperer*? He was like a woman whisperer.

My love life before Nash was Jon (workaholic, mountaineer), three Pauls (they all run into each other now) and after that, years of nothing. I was forever single in London, possibly the cruellest city in the world for a woman on her own – or a pigeon. When Suzanne dragged me along to the pub after work saying that an interesting man would be there it was hard to feel inspired. Nevertheless, Nash was more than interesting. And to say it was good with him at the beginning is an understatement. It was bloody incredible.

Now it just feels like hard work pretty much all the time. I wonder how long you have to slog away before you know it's time to give up?

Hopefully we won't have to find out. That's what Australia's for. I dream that Australia will be like a born-again baptism for us. New country, new life, new beginning. We can wash the last year in London off our backs – not to mention all the tomato sauce off our shoes – and start all over again.

Once we get to Bondi Beach we'll rediscover each other, recycle the relationship and make sure we never have another conversation about the Swiss Cottage International Travellers Hostel. I wonder if we'll swim with our arms around each other when we get there? That's one of the daydreams that keeps me going at the moment: Nash and I swimming with our arms around each other at Bondi Beach (not sure how we'll stay afloat, but anyway) and frolicking like young dolphins.

Dr Ray Stein, the author of *Should I Stay Or Should I Go?*, also wants to know what we once did together that made us feel close. That one's easy. I worshipped Nash. He wanted to be idolised and I did it. I actually sat at his feet while he strummed his guitar, like some 1960s babe in a beret. The fact that Nash could say sentences like 'I love your earlobes' in Italian was part of it. So was his funniness. I wonder if he's still as funny now as he was then, and decide he probably is. The problem is more likely to be me. At the moment I'm not finding this map-reading thing very funny at all.

Heidi comes out of her office and calls us in. Nash gives me a look and puts his G'day Australia pack away.

I try to work out how Nash is feeling and realise I don't know. He's as cool as ever, despite the fact that this is a life-changing moment. Very little shows on Nash's face. He's laidback, chilled, born in an ice bucket, cooler than the fish fingers at Asda. Perhaps that's why it's my challenge in life to make him happy, or at least make him passionate about me again – just so I get the satisfaction of watching him crack.

We follow Heidi into her office and see all the documents on her desk.

My God. This is it. We're actually going.

Nash gives the smallest sigh of relief. He *must* be feeling it now.

My own heart is thudding, and the whole thing feels slightly unreal, as if I'm watching myself watching myself.

'Hi, Alice.' Heidi shakes my hand. 'Hi, Nash. Is it still raining outside?'

Heidi always asks us about the weather, basically because she never knows what's going on outside in the real world. Australia House is like a hermetically sealed tomb.

'Can't wait to get to Bondi Beach,' Nash says with a smile, and she smiles back, going a bit fluttery.

'Not long now,' she reassures him, and Nash and I exchange looks. 'Everything's ready to go for you, guys. I just need a couple more signatures and then we're done.'

She always calls us 'guys'. Nash says it makes him feel as if he's in a Western.

When Heidi thinks we're not watching, she checks her watch and I realise she's probably dying to go home. She lives in Wimbledon. At this time of day that's like travelling to Serbia. She excuses herself to go and find an extra bit of paper that I appear to be missing.

'We should celebrate after this!' I squeal at Nash. 'Let's go and get some champagne!'

'Okay,' he says calmly, and hands me some coins. 'That's our budget. I believe that's enough to buy one can of lemonade. Let's go crazy.'

What is it about Nash today? I can normally cope with his ice-man approach to life. But this is practically polar bear.

'This is the most important day in our relationship since we moved in together,' I tell him, 'and you want to go home to the horrible hostel and eat baked beans.'

'We're eating baked beans because you don't have a job,' he says.

'Shut up. I do have a job. I'm trying to create my own label.'

'Maybe. Wait until you get to Australia and earn some money. Then we'll have champagne.'

'When are you ever going to understand the fashion industry? It doesn't happen overnight.'

'I know, I know. We've been through this.' He affects a bored look.

Heidi strides in with the missing bit of paper and we both clam up, like naughty children.

'Alright, guys?' she enquires.

Despite my worries about Form 80 it seems we are in the clear.

'Well, I hope you'll be very happy in Australia,' Nice Heidi says, remembering her script as she hands us our visas and documents. Then she weakens and adds, 'Say hello to Bondi for me.'

'My God,' Nash says as we go down in the lift, 'I think Heidi actually had a tear in her eye when she told us to say hello to Bondi.'

'She must miss it. I would.'

Nash laughs at me. 'You've never even been there.'

'Yes, but I sort of know. I know that I'd miss it if I was from there and I was stuck here.'

We walk back along the Strand in the rain and share Nash's umbrella again, and I ask him one more time if we can have champagne to celebrate. If nothing else, it will numb the slight shock I feel. After all this time, I can't believe we're finally ready to go.

'Alice! We're broke!' he protests.

'Just a glass of wine then. We can share it in front of a fire somewhere.'

No reply.

'I'm not going home with you!' I hear myself shouting. 'I'm going to Trafalgar Square!' Then I storm off across the street, without looking back.

I doubt Nash will come after me, but just in case I use the backstreets so he can't find me. Then I stand under my umbrella in the rain, taking a last look at the lights, the lions and the fountains. Of course, it may be one of several last looks at London – we still have two months left. But what if we're too busy with other things? This could be the last time I see Trafalgar Square for two years. Maybe even longer, if we stay in Australia.

If it all goes well.

I stand in the rain and try not to cry. When I was a kid, Dad used to bring me to Trafalgar Square all the time. I suppose millions of people must stand here and remember their childhoods.

I'm feeling guilty that I haven't told my mother. I should have rung her as soon as I knew we had this final interview with Nice Heidi, but I couldn't face it. Nash hasn't told his parents either. We agreed that we would wait until the visas were in our hands, just to make absolutely sure it was happening, but we both know we're being cowards. Neither of us really knows how to tell our parents that we're leaving them. How can I tell my mother I am moving to the other side of the world when she no longer has anyone left except me? How can I tell my mother, that great lover of all things English, that I have simply had enough?

The rain is falling in front of the floodlights around the square, making the kind of dash-dash-dash pattern you see in cartoons. Robyn says the rain in Sydney is quite different. It's usually torrential and often warm.

Oh, England. It's all very well to talk about a lovely new life in a lovely new place, with a lovely fresh start – but the reality is, we're dumping this country and everyone in it. I've tried my hardest to live here and be happy all my life, but it just hasn't worked. *Dear England, I'm sorry – but it's not me, it's you.* It feels exactly like dumping a boyfriend. The churning fear and horrible guilt are about the same.

In one of the quizzes in *Should I Stay Or Should I Go?*, you're supposed to find out if the problem with the relationship is in your environment or in you. Amazingly,

I managed to get Nash to fill that bit in. I've still got the piece of paper in my handbag.

I look at it now, in the floodlights.

Alice fed up with England due to cost of living – cannot pay for leg waxing. Embarrassed about constantly being filmed with hairy legs on thousands of CCTV cameras across London.

London so expensive had to sell motorbike. Now have to catch bus and train to work – Dante's bloody inferno. Nine concentric circles of hell etc.

Backpackers at hostel complain about guitar coming through walls. Forced to live in cheap, non-soundproof hostel because of extortionate London rents. Cannot afford to move because promotion chances tied to London school.

What Nash and I need is sunshine, sea, music, flowers and enough money to buy a glass of white wine at the end of the day. It's not much to ask – is it?

Mum has always wanted us to move to Sussex, to be near her, but I don't think the answer lies there. Nash and I need to go somewhere so big it will make our problems seem small, and so far away that our differences will fade into the distance. We need a really, *really* big leap.

I look around Trafalgar Square at the hoodies. Honestly, it's like standing among a bunch of novice monks. I take one last look at the lions and the fountain, in case it really is my last look, and cross the road to St-Martin-in-the-Fields.

A service is in progress so I go inside to absorb all the Englishness, to get a better idea of what I am about to lose. The church smells of mould and candles, just as it always has. It's also full of non-believers, like me, who are only here to get out of the rain. We all sit at the back, partly because we feel too embarrassed to sit at the front and partly because it's the best place for a quick exit if it all becomes too . . . religious.

The Bishop of London begins his sermon. He lets us know that they're getting a real donkey for their Christmas service. I give him ten minutes before I escape. I went to an Anglican school but none of it really stuck. Besides, I've been looking for England here, rather than God, but the Japanese tourists with their Burberry brollies make it impossible to find.

Maybe I should give up on this forced farewell to London and catch the tube. Nash must be halfway home by now. Suddenly, a man on a penny farthing bicycle honks his horn at me and wobbles from one side of the road to the other, with various drivers honking him back. He's wearing a tweed suit, bicycle clips and a deerstalker hat. He is also about 250 years old.

A group of girls on a hens night yells at him. They are drunk, screaming and dressed like red devils. The bride is also wearing a Viking helmet and a giant pair of fluffy monster feet. Maybe this is God's joke. I went looking for England in a church, and it has decided to find me instead. People get it wrong when they say the English are eccentric. We're just escape artists.

It's only now I'm leaving it all behind forever that I really notice the madness. That group of people standing under a tree, dressed as hedgehogs and doing the Hokey Cokey – would I have paid attention to them before? It appears to be a sponsored Hokey Cokey in aid of a hedgehog sanctuary called Mrs Tiggy Winkle's Orphanage. They are roaring drunk, soaked to the skin and all their quills have gone floppy, but they don't seem to notice.

I'm fairly sure this sort of thing never happens in Sydney.

A woman in a pillbox hat, fur coat and high heels teeters up the street towards Soho like some 1950s film star. Will there be any mad, exotic creatures like her on the other side of the world?

I fold up my silly tartan umbrella and let the rain fall on my face so people won't see me cry. It's pathetic, but the tears are hard to stop now I've worked myself up. Dear England. Where else in the world will I see giant pissed hedgehogs doing the Hokey Cokey? Goodbye, London. Goodbye to people flapping their smelly pizza slices in my face on Shaftesbury Avenue. Goodbye to all the simply marvellous plays in simply marvellous theatres that Nash and I can't afford to see. Goodbye to Gap and Coca-Cola. Goodbye, Eros. I have never arranged a romantic assignation beneath his bow and arrow and now I never will.

I feel for my purse in my pocket, but it's gone. Bloody pickpockets. I could kick myself for being so stupid. I kneel down on the pavement to rifle through my bag and find my make-up, keys, antique tampon collection and overdue library notices, but no purse. Well, I hope they enjoy it. They picked the wrong woman if they were looking for platinum credit cards.

There are no police anywhere. There never are. The only thing I can do is ring Nash, except my phone's still out of credit and there's no money in my pocket to recharge it. Then I realise the battery's died anyway. Great.

I don't even have enough money for a phone box. Not even a lousy 20p.

Walking home to Swiss Cottage isn't impossible. Nash and I have done it before so I know I won't die; it's just that it was summer then, and now the winter wind is physically painful – the kind that gives you weepy eyes and sore ears. My tartan wellies and umbrella are useless against it.

A couple in evening clothes step out of a taxi, on their way to some event. She is wearing a tiara and silver shoes and he's wearing a black cape and bow tie. They look like characters from a fairy story, but I know that if I did a fairy-story thing and asked them for money, they would just ignore me, or possibly even use me as puddle-coverage.

Then I see her. Nice Heidi. I look away, but something makes me look back and I see that she's waving so I go over. Sometimes it's best to ask questions first and think about it later.

'Heidi!' I launch myself at her. 'My purse has been stolen. Could I borrow some money for a phone call? I'm sorry. I just need to call Nash.'

'You dropped your purse outside the lift,' she says, and pulls it out of her handbag. I am torn between huge relief and embarrassment because it's such a pathetic purse – a silly little tartan plastic thing that matches my wellies and umbrella. What if she's looked inside it and seen that all I own are two pounds and an Oyster card? And what if she saw the Glastonbury condom that Nash bought last year?

It looks like some ancient relic from an archaeological dig, lying there covered in fluff at the bottom of my purse.

'I called you but your phone wasn't answering,' she says. 'Then I called Nash and he said you'd gone to Trafalgar Square. You look like a drowned rat. Do you want a drink?'

'Oh no. That's alright.'

'Come on. You're moving to Oz! Let me buy you a drink. I've got some time to kill before the theatre. I'm way too early, I got the time wrong,' she says.

'Actually – yes, please.'

Heidi has kind eyes, and I'm sure she's telling me the whitest of all white lies, but why argue? I am freezing cold and running out of tissues to blow my nose. I can think of nothing better than sitting in a warm, dry pub with a glass of wine and a packet of peanuts.

We find a place just off Covent Garden with a table near the window, and sit down. Water trickles down my legs and into my wellies. I bought them, the purse and the matching brolly at Glastonbury. It was supposed to be a romantic weekend for Nash and me, but we argued so much that we ended up sleeping on opposite sides of our two-man tent, so far apart that our bodies bulged out at the sides.

'Let me tell you a secret,' Heidi says, once she's bought us a bottle – not two glasses – of wine. It's from Margaret River, she explained, which is the best wine region in Australia.

'What secret?' I ask.

'You were fast-tracked. We had a note from someone in head office in Canberra. You must have good connections.'

'I thought it was because of Nash's job.'

'Nah,' she says, gulping her wine down, 'you might not have got in so easily without help.'

'Because of my application? Being a woman with a key in my back?'

'Sort of.'

'I knew it.'

Heidi finishes her wine, pours herself another, and tops up my glass.

'Your cousin Robyn is probably the reason you got through,' she says. 'She manages one of the hotels all the public servants stay at so I bet she's got great connections. But who cares? You're in.'

I decide to own up about the fight with Nash.

'I thought there was something going on,' Heidi says.

'I wanted champagne to celebrate and he didn't. Thank God you picked up my purse,' I say, and thank her again. 'I've just been to church actually. St-Martin-in-the-Fields. Maybe it's an act of God.'

Heidi nods sympathetically, even though I must sound like some dribbling madwoman.

We keep drinking the wine, in a new-best-friends kind of way, and talk about the pelicans in Australia – which, unlike the cruel London pelicans, do not attempt to swallow pigeons whole. Heidi misses feeding the pelicans in Byron Bay where her aunt lives, and she also misses the sound of cicadas, whatever they are, and the smell of the gum trees, and the fact that you can ring the local doctor and see him the same day. Not like farking London, she says, where you can wait two farking weeks for someone from the NHS. Heidi talks and talks. I have never heard such homesickness pouring out of someone. Most of all, she hates English post offices. In fact, when she talks about them, she grabs her hair and pulls at it as if she's going mad.

'The queues go out the *door*!' she squeals. 'There's a class system for the *stamps*!'

I change the subject back to Byron Bay. 'What's it like for jobs there?' I ask.

'Not bad. What sort of jobs?'

'Not public service jobs. I'm useless at that kind of thing. Well, you saw my application form.'

'Oh well,' Heidi says in her kind way.

'I can do basic jobs though. Cleaning. Waitressing. Cooking. I've run market stalls. I can walk dogs – that kind of thing. I really want to be a fashion designer, of course, but . . .'

Heidi nods. 'I remember. What sort of clothes do you want to design?'

'I want to recycle old fabric, like the stuff you find in charity shops. But I also want to use vintage clothes so that's why the label will be called Vintage Alice. And I'm going to use real women to make the clothes – not kids in India – and they're going to be paid real money.'

'Wow,' Heidi says. 'Will the clothes be for real women too?'

'Oh yes. The sizes are going to go up in ones not twos.'

'So could I be a size 13?' she asks. 'Because I'm never a size 12 in half the shops, but I'm never a 14 either.'

'Absolutely. You'll be a Vintage Alice size 13.'

'I want you to make me something now!' Heidi shrieks.

'Well, I could, except –'

'You're going to need a job to get the business started,' she finishes for me. 'Hey, do you like dogs?'

'Most of them.'

'My Auntie Danielle has a boarding kennel in Byron. She's always looking for staff. You get your accommodation thrown in – you just have to walk the dogs and feed them.'

'Great.'

'Here.' She writes a name and phone number on a piece of paper. 'Her name's Danielle Coles. We're both called Coles. The boarding kennel is called Bark's of Byron Bay.' She pulls a face. 'I know. She thought of it, not me.'

'Thanks. Really. This is great.'

'It's a long way from Sydney though.'

I picture a two-hour commute morning and night and tell her I can cope.

'It's a full day on the train,' she says. 'Like going to Europe.'

'Ah.'

'If Nash is working in North Sydney you might have to live apart for a while, till you earn some cash. There's no way you can commute every day. Then again, you might need a break from him if you're having domestics all the time.'

Heidi's voice goes up at the end, just like the people on *Neighbours*.

'Thanks, Heidi.'

She glances at my silly tartan purse. 'Here. Buy yourself some champagne and take it home to your boyfriend,' she says, putting a pile of notes in my hand.

'I can't.'

'Yeah, you can.'

She smiles and leaves quickly through the side door. I'm still sure she was making it up about going to the theatre. And look – she's just walked out of the pub in her lovely pencil skirt and lacy tights without a single man looking up. The men in London can be so thick sometimes.

I don't use Nice Heidi's money to buy champagne. Instead, I save it for the next great cash emergency in my life and spend the last of my coins on the ladies' loo at Victoria Station where I know there are big, strong, reliable hand-driers – unlike the broken ones in the pub. I don't care if I miss a train and it takes me twice as long to get home – I just have to stop feeling so soggy. I get maximum value for money by shoving my entire head and body under the hand-drier for twenty minutes, flipping my hand backwards and forwards to keep the machine on, then using every last paper towel to dry off my legs. Then I dry my wellies, my umbrella and my handbag.

In the unlikely event that I ever get any money at all ever again, I will send Heidi Coles the biggest magnum of champagne known to womankind. I wonder if they're all like her in Australia. I hope so. I feel as if an angel has just flapped her wings at me.

I find a phone booth and call Nash, who doesn't pick up, so my call goes straight through to my tired old answering-machine message from last year. It was about that time that we began talking about moving to Sydney.

I look at my useless tartan boots as I sit on the tube on the way home. I should never buy my footwear at music festivals. I had a good T-shirt stand there though – it was the only reason Nash and I got tickets. Women loved my T-shirts because they had lovely flattering necklines and long sleeves you could push up and I'd decorated them with cut-out laminated pictures of all the bands. They were like fan-club T-shirts from the '80s. I sold the lot, and bought the wellies, the purse and the brolly with the profits. Then I gave the rest to the bank before they could send debt collectors to the hostel to repossess everything I owned.

Now the bank debt has become a Nash debt and a Mum debt. I added it all up last weekend to see how long it would take me to waitress my way to solvency once I got to Sydney. I should be in the clear in eighteen months if I only eat protein in the form of eggs and stop crazy luxuries like coin-operated public loos.

I feel Heidi's money in my pocket and think about my cousin Robyn and our fast-tracked application. The photo I have of Robyn in my bag shows her wearing a diving mask, a snorkel and flippers and waving a dead eel. I have more sensible photographs, but I like this version of her and it's the one I most expect to see when we finally meet. In the meantime, it seems Nash and I both owe her a huge favour. I just hope she didn't have to sleep with some horrible old ambassador type to get us to the front of the list.

two

My mother's name is Penelope Templeton. My dad called her Penny. Nash calls her Lady Penelope, because she has a blonde bob, like the *Thunderbirds* puppet, and because she drives a Jaguar. He thinks she's posh. There's no point in telling Nash that the real Lady Penelope had a Rolls-Royce, or that my mother only has a Jaguar because Dad used to own a car business. Nash made up his mind about my mum the first time he met her, and that's it.

I am on the train to Hove to spend the weekend with her when Nash rings.

'Can you ask Lady Penelope if she has any old suitcases we could take to Australia?'

'Yes, I'll ask my *mother* if she has any old suitcases we can take to Australia.'

'Once you've done the shock-horror Australia news bit, of course. I've just been testing out this suitcase and the lock's broken.'

'Whatever. I'll also apologise for the fact that you're spending the whole weekend at home working on your school Christmas concert, although this is obviously twaddle because the kids already know the carols. You're just going to drink beer and read Bob Dylan books.'

'Bollocks, Alice. I'm going now.'

'Yeah, bollocks to you as well. And Australia is not shock-horror news. It's our future, Nash. Try to be a bit more optimistic about it.'

My mobile phone seems to have a sensor that reacts to the amount of heat generated in my conversations with Nash. The more irritated we both become, the hotter my phone becomes, until it feels as if it's going to scorch the side of my head. Right now, I feel as if someone's been ironing my ear.

I turn the phone off and look at my G'day Australia pack again. I'm going to leave it with Mum in the vague hope that she may start to understand what we're doing and why we're doing it. At the very least, she may get a better sense of where we're actually going. Geography has never been her strong point.

The last two weeks have been impossible. I've picked up the phone to tell her so many times, then put it down again. Nash hasn't done anything about his parents either, and we still haven't been brave enough to tell any of our friends. We are breaking up with England, and breaking up is hard to do. Every time I try to find the words to tell people, I just can't. And every time we decide to organise a farewell party it never happens. There was a vague plan to have a spontaneous gathering for Bonfire Night on Primrose Hill, but in the end we just stayed home and watched TV.

The only time I've discussed Australia with my mother was months ago, when we posted our application to

Australia House. She kept mixing up New South Wales with Wales, because Wales was our idea last year, before we settled on Sydney.

My relationship with Nash has always been full of vague plans and mad ideas. The Wales scheme was one (although we were going to travel round the country by motorbike first). A possible move to Canada was another. My mother has been told about all of these ideas over the last two years, then forced to forget them just as quickly. I suppose she thought the Australia plan was another non-starter. This time, though, I'm going to have to show her the letter from Immigration and Robyn's keys, and pour her the largest brandy of her life.

I have drawn big gold circles using my favourite Christmas card pen all over the giant map of Australia to help my mother get her bearings. There's a giant circle for New South Wales, a smaller one for Sydney and a gold blob for Bondi Beach. I've also added a gold arrow in the ocean pointing to the location of the real Wales, just in case. To avoid the chance of any further confusion, I've illustrated the arrow pointing to Wales with big wooden spoons and pictures of women in black stovepipe hats.

Just looking at the map of Australia makes me feel overwhelmed. It's so big you could fit England, Scotland, Ireland *and* Wales into it about fifty times. How am I ever going to find my way around that?

Nash has given me a bag of barley sugar for the train journey and I catch myself mindlessly crunching one sweet after another, feeling more and more nervous about seeing my mother.

When I arrive, she's waiting for me on the platform wearing what Nash calls her Princess Anne headscarf. Mum has always worn it, and I never notice it, except when I'm worrying about what Nash thinks of her. Occasionally, I tell myself that I'm going to make jokes about his parents' chunky matching cardigans. They live in Cambridge and own an art gallery, and their cardigans always have such big toggles I have to fight off a secret urge to yank them.

The car (which my mother always refers to as *The Car*) smells of her cigarettes and there are library books all over the back seat as usual. She reads the same Georgette Heyers over and over again, to the point where she can detect her own fag ash in the binding.

'How's Nash?' she asks.

'He says hello. He's doing the Christmas concert all weekend.'

'They work him so hard, don't they.'

'How are you?'

'Actually, I've just finished that wall-hanging for you. For Christmas.'

Oh God. The embroidered wall-hanging with pictures of Labradors savaging ducks. How am I going to fit that into my luggage?

'And I thought I'd give you my old watch as well. I decided I'd get another one in the sales.'

We both look at my watch-free wrist, and I immediately feel guilty about the other watch she bought me, five birthdays ago. I sold it last year so I could buy Nash a Christmas present.

'Are you excited about Australia?' My mother lights a cigarette and winds down the window.

'What!?'

'Nash rang just now and said you were going in a few weeks. Or have I gone off half-cocked and got it wrong?'

'No. Oh my God. Nash *told you*?'

'Just then, when I was waiting for you at the station.'

My mother takes a huge drag on her cigarette and throws it out of the window. Then she lights another one. Oh God. She's driving too fast. I think she may be having some kind of attack. She's going to kill us.

'He was ringing because he's lost his reading specs and he thought you might have moved them somewhere. He tried calling you on the train but you kept going through tunnels. Anyway, do you have them?'

'No, I bloody don't! I can't believe that Nash told you about Australia before I did!'

'It's really fine, darling, please don't worry about it. He was confused, that's all. He thought you were already off the train and you'd already told me. I just mentioned that he might like a nice big jar of Sussex honey for Christmas and he said it might be too hard to get through Australian customs. So then the cat was out of the bag. Where are you off to again? Something Wales, isn't it?'

'New South Wales. We're going to Sydney after Christmas. To Robyn's flat at Bondi Beach at first, and then we'll look for a place of our own. God, Mum, I'm so sorry. I meant to tell you myself. It's all happened incredibly quickly. That's why I came up to see you.'

I feel the angelic Heidi's money in my pocket; the sole reason I can afford to be here today. I cannot possibly borrow any more money from Nash.

'Absolutely no problem at all,' my mother says, lighting another cigarette as we screech around another killer corner.

I am trying to break up with Mum – and England – as sensitively and carefully as I know how, and now look. Her hands seem to be shaking as she grips the wheel of the Jaguar and her cigarette ash is dropping all over the gearstick. Thank you, Nash, you complete wanker.

'Sorry, Alice, I'm really going to have to pull over.'

We lurch into a disabled parking space near the supermarket, and then Mum remembers this is immoral, so we lurch out again and finally end up parked under a tree near the station, where we started. My mother is the only woman I know who can cry and smoke at the same time. She did it at Dad's funeral, and she's doing it now. I hold her hand, and realise she's wearing the same red leather gloves she has owned all my life. It's all I need to make me cry as well, and soon we're both sobbing like idiots.

'So you're definitely off then?' she asks, after she's taken off the gloves and blown her nose.

'Yes.'

'You two never got on with London, did you? I can understand Nash not liking it because he's from Cambridge and they've never liked the competition, have they. But you were born there! You know, you could always have moved down here. It's so different near the sea. And I'm sure Nash could have found a good school near Brighton.'

'I thought we'd sort of talked about this. Staying in England isn't really going to work.'

'So you've had enough of this country. Well, many people have.'

'That's not the only reason we're going. It's complicated.'

Mum dabs at her nose. 'I'll have to come out and visit you over there,' she says, trying not to cry again. 'If you can bear an old fuddy-duddy like me following you halfway across the world.'

'Mum. Stop it. We'll come back and visit you here as well. We're not . . . dead.'

Oh God. Bad choice of word. I bet she's going to get even more upset now, because of Dad, and sure enough, she does.

'I know you'll visit. That's fine. Honestly, I'll stop blubbing in a minute. But, Alice, are you absolutely sure about this? It's just that I've always thought Australia is one of those places where you might become a cropper.'

'I've talked it through with Nash a million times. And Robyn's been so amazing too.'

'Oh, Robyn's been helping you! Well, that's nice to know. Her father was always a very kind sort of person. Mad as a hatter, of course, but never mind. Did Robyn tell you anything about him? I haven't heard from that lot for years. In fact, the other day I realised I don't even know where to send the Christmas cards.'

'All I know is that Roland's in San Francisco. And they're all fine, I think. Robyn's managing this hotel at Bondi Beach I told you about. Roland's retired and living by himself, Joel's in India working for a charity, and Aunt Helena's in Jamaica with her new boyfriend –'

'Hippy Helena,' my mother interrupts me. 'That family really did spread itself far and wide, didn't it? They were so adventurous. Roland was always much more bohemian than your father was. I remember, on the day they all left England, *the whole family* was wearing these enormous clogs.'

I laugh and blow my nose. 'I remember. I'm glad Robyn stayed in Australia though. If she hadn't, I'm not sure it would have been this easy for us to move.'

'Oh, well,' my mother sighs. 'As long as you're sure about it all.'

'Yes,' I hear myself saying, although I know that later on tonight, when I'm lying in my old bedroom with its pink curtains and the view of the English Channel, I may well get the Aussie wobbles. That's what Nash's been calling it all week – The Big Aussie Wobble.

After we've both gone through all the hankies she possesses, my mother drives us home, through thick traffic jams and heavy fog.

'Apparently there's no traffic in Australia at all,' Mum says. 'What a relief for you. It's hell here. Especially now everybody does their Christmas shopping in November. And, of course, they all descend on Brighton and try to park their cars in Hove. All those cars looming out of the fog. Brrr! It's like a horror film, darling. It gives me the heebie-jeebies.'

She is already cheering up. I've forgotten how quickly she can bounce back – my father used to call her the trooper. I'm worried about the number of cigarettes she's smoking though. When she coughs, it extends for five minutes. My mother's the sort of person you don't ever want to let into a live television audience.

Mum starts on her newspaper crossword as soon as we get home, and after a few more polite questions about Robyn's flat at Bondi Beach and Nash's new school in North Sydney there's no more talk about Australia for the rest of the night. Instead, Mum and I watch a program about stoats.

'When alarmed,' the commentator tells us, 'stoats release a powerful musky smell from their anal glands.'

'How awful for them,' my mother murmurs.

Oh no. I can't believe I'm feeling emotional about stoats, but as the final credits roll, with their moody shots of stoats and their anal glands frolicking across the green English hills, the tears are pouring down my face. Everything seems so richly British these days, and instantly sets me off. The chunky Kit-Kats I saw on sale at the station this morning immediately made me feel homesick. So did the spotty teenage Goths who got on the train at Haywards Heath. Every time I notice something else about England, I start missing it. And I haven't even got to the airport yet.

Suddenly, Nash texts me: SORRY ABOUT TELLING LADY P.

I switch my phone off. I am so angry with him that I'm not sure what to do about it.

The program about stoats is replaced by a real-life crime show, which Mum immediately switches off.

'Absolute cobblers,' she says.

'I might get an early night actually,' I tell her.

'Yes, of course. See you in the morning.'

Everyone we know hopes my mother will get a new partner, but we can't count on it. She looks so lonely sitting in front of the fire with her solo possessions around her. One brandy glass. One Georgette Heyer book. One packet of Silk Cut. One embroidery kit. One packet of cards with horses on the front. Maybe I could find her an Australian man and send him over. There must be someone for her over there, in Delicate Nobby perhaps.

I go up to my room and pull my copy of *Should I Stay Or Should I Go?* from my bag. Okay. One more time. Are my memories of the really, really good bits with Nash still enough to make me feel wonderful? Yes. There is no substitute for the memory of a long bike ride into the country on an autumn day, followed by an afternoon of passion on a tartan blanket. Wearing my own homemade silk slip, of course.

The next question in the book is rather shocking: Has Nash ever hit me? What? Yes, apparently I need to think about the amount of violence there has been in the relationship.

The answer, of course, is no. Unless you count me threatening to hurl my sewing machine at him when we were having an argument about Bob Dylan.

I move on to another question, propping up my head with one hand, while outside the window the wind howls across the Channel. *Are you already spending time or money on a subtle escape route from your relationship?*

What? I really shouldn't have had that second brandy while I was watching the program about stoats. Reading this book is like taking an exam. And yet, I want to pass. I want to know things will be alright.

Except I'm not going to pass. Because I certainly have planned an escape route. Three days ago, I secretly applied for a part-time job at Bark's of Byron Bay Boarding Kennels with Heidi's aunt, Danielle Coles. It includes board – a self-contained flat – and Nash could visit on weekends, but that's all. If I'm going to work there, we'll have to live apart.

And . . . Nash hates dogs. He really, really hates them, because he was bitten in the face by a Rottweiler when he was a child and still has a scar beneath his ear, which he's permanently embarrassed about. Hence the slightly-too-long-but-sexy curly hair. If he wasn't such a brilliant music teacher, his school would have made him cut it years ago. Perhaps if I get the job at Bark's, I'll never see Nash at all.

I am crying again. Oh God. They never tell you about this at Australia House. You might be among the lucky few to make it into the Lucky Country, but every day during your last weeks in England you weep a river of tears.

Danielle Coles is bound to prefer one of the oodles of Australian trainee vets who'll apply over me. Nevertheless, the letter has gone – and, without even admitting it to myself, I have already put hundreds of miles between me and Nash.

When I was at the University of Huddersfield, failing my arts degree, I walked a fox terrier called Goggles who had patches over both eyes and was owned by an old lady who used to leave a few pound coins in an envelope for me in Goggles' dog basket. His speciality was going into a trance. One minute he'd be trotting along on the common perfectly normally, and the next he'd plonk down on the grass with a strange, glazed expression on his face. One day, I poked Goggles with my finger and he fell over sideways, dead. I had to carry him back to the old lady in a plastic bag – and that was the end of my dog-walking career at Huddersfield University, although I will never tell Danielle Coles any of this.

My only other canine-handling experience consists of feeding and walking our old Labrador, Charlie, who used to wander into this bedroom and shred my school shoes. He was also known as Yeller, Feller and Smeller and sometimes Yeller Smeller Feller. I should have got him to put his pawprint on a reference for me while I had the chance.

I can hear Mum snoring next door now, and I think about Dad again. While he was in hospital, he told me he'd look after me, because life was too short to be worried about money. He did his best, but the money he left Mum and me in his will only just covered his medical bills and taxes. This house is all Mum has now, because even after we sold the business, there were still debts. She had to use up a lot of her own savings to pay them all off.

I sometimes think about my school fees, and wish I could have talked my parents out of it so they could have saved their money for my mother's old age. But, no. I cost them a fortune and now she's paying the price. She even dyes her own hair these days, after a lifetime of going to the same hairdresser in Hove. I saw the bottles in the bathroom. Mum shouldn't have to do that.

Dad once told me that marriage wasn't about sums, and that I should never try to do any. That was probably true for him and Mum, but when I think about Nash these days,

I just remember all the money I owe him. Nash and Mum took over where the bank left off. He lent me £10,000 to get the bank off my back (and stop the nasty letters from their debt collection agencies) and she lent me another £10,000 to live on while I was at college. The relationship between Nash and me was never supposed to be run along such venal lines, but on reflection, who on earth were we kidding? Every couple we know in London, married or unmarried, thinks about money all the time.

The bank took me back eventually, of course. And that's where my other debt comes from – the scary £2000 overdraft that won't go away, the last trace of my student loan. Oh, and then there's my credit card.

Thank God Robyn helped to fast-track our application. I'm sure the Australians have no idea what a dribbling pauper they're letting in.

The rain pours down while I make plans. If I get a part-time job at Bark's of Byron Bay, I could get a second job as a waitress, so I'd have two lots of money coming in. Maybe I'd even get tips from both jobs, and I could post some back to Mum every month and put a chunk aside for Nash in a jam jar. Two smaller jam jars would take care of the bank and the credit card.

My father would put his head in his hands if he could see me now. For my entire life, my finances have revolved around jam jars. So much for all those talks about comparative interest rates.

Our local corner shop is run by an Indian family whose son has installed a second-hand PC in the corner. It's connected to the world's slowest modem so they don't charge much. Just lately, I've been sitting on it for two hours a day, looking for jobs in Australia and using a currency exchange website to turn pounds into dollars and dollars into pounds, just to see if I'll be a richer waitress over there. I won't be. But I'll be able to live on fruit.

According to Australian Google, denim's $6 a metre. So I could make some really groovy denim culottes and sell them, all for the price of a single journey tube fare. Oh God. I've got to stop designing denim culottes in my head. It's 4 am now. How did that happen?

There's a knock at my door. Mum can't sleep either.

'Alice, do you want a hot drink?'

'Cocoa.'

It's out of my mouth before I've even thought about it. I suppose being in my old bedroom has sent me straight back to childhood. I don't think I've had cocoa for years.

'I was woken up by my own revolting snoring,' Mum says as she goes off to the kitchen. 'Your father always said I sounded like something with flared nostrils that you might see staggering around at the Grand National.'

When she comes back, she says she wants to talk to me about Dad's will, and sits on the wobbly wooden chair next to my bed with a shoebox full of his old notebooks on her lap. My father wrote everything in block letters and it jolts me to see his handwriting again.

'I have a funny feeling you're lying here worrying about money,' she says.

'Sort of.'

'Nash did vaguely say you were both worried about money when he rang.'

Bloody Nash. 'I wish he hadn't.'

'Alice, is everything alright between you? You had a face like a boot in the car today.'

'It's alright. We're going to Australia. We're going to have a fresh start.'

'Anyway,' my mother pats the shoebox, 'what I meant to say was, there *is* money. Your father had it tucked away in a different account, and before he died he told me it was just for us. A sort of emergency fund. He forbade me to touch it for any other reason. Not even to pay bills. And I woke up just now and thought, stone the crows! This really is a sort of emergency.'

'No it's not, Mum. I don't need it. You hang onto it.'

'Well, I was rather hoping we could sort something out. It's quite a lot of money, Alice. Almost £50,000.'

'Really? Is it?' (I must not look excited, I must not look excited.)

'Tell me why you're really moving to Australia.'

'Because I want to design clothes. Because the exchange rate means we'll have money again and I can pay everyone back. Because Nash can get a motorbike. Because we can move into a proper flat. Maybe even a little house with a garden. The weather's better over there, Mum. No more tube. No more rubbish. No more zillions of people. No more CCTV cameras everywhere . . .' I pause for breath. 'No more pigeons.'

'But pigeons are very brave – they won the war for us. They were attacked by German hawks, you know, and Nazi marksmen, and they still flew straight and true with their messages tied to their legs.'

'Mum! It's four o'clock in the morning. Why are we talking about pigeons' legs?' I yell.

'Why are you really moving to Australia?'

'Oh God. If you must know – to stay together. If Nash and I don't do something drastic, I'm worried we'll break up.'

'I see. Look, Alice, I may be using a sledgehammer to crack a nut here. But what would you say if I asked you not to go?'

'But we've been accepted. And they're waiting for Nash to start his job.'

'This is your father's vital emergency money.' My mother pats the shoebox. 'And I think he'd see this as a vital emergency. You're leaving England. Quite possibly for the wrong reasons. Sometimes, Alice, it's better to travel hopefully than to arrive.'

'What does that mean?'

'It might be a different kettle of fish once you actually land in Sydney.'

'Maybe.'

'If you and Nash would like somewhere nicer to live, that's fine. I quite understand. He should never have let you take that job at the hostel in the first place. And if you'd like to set yourself up in the fashion business, that's fine too. It will be a feather in your cap. But you don't have to leave good old England to do it.'

'I think Dad meant that money should be put aside for you, if you were ever ill.'

'Not necessarily, darling. Anyway, if I am ill, what use will it be if you're in Australia? Before you can say Jack Robinson, I could be in the deep-freeze in Hove with my poor feet sticking out of a sheet.'

Perhaps my mother is like Lady Penelope sometimes. Although it's my strings that are being pulled here, not hers.

'I can't think about this now, Mum. It's too late.'

'Okay, darling. Just remember – there's money here if it's required. You don't have to take such drastic measures to help fix things with Nash. And I'm really, truly sure that your father would see this as an emergency. Heavens to Murgatroyd, Alice, you *know* it is.'

Eventually, she goes back to bed – and the awkward question about my own debt to her is left hanging in the air.

Counting the wallpaper roses in this room has been a reliable cure for insomnia since I was small. Perhaps it's worth trying now. I have forgotten how pink my childhood bedroom actually is – the lamp still turns everything rosy. I stick my leg up in the air, examine my toes and decide I want a pedicure. My life is all charity shops, canned soup, baked beans and cheap shampoo. I am fed up with feeling guilty about the money I owe Mum. I am sick of worrying about the money I owe Nash. Dad's money would fix everything and it's the most tempting offer in the world. But I can't do it. I can't stay in this country. My dreams about the future in Australia are too far gone.

I listen to my mother coughing next door. If she keeps smoking a packet of fags every two days, she will probably have a stroke. Then they will ring me in the middle of the night in Australia and tell me she's dying and calling my name. There'll be a desperate rush for the airport in Sydney, followed by a lecture from her – on her deathbed – at the other end in England.

It's now 5.30 am, according to my old plastic clock. Great. Once I'm in Australia and she's on the other side of the world, will I ever actually sleep again?

three

Some time ago, Suzanne (my oldest friend, and my unofficial relationship counsellor) suggested that Nash and I find a new hobby to share. She thought it might help us forget about our other problems. Or, more specifically, my problems with Nash. The way he expects me do most of the housework, even though I spend half my life cleaning. The way other women always get the compliments, not me. The fact that he seems to spend most of his time living in Nash World – which means Alice World doesn't really matter.

We spent a whole night coming up with unlikely options: joining a fox hunt saboteur group; learning to cook Italian food; exploring the little-known world of Tai Chi. In the end, though, Nash beat us to it. Because his mate Richard fancied Suzanne, he roped us all into the same pub quiz team at The Bell and Dragon.

Richard is the drummer in Nash's band, The Believers. Thus, it would have been extremely convenient for everyone if Suzanne had fancied him too. However, she made it as far as Richard's bedroom one night, then saw he had a metal clothes rack and pulled back. Suzanne is extremely wary of men in their thirties who still have tubular metal clothes racks.

Our quiz team is called The Believers, just like Nash and Richard's band. Their singer, Lisa, is also in the team, along with Michael, a teacher at Nash's school. As well as singing in The Believers, Lisa is also head of music at Romney College in Windsor, where she seems to spend her days playing the harp on the lawns for the girls and floating around in the school swimming pool wearing a straw sunhat. Suzanne and I know this because sometimes she brings photographs of herself to show us. Suzanne thinks Lisa might be trying to get a job as a model on her magazine.

Lisa is also a friend of Nash's ex-wife, Sarah. When they both turned up to The Bell and Dragon last year looking all floaty and sensitive together, it was one of the most terrifying nights of my life. They were all doing some sponsored charity swim for their various schools, so I couldn't protest when they went out together afterwards. But when Nash failed to come home at the designated time, I was very glad I had Suzanne to look after me.

Sarah floated off again (she teaches in Cornwall) so only Lisa remains to remind me that Nash has a past. Lisa laughs in a tinkling feminine way – not like my awful honking and Suzanne's raucous snorting. She also has hair she can sit on. It's the kind of hair that makes you think about Lady Godiva, and I can see why that would get Michael going. Even though he's married to another teacher from Nash's school, I'm sure he's secretly in love with Lisa. He's practically salivating all over the table tonight because her nipples are pointing at him through her shirt.

There are some Australian questions on the quiz sheet, which provides Nash and me with the perfect excuse to tell everyone about Sydney. Our departure date is looming.

Nash has finally told his parents, after telling Mum. That means it's only a matter of time before the news starts trickling back from Hove and Cambridge, all the way to London. Nash says his parents told him they were happy we were going. 'They said they nearly emigrated back in the '80s. It's just that the art scene wasn't really happening in Australia then.'

I love the way his parents think they're in any kind of art scene. They run a gallery and gift shop in a little street in Cambridge selling woven wall-hangings and teapots with lids in the shape of root vegetables. I think I'm allowed to have mixed feelings about his parents. In my darkest financial hour, I asked them to put some of my T-shirts in the shop and they wouldn't.

I haven't told Nash that Mum tried to talk me out of leaving. And I haven't told him about the £50,000 emergency money either. The less I think about that, the better.

'So are we actually going to see your mum and dad before we go?' I ask Nash as we sit with The Believers, ticking off questions on the sheet.

'There's a big lunch on New Year's Day at the gallery, if you're interested. They said to ask Lady P as well.'

'My mother is not called Lady Penelope. And you know she can't come to Cambridge. The trains are useless and she doesn't like driving in this weather.'

Nash shrugs. 'Okay.'

It says a great deal for our relationship that the other Believers – Suzanne, Lisa, Richard and Michael – have reached the point where they no longer notice our gentle bickering. I suppose it's become like a pub soundtrack to them, like the pinging of the fruit machines.

The Bell and Dragon is packed tonight because the jackpot prize has gone up again. While our team wrestles with the Australian questions, I wrestle with our vague Australia-announcement plan, made up on the spot this evening while Nash and I were eating baked beans on toast for dinner yet again. The idea is that we'll tell everyone on our quiz team tonight, which should take care of most of the people we know as Lisa, Suzanne, Michael and Richard can be counted on to spread the news far and wide.

The plan is I will organise a big drinks night in a few days' time in the pub's back bar. Anyone who doesn't hear about it on the grapevine will be telephoned, once I find the jam jar with all the 20p pieces that I hid last summer and recharge my mobile phone.

My God. It's like a military operation just getting to Heathrow. And Nash and I haven't even started packing yet.

I tune back in to the quiz discussion. Question Four: Which Aussie won the 2005 Nobel Prize for Medicine? Easy, according to Richard – a bloke called Barry who discovered a bacteria called Helicobacter pylori.

While we're on the subject of Antipodeans called Barry, did we mention we're emigrating to Australia?

'Yass,' Lisa's saying to Richard. 'Yass, you're absolutely right about that bacteria.'

Lisa is dating a barrister, but nobody has ever actually seen him. He's always working, apparently. I'm not jealous of wafty Lisa. She's just an irritant – a reminder of Nash's clever, sensitive, ethereal ex-wife as much as anything – and soon she'll be a dot on the landscape, just like all the tiny houses that you leave behind the moment you take off from Heathrow.

In a way, Lisa's a fair swap for Sarah. It's so much better having to put up with her than the woman he once married. Sarah and Nash exchange Christmas cards and birthday cards, but that's it. I must have read them a hundred times, looking for scary signs of intimacy, but she always just signs them *Best Wishes, Sarah*. Nash seldom talks about her.

I look out of the window and watch the smokers struggling to light their cigarettes in the wind. Part of me is longing for that holidayish, Bondi Beach feeling of escape now. You can run away from your life all you like by trying not to think about it, but there's no substitute for a great big 747 and a lot of tiny dots below.

We tackle a question about the most common pub name in Great Britain. Is it a) The Green Man, b) The Dog and Duck, c) The Queen's Head, or d) The Dog's Bollocks?

Nash says that he'll miss English pubs most when we leave. I don't think I will. The basic elements will be the same in Australia, won't they? Sticky tables, smelly carpet, a ladies loo with a silhouette of a woman from the 1950s with a powder puff . . . The last time I checked on the internet, the pubs over there looked the same as pubs anywhere else. It's the other things I'll miss. Morris dancers. Dead old kings called Svein Forkbeard and Harald Harefoot. And sundials . . .

The sundial on the Hove seafront reads *Non Redibis – Thou shall not come again.* My mother and I tried very hard not to look at each other when we noticed it as we walked along the beach on my last night. I'm sure she still thinks I'll change my mind at the last minute. Just imagining her disappointment when we don't makes me feel teary.

It's Lisa's round, so she goes to the bar with Nash in attendance. He's always her wine waiter on these quiz nights.

'How was Twad today?' I ask Suzanne. She hates her job and her nickname for the magazine she works on is Meaningless Twaddle, usually abbreviated to Twad.

'Nightmare. We're doing how to be pregnant and stylish. Well, the model's definitely pregnant but none of the clothes fitted. We're trying again tomorrow.'

She sticks her leg out from under the table. 'Remember these trousers you made me?' She's wearing a pair of purple velvet flares I made for her years ago. They still look great, though it took me ages to get the waistband right. 'Everyone at Twad wanted to know where I got them,' she says, and nudges me. 'We've got this stylist from New York here at the moment – Vera Van Der Meer. She *loved* them.' I change the subject back to the quiz. I know Suzanne is throwing me the most enormous opportunity, but the truth is, I'm so broke I couldn't afford a phone call to Vera Van Der Meer, let alone run her up a pair of trousers.

'I have a cunning plan to fix that,' Suzanne says, reading my thoughts. 'I'll tell you later, once we've finished this round.'

Our team presses on with a question about Britain's most loathed dish. Do we think it is a) Tripe, b) Deep-fried Mars Bar, c) Jellied eels or d) Fruit and vegetables. The last one gets a huge laugh.

Where the hell are Lisa and Nash? They seem to have spontaneously combusted by the bar. They finally reappear – I suppose Lisa went outside for a cigarette – and she immediately answers an extremely long question about the Scottish National Party, which is exactly the kind of boring thing she knows about. Then I notice something. Lisa has been crying. And over-smoking too, because I can smell her from the other side of the table. I expect she and Nash have said their last goodbyes.

I look carefully at Richard and Michael. There's nothing in their faces to suggest they know anything about us leaving for Australia yet. Their main concern seems to be choosing between b) Deep-fried Mars Bar, and c) Jellied eels. So Nash hasn't told them yet, just his great mate Lisa.

Lisa says nothing for the rest of the round, even though there are questions about Plaid Cymru and Sinn Féin – the kinds of things she can be counted on to know about. Meanwhile Richard and Michael argue about the most loathed dish question.

It's my turn to get the drinks. That means I'll have to borrow some money from Suzanne, because I only have coins left in my purse now and someone (Lisa?) might go mad and order something that isn't house wine. I put my hand in Suzanne's pocket under the table, which I hope is a heavy enough hint. It isn't though, because Suzanne is transfixed by Lisa – who is openly sobbing now.

'It's not that far,' Nash says, leaning over and comforting her. 'It's not the moon, Lisa. We'll be back. You should come over and visit us sometime.'

'What's not that far?' Suzanne asks loudly.

Lisa is snuffling into a tissue. It seems Nash has just broken the kind of news that has destroyed at least one big dream, and possibly more. She apologises and runs out of the pub.

Suzanne tries again. 'What's going on?'

'We're moving to Australia,' I hear myself saying, because Nash doesn't seem able to speak. 'Nash's got a job teaching music at a school in Sydney and I'm going with him. Sorry, we've been waiting for the right moment to tell you. We're leaving in January.'

'I'll just see if Lisa's feeling okay,' Nash says, and follows her outside.

'Drink!' Suzanne commands, and steers me to the bar.

'Sorry, sorry, sorry,' I tell her. 'I meant to tell you before but it's all been so mad. We didn't expect our visas to arrive this quickly.'

Suzanne produces a £20 note, which she flaps at the barman. Not surprisingly, he races straight over.

'Two treble lemon vodka, lime and tonics,' she instructs him, then turns to me. 'I know I told you to get out of London to save your relationship, but I didn't mean scarpering to the bloody Antipodes.'

'Mum doesn't want me to go.'

'I'm not surprised. *I* don't want you to go.'

'I'm sorry.'

'Don't be so silly!' Suzanne gives me a shove. She has huge silver rings on her fingers, like gangsters' knuckledusters. 'Look, I don't want you to go anywhere. But Australia's going to be the making of you, Alice. It's the best thing you've ever done. Nash is going to be a *changed man*.'

Whatever I was expecting from Suzanne it wasn't this. I suddenly feel a wave of gratitude. I had forgotten how brilliantly encouraging she can be. It's like standing in sunshine.

She hugs me, long and hard, and tries not to cry. Then she takes both our drinks and leads me back to the table singing 'Waltzing Matilda' in a tuneless voice and getting it wrong.

'*Once a jolly jam bloke, camped by a bongy thing, under the shade of a kangaroo beast . . .*'

When we sit down, Richard pokes me with one of his drumsticks. 'So why are you going?'

Bugger. I knew it would be like this. We're about to get the third degree from everyone we know.

'Had enough of us, have you?' Michael adds.

I look down at the carpet and see that Lisa has left a plastic bag of shopping behind. It contains things like mineral water and proper moisturiser. I can't remember the last time I bought anything so civilised. Everything we eat comes from the markets. Everything I wear is recycled from a little charity shop in Finsbury Park that helps donkeys. Nobody goes there so it always has black tights, even if you have to sniff them before you buy them. They often smell as if the donkeys have been walking around in them.

Why are we going to Australia? It's so hard to list all the reasons that I can't answer. Instead, I pretend I'm really interested in the next quiz question. *No whales or sturgeons washed up on British shores may be disposed of without the consent of the monarch: true or false?*

Richard and Michael say it's false, but I think it's true. It's like swans – the Queen owns all of them as well. Meanwhile, the rest of us are wearing tights that smell of donkeys and panicking about our tax.

'I'm going to Australia because I'm fed up,' I tell Richard at last, feeling the vodka hit my brain. 'I'm not sure about Nash. You'll have to ask him. Obviously, when he's finished cheering up Lisa.'

'Steady, Alice.' Suzanne puts a hand on my shoulder, but the drink has hit some angry part of my brain that was switched off before. I leave The Believers to it, go to the loo, slam the door, throw the lid down and sit on it until I have calmed down again.

Then I hear the familiar sound of Suzanne's platform shoes clumping across the tiles.

'We need a frock for our pregnant model tomorrow,' she says through the door. 'Vera Van Der Meer just rang me. There's a flap on. The model's measurements were all wrong. She's about ten times as big as she was two weeks ago. Do you think you can do one?'

'I'm not sure.'

'Vera loved your purple trousers. Anyway, I told her that you run a very cool indie label and make bespoke clothes for real women.'

'Shit.'

'Stop thinking about Nash and Lisa! Think about this instead!' Suzanne thumps the door. 'I want you to bring your sewing machine and scissors over in a taxi tomorrow at 9 am and make a frock. I'll get the fabric. Don't argue, because I know tomorrow's your day off.'

Two pieces of paper suddenly appear under the door. A taxi charge voucher and the scrawled address of some place in Soho.

I take a few deep breaths and calm down. No wonder the Russians are so militant – it must be the vodka. I felt so angry just now about Nash and Lisa, I could have bitten a chunk out of my own glass.

'There.' Suzanne slaps me on the shoulder as I emerge. 'Come and help us out tomorrow. It's a photographer's studio. Big loft place. The model will be there from nine, and I'm picking her up so I'll be there too. If we can both fit in the cab. Apparently she's *enormous*.'

'Can you get me some stretch jersey?'

'Oh, I've got something better than that. From the stall.'

As well as working on Twad, Suzanne runs a vintage clothing and fabric stall on Saturdays at Camden Market. A lot of the material I've used for my designs has come from there.

'I've got some very nice dark green stretchy wool,' she goes on. 'Very light, but also *very* warm. This factory closed down in Milan and I got the lot. However, I've *also* got this beautiful old tweed coat from Biba I think you could do something with. I want this model to look fantastic, Alice.'

There. Suzanne has had the instant sunshine effect on me again. What is it about her that she can suddenly make everything seem alright?

We return to our table. Perhaps Nash will be back by now.

He isn't. But Lisa is.

'He's just gone to the cashpoint machine,' she sniffs, and fiddles with her hair.

Richard and Michael plough on, trying to answer a question about James Bond. They are clearly miffed about the Australia news, but I'm not going to say any more. That's Nash's job. Eventually, he comes back and sits next to Lisa. Richard and Michael go into a huddle over the James Bond question with Suzanne, while I look sideways at Nash and Lisa and find myself thinking the worst.

It's hard not to. I try to see Nash as Lisa might have seen him all this time – cool, sexy, distant, a bit funny, undeniably fit (from the school football coaching), curly-haired, multilingual, pale, interesting, a musical genius (obviously). And, above all, a woman whisperer. Lisa went to Nash and Sarah's wedding. There are photographs of her looking wistful, waiting to catch the bridal bouquet. She probably secretly fancied Nash the whole time. Lisa is the kind of utterly wet female you can imagine nursing a hidden crush on someone for about 500 years.

Suzanne once told me that you either sort relationship problems out right away, or you pretend you're Winston Churchill and plot the right time and place for a strategic attack. In the early days of my relationship with Nash, I used to try to fix things immediately. These days, I tend to wait so I can blow up bridges later. The Lisa thing can be put off until I'm good and ready. I'm sure they've been up to something behind my back. In the meantime, I'll sit on the explosives.

Nash speaks at last. 'I've just been telling Lisa the news. Alice and I are moving to Australia.'

'We heard,' says Michael, looking as if he's just ingested a deep-fried Mars Bar and jellied eel at the same time.

'Bloody fantastic news!' Suzanne pumps Nash's hand and then mine. 'I'm going to miss you like hell but it's the best thing you've ever done. You'll love it. Trust me. You'll never, ever regret it.'

'Have you actually *been* to Australia?' Richard asks pointedly.

Suzanne pouts. 'No.'

The quiz goes on. I hear none of the questions, because all I can think about is Bark's of Byron Bay. Danielle Coles wrote to say there may be a vacancy for me if I'm prepared to start on a trial basis. I was so excited when I read her email at the Indian corner shop, I even paid for a printout so I could hold it in my hand. Bark's of Byron Bay isn't much – but it's something. And I desperately need *some* kind of something, even if it's my secret.

When it was very bad with Nash – around the time I gave up fashion college – I became very good at living in the future. It was the best way I knew to get past our problems. The way he always made me feel, very slightly, invisible. The constant put-downs about my lack of job/money/general life skills. Some of the problems were very small, and some of them were very big, but I always longed for an escape. The more I encouraged Nash to daydream about where we might live, who we might become, what we might have in life, the more it seemed to help our relationship. That was when the idea of living in Wales or Canada started to appeal to us. Australia seemed too remote then – but as things got worse, we both found we needed a really big dream.

My cousin Robyn was the key. She was like a mythical creature to me, living in a far-off, upside-down place. We were penpals for a while, when we were both at school. I still have her letters. She used sunflower writing paper and I used a purple notepad with a teddy in the corner. Our handwriting was identical, because we both used to write big, round letters on the edge of a ruler.

Robyn's brother, Joel, is a few years older than Robyn and me. My most recent photograph shows him at the age of seventeen or eighteen, riding a horse in his bare feet. I wonder what he looks like now. Joel went to India years ago to work for a Tibetan charity, and since then he's sent Mum and me the occasional postcard, but that's all. He doesn't do email, according to his sister, and the two polite letters I sent were returned by the post office.

I suppose the other Templetons, as my mother calls them, had big dreams too, like Nash and me. They left England in the 1980s to go travelling, but then a few years later Roland and Helena divorced. She stayed in Sydney with my cousins and Roland ran away to America. Eventually, only Robyn remained in Australia. She told me she loved it too much to ever leave. None of these other Templetons have ever felt as if they belong to me, but as Australia comes closer – and even Jamaica, India and San Francisco too – I am beginning to feel as if I have acquired a new family, even if they are scattered all over the place.

The quiz seems to be over. Whoops. How did that happen? I usually manage one or two questions, but the vodka has made me drift off.

Richard and Michael are talking animatedly about the Australian Nobel Prize winner. Lisa is staring out of the window, still gently weeping, and Suzanne is flirting with a man at the next table. Nash is in his world, and I am in mine.

What a disastrous night. It's definitely time to go home.

Nash and I have the same idea at the same time and stand up together, ready to say our farewells. Richard looks as if he couldn't care less that we're moving to the other side of the world, and Michael just looks furious.

'Quickly, before you go . . .' Suzanne kisses me on the cheek and presses three £50 notes into my hand. 'That's for tomorrow, in case you need to get any cotton or anything.'

'Wow. Thanks.'

Never mind cotton. That's enough to live on for the next three weeks. What on earth would I do without Suzanne?

'Come on,' Nash says, sensing another long conversation starting up. 'See you later, Suzanne.'

Once we're outside I tell him the good news about the job. 'I'm making a dress, for the magazine – for Suzanne. The model's pregnant and the clothes don't fit, so I'm going to make something on the spot.'

'That's great, Alice, really great – but we need to talk.'

Nash hails us a taxi. I am amazed. He never does that.

We sit in the back of the taxi and I watch him searching for the right words to use in his talk. All the time, I am thinking about Bondi Beach. Whatever he's about to tell me, I have a horrible feeling I'm never going to see it now. I also think about the way Lisa ran off tonight, and the way she cried at the table.

'I borrowed a library book about living in wartime,' I tell Nash, to fill the silence as we lurch towards Swiss Cottage.

'But we're not living in a war,' Nash says, as if he's talking to an idiot.

'It's a book about growing your own food, about gardening and cooking during war. I can plant spinach, then bake homemade spinach pie – in Australia. When we get our own garden.'

Nash stares out of the window at a red traffic light. Whatever he needs to tell me, it seems impossible for him to articulate. The journey finishes in silence.

'So what are you thinking about?' Nash asks as I unlock the front door of the hostel.

'Funny, I was going to ask you the same question,' I reply as we trudge upstairs.

He vanishes into the bathroom as soon as we go inside. Suddenly Suzanne calls me. She's just made a mad decision to go away for a few weeks over Christmas and into the New Year. Is there any way I could look after her stall? 'I'll pay you upfront,' she says. 'I can give you the money tomorrow.'

'Suzanne, you have no idea how amazing that would be.'

'I thought you might want some dollar dosh before you go.'

I want to tell her about what's just happened – or not happened – between Nash and me, but I can't. If I start talking, I might not stop. And besides, he can hear every word. That's one of the most horrible things about where we live – the walls are so thin that every backpacker grunt, groan and moan is audible.

'So anyway,' I say, once I've finished the call with Suzanne and climbed into bed with Nash.

'Anyway what?'

'About Lisa. She seemed so upset. I mean, nobody else started crying when we told them we were going.'

Nash waves me away. 'She's a bit sensitive.' Then: 'Tired,' he adds. 'We do need to talk, Alice, but I've got to go to sleep.'

With that, he pulls up the eiderdown I made at college, gives a theatrical yawn with one arm stretched up in the air and his fist over his mouth, and goes to sleep, leaving me to worry about Lisa.

I try to think about tomorrow's job for Suzanne instead. And the stall. Sometimes I find comfort in thinking about fabric, and tonight is one of those nights. I've been stitching and re-stitching a 1980s nylon suit lately, and all it needs are houndstooth checks. I fall asleep seeing houndstooth checks in my head.

four

I find out all about Lisa at breakfast the next day.

Nash and I eat downstairs in the dining room at 7 am, before the backpacking hordes are allowed in at 7.30 for their bread rolls and packets of jam. Because we are staff (at least, I am) we're allowed to use the microwave in the back kitchen. Honestly, there is nothing the owners of the Swiss Cottage International Travellers Hostel won't do for us.

Over a bowl of porridge, Nash tells me that Lisa has just lost her job as head of music at Romney College.

'Is that it?' I say. 'I thought you were going to tell me you'd been having an affair.'

Nash shovels down his porridge. 'What? Thanks very much, Alice. She's terrified,' he says. 'It's the first time she's ever lost a job. And she's not sure she can get another one easily. Apparently the headmaster's been a bit of a problem. She's worried about her reference. She got the bad news just before she came out last night for the quiz.'

'I'd have stayed at home if I was her.'

'I think she wanted to tell me herself.'

'And then you told her you were leaving the country. That must have really finished her off.'

'Why are you using that tone of voice?'

'What tone of voice? I'm eating porridge. How can I have a tone of voice? When you told her we were moving to Australia she bawled her eyes out.'

Nash shrugs. 'Not interested in starting an argument.' Then he takes his leather jacket off the back of the chair, picks up his school briefcase and walks out.

Our two rooms – the studio as it was called at my job interview – are freezing because the owners ration our heating. Thus my sole source of warmth is a Nag Champa incense stick, two tracksuits and two pairs of socks. I lie on the bed with one of Nash's old sheepskin coats over me and think about the day ahead, trying not to panic about the job for Suzanne. I have never made a pregnancy dress in my life. I'm just going to have to take everything I know about the female form and adapt it. Thank God I had all that practice at fashion college creating between-sizes (like the size 13 that Heidi got so excited about).

Someone is gargling and spitting in the bathroom next door. I ram my fingers into my ears. I suppose they'll leave me a small woven mat of pubic hair in the plughole as well. With Nash rushing off like that, I've completely forgotten to wash up our breakfast things downstairs. Because I work as a cleaner here, Nash just assumes that his mess is my responsibility, so I end up doing our dirty dishes, and washing his shirts in the sink, and hanging up all the coats and jumpers he leaves piled on the bed.

I stare up at the ceiling. I know it so well. There's a rusty brown stain in the shape of the letter B in the right-hand corner, above our shelves. There's also a chipped plaster posy of flowers around the light bulb, which lost its shade months ago when Nash threw a book at it. There have been so many episodes like that in the history of our relationship that I can't even remember what he was angry about. Has my boyfriend hit me? asks Dr Ray Stein. No, he hasn't. But he's chipped an awful lot of Victorian ceiling plasterwork at the Swiss Cottage International Travellers Hostel.

I should really be getting my sewing kit together for Suzanne, but instead I find myself returning to *Should I Stay Or Should I Go?*. It's now two weeks overdue from the Swiss Cottage Library, but it is also my sole source of guidance at the moment.

New question. *If all my friends and family staged an intervention and told me it was fine to leave Nash, would I do so?*

My God. The relief would be incredible. Yes, yes, yes!

I wonder if I got that question right or wrong.

And I wonder what my mother would say if I told her about Lisa.

Lisa was one of the reasons Nash and I spent the whole of our Glastonbury weekend arguing with each other. She was there too – not with her mysterious barrister boyfriend, of course, but with a group of friends. Nash and Lisa spent a lot of time lying side by side in a dugout on the Green Fields. It was supposed to be a copy of an Ancient Briton camp, and had seats made of earth and a little stove at one end. Their hands were just – only just – touching in the mud when I found them.

They were listening to a man playing the piano on a wooden platform, and smiling. They looked as if they were stoned, but I don't think they were. They were just happy.

That was what hurt me the most – the intense happiness and the smiling. And the fact that Nash was prepared to do such a woo-woo thing with Lisa when he point-blank refused to go and see the fireworks with me. I was dying to see the fireworks. They were inside willow-tree sculptures on the hill, and everyone was talking about them. Not Nash though. He thought they were bollocks.

The Believers did some busking at Glastonbury (because they couldn't get a proper gig) and drew a small crowd. Nash and Lisa were in their element then too. Here's my deep, dark secret. I don't really like The Believers. They make the kind of music that you can't dance to, or sing along with. Instead, you're just supposed to sit on the floor with your legs crossed and *listen.*

Nash loves people who listen. That's why he likes teaching. It's a captive audience. If the boys don't give his brilliance their full attention, he marks them down. He's got them exactly where he wants them.

The one word that Nash uses most in our relationship is 'Listen'.

'Listen, Alice . . . can you just listen? Listen to me! Are you listening?'

I know very well that's why he likes Lisa. She's a listener. She just wafts around and receives. The only time she says anything is when she opens her mouth to sing – and even then it's other people's words.

Oooh, I desperately need a good bitching session with Suzanne. She's the only person who knows me so well she won't be horrified by my character assassination of Lisa and Nash. And it'll get me to the photo shoot on time.

I look at my cab voucher and the £150 Suzanne gave me last night. The temptation to go straight to the nearest beauty salon and treat myself to a pedicure is extreme, but I resist. Instead, I lay out my clothes. It's been such a long time since I dressed for a proper job that I've almost forgotten how to do it. I have to impress the people from Twad though. Last night Suzanne told me we'd be working with a veritable circus of glamour; not only Vera Van Der Meer, but a hair and make-up artist, a photographer, a photographer's assistant, and even a work-experience girl who's to be our minion.

The thermal underwear I dyed last winter might work – if it's layered under a mad denim skirt I made at college. There's also a boxy tartan jacket from the charity shop, which I customised. I love laying out my clothes like this. The clashes – of colour, texture, shape – are always more interesting than the matches. My hand-knitted mohair cardigan with seashell buttons, placed next to the skirt I made from an old 70s kaftan looks great. Especially when I add an old leather belt of Dad's. Biker boots (from one of Nash's motorbike shops) and an amazing crocheted cap from Suzanne's stall should finish it off. At least the cap will cover up my one-quid hair.

I apply my make-up in the taxi, resting one foot on my sewing-machine case while the other holds down a cardboard box full of trims, scissors, thread and glue. That's one secret they never tell you at fashion college – when all else fails, you can wing it with a big tube of adhesive.

* * *

Suzanne is fizzing with panic and too much caffeine when I arrive at the studio in Soho. It's a loft on Lexington Street with a high glass ceiling and polished wooden floorboards. There's a bunk bed in one corner – I suppose that's where the photographer sleeps – and a tiny kitchen. You probably don't need a big kitchen when you're working with Twad models. The last one Suzanne introduced me to told me she was an American size zero and she lived on sushi and water. Suzanne described her as a ping-pong bat with earrings.

Suzanne spirits me away to sit on the bottom bunk of the photographer's bed surrounded by bags of camera film and piles of magazines. 'Now, Alice,' she says, 'stop thinking about Lisa and Nash.'

'How did you know I was?'

'You've got bags under your eyes. Did Nash tell you they'd had it off then?'

'He says they didn't. She was crying last night because she'd just been sacked. She wanted Nash's shoulder to cry on.'

'Pesky old Lisa!'

Suzanne rubs my shoulders and I smell her scent. She always wears the most fantastic perfume, thanks to all the free bottles that arrive at Twad.

'I'm a bit wobbly,' I confess.

'Right then, Miss Alice. You know who's really wobbly this morning? Natasha. She's the pregnant model. The very *naughty* model who fibbed about how big she was going to be.'

I glance over at the beautiful red-haired woman sitting patiently in a chair while the hair and make-up artist squeezes her eyelashes in a painful-looking metal curler. She is, indeed, enormous. Maybe she's having twins.

Suzanne reads my mind. 'Looks like she's having twins. Anyway, here's your dosh for the market stall. I'll be back some time in January – before you go off to Australia anyway. Is that alright?'

She presses a fat envelope bulging with £20 notes into my hand, then guides me over to the corner of the studio where all the people from Twad are. They're all freelance, but Suzanne works with them all the time and calls them her Meaningless Twaddlings. Nobody seems to mind.

Vera Van Der Meer is extremely loud, as if she spends her whole life trying to CALL CABS in New York over the top of the traffic. I instantly want to take her plum-coloured coat-dress off her back and examine the stitching. It's a brilliant piece of work, right down to the tiny little padded shoulders.

The work-experience girl is better dressed, better spoken and far more confident than me. Suzanne tells me she's fifteen years old.

'Honestly, London teenagers! They're the next bloody master race,' she hisses.

I start cutting the beautiful stretchy green fabric Suzanne's brought along. 'I'm going to channel BodyMap from that old copy of *The Face* we were looking at the other day,' I tell her. 'Is that alright? Do you know what I mean?'

'Absolutely,' Suzanne says. She holds the gorgeous old Biba coat up to the light. 'What are you going to do with this then?'

'Cut straight up the seams and take off the buttons. They're going sideways across the skirt.'

'Vera brought a stack of stuff just in case,' Suzanne reassures me, 'so don't panic. Then again, what she found was basically rubbish, so I don't think we'll be using it.'

Natasha glances over at us. She is beginning to look beautiful and other-worldly, like some wild woodland creature. Her dark red hair has been crimped into cascades of waves, and her skin has been powdered pink and white, like some expensive peach. Everyone is staring at her – and smoking around her at the same time. She fans the smoke away.

Vera puffs her cheeks out when she exhales, like a hamster. She has tufty, pale orange hair and slightly buck teeth, which makes her look even more pet-shoppy. She puts her cigarette on the windowsill and pumps my hand.

'You're Vintage Alice? I love the sound of what you're doing.'

I try not to blush. If only she knew I can't even afford zips.

'So what *are* you doing?' she adds.

'Well . . . because Natasha has such a beautiful long neck and sculpted collarbone, I'm going to shape the neckline of the top around that. Then I'm going to sew together a kind of second-skin tubular dress that fits over the top and skims the floor. The Biba coat will become an angular, boxy jacket and the buttons will draw the eye up to Natasha's tummy. The whole point of this photograph is to show her pregnancy off, not to hide it.'

'She's channelling BodyMap,' Suzanne adds, and Vera immediately shuts her eyes as if she's having a religious experience and makes mad little humming noises of approval.

Close up, Vera's coat-dress is even more wonderful. It's all I can do not to stick my hand down the back of her neck and pull out the label.

'Break, everybody!' the photographer's assistant yells over the deep dub reggae pouring out of the speakers. It seems Natasha is feeling nauseous from all the smoke and must go up onto the roof immediately for some air.

'Right then.' Suzanne stands with her hands on her hips, taller than everybody in her huge platform shoes. 'Cigarettes out *permanently*. Natasha, time out on the roof – don't fall off for God's sake – and we'll see everyone back here in half an hour.'

The place empties and we're left alone. There's a loud buzz at the door, which Suzanne answers. A few minutes later, a courier comes up with an enormous bunch of flowers. To my surprise, they're for me – from Nash! Nash never writes long notes, and this one simply says *Sorry. Good luck today*. But at the moment, that's enough for me. I'm filled with love and forgiveness. Is this the start of our Bondi Beach born-again baptism?

I eye the photographer's TV. Robyn has sent me a homemade DVD about Bondi Beach. There's a note taped to the cover – with her customary four kisses – explaining that although she's very bad at using the camera and her hand wobbles a lot, she's tried to film all the important things in Bondi, so Nash and I will get a better idea about our new home before we land.

'Can I watch my Bondi Beach DVD in here?' I ask Suzanne. 'It'll help me calm down. I can cut while I watch.'

Suzanne puts the DVD in while I start cutting up the Biba coat. Robyn certainly has a bad case of shaky hand – unlike me, fortunately – but she's also typed perfect opening titles (in Helvetica bold). I'm excited. I know it's ridiculous, because I'm so far away, but – look! There's a sign saying 'Bondi Beach'. And look! That must be Robyn's flat.

'Noice,' says Suzanne in a bad Australian accent.

Robyn walks around the bathroom first, showing us the bath, the loo and the spa. *The spa.* After that she shows us the balcony, where she has barbecues in summer. I know this because she's sent me photographs of them. They involve dozens of ridiculously attractive Australians standing around eating very little and wearing baseball caps and almost no clothes. All of them have white teeth, just like Robyn's.

The flat is amazing – more like a house high up in the sky. Then, when Robyn turns the camera towards the window, I suddenly see what looks like the biggest beach in the world lying in front of me.

Robyn must have squashed her hand over the microphone for most of the filming because her running commentary sounds like someone squeaking from the murky depths of a sock.

'Icebergs,' she mumbles, and the camera wobbles over some amazing restaurant on top of a cliff and then down to a brilliantly blue swimming pool. There seems to be just three people using it. Only three! They also appear to be quite old and a bit saggy and wrinkly. Whoops. Unbeautiful Australians. The camera moves quickly away.

'Surfers,' Robyn comments as she films some tiny human dots in the distance, pinned against a series of enormous waves.

'Drongo waiter,' she laughs, as the action cuts to a man's large, hairy hand stabbing her with a fork while she tries to eat a huge breakfast. 'Stop it, Jason,' she says and there's a fight over the lens cap.

Suzanne and I stop the DVD and count all the things on Robyn's plate at the Bondi Beach café. Scrambled eggs. Bacon. Tomatoes. Parsley. Chives. Bagel. Avocado. Avocado for breakfast? Robyn must be showing off, I think. Mornings in Australia can't possibly be this decadent. Then I see that the café is packed. The clock says it's 8 am. How can everyone be eating breakfast outside at 8 am? Some of them have work clothes on – are they having meetings?

The camera sweeps over the menu. Everything is $9. About the same price as going one stop on the tube in London.

The Twad people eventually drift back into the studio and the hair and make-up artist gives us Natasha for half an hour so I can pin her into the jacket and what will become the elongated tube dress.

The work-experience girl asks if she can rewind Robyn's DVD, and soon everyone is watching my cousin's hand-held version of Australia and engaging in a game of one-upmanship as they all claim to have been to Sydney's most glamorous bars and clubs.

'I went to Cate's hairdresser when I was there,' the photographer's assistant boasts. I suppose she means Cate Blanchett.

'Did you get up to Byron Bay?' the photographer fires back, looking impossibly smug.

'I went horseback riding with Sass and Bide,' Vera trumps them, and puffs out her hamster cheeks.

Suddenly I realise I'm not going to some funny upside-down country after all. I appear to be moving to one of the hippest destinations in magazine-land. If I confessed I'd just secretly applied to be a dog-carer at Bark's of Byron Bay, they'd probably make a mass exodus.

The DVD finishes and the work-experience girl puts on more deep dub reggae and starts dancing around in her ballet shoes.

Natasha is beginning to look like a cross between a heavily pregnant Celtic seductress and a beautiful tree, which is the way I pictured her.

'No sketch?' Vera Van Der Meer asks.

'Alice doesn't need to sketch,' Suzanne explains for me. 'She just goes by feel. You should see the clothes she's made for *me*.'

I check Natasha's face in the mirror to see if she's feeling tired from her pregnancy, but she looks dreamily content, and so she should. Her face is immaculate. Her hair is wild, red and impossibly romantic.

'Wow,' the work-experience girl says when she returns from a coffee run. 'She looks fantastic.'

What I've done with Suzanne's coat is not what Barbara Hulanicki would ever have envisaged during her time at Biba, but I'm happy with the way it balances Natasha's proportions. I've woven the light, deliciously stretchy green wool as gently as I can around Natasha's bump, and then cut the skirt so it's comfortable enough for her to move freely in, even though it looks tight and sexy down to the ankle.

'Clever,' Vera says as she pinches the fabric.

Soon it will be time for a final hair and make-up touch-up, and then the photographer can begin the shoot.

'I think we'll go back up on the roof,' he muses, and tells his assistant to drag out some plastic trees from an old *Vogue* shoot last year. The work-experience girl is dispatched to buy boxes of mushrooms at Berwick Street Market by Vera, who says she is 'feeling the Welsh woodlands'. I suppose the photographer can microwave them for breakfast tomorrow morning.

The day flashes past and I am so caught up in my work – and the excitement of the shoot – that I forget I need to go the loo.

'You'll keel over standing there like that with your legs crossed,' the photographer tells me.

But I'm not listening. Vera Van Der Meer wants me to give her a call when I get to Sydney. Her business card is the palest off-white, very thick, very expensive and engraved in hot pink copperplate. If Vera isn't careful I may drool on it and leave little saliva marks all over her VV logo.

'If you can make a pregnant woman look hot, you can make anyone look hot,' Vera says.

'See?' Suzanne squeaks at me in the privacy of the loo later on. 'It's happening, Alice! Australia is already happening to you before you've even got there. Vera is *huge*.'

The fashion industry is a funny business. If you're actually huge or massive they can't cope with you, but if you're *described* as huge or massive, you know you've got it made.

five

It always takes ages for Twad to get a fashion story to print, Suzanne says. Therefore I should stop rushing into every newsagent I see and getting disappointed when I'm not in the magazine.

The Saturday morning after our farewell drinks for everyone at the pub, I wake up in Nash's arms. I hadn't realised we'd been sleeping together like that, all night, but it's a nice surprise, like suddenly remembering it's Christmas, or finding something velvet at the charity shop.

'Nothing like hangover sex,' Nash says, as he gets down to business.

I lie in bed for as long as I can after that, then Nash says he's going to pick up some overdue marking from his school so I begin to get ready to meet Suzanne at her Camden Market stall.

There was no sign of Lisa last night. She had the flu, according to Nash and Richard, so she stayed at home with her boyfriend. It was a relief, really, after Suzanne and I had spent so much time talking about her behind her back.

Suzanne was in a class of her own last night, forcing the DJ to put on Adam and the Ants then doing her own version of 'Ant Music', on her back, wriggling her legs in the air. Then she sprayed herself with imaginary insecticide and flopped on the carpet.

Today, she's showing me the basics of managing her stall and introducing me to the other stallholders. I've looked after the stall before, but she has more stock now and new rules – since she realised that all her best vintage pieces were being snapped up by dealers. I meet her outside Camden tube station and admire her leather bomber jacket. She's paired it with red jeans, stripy socks and strappy sandals. She's dissolving a vitamin B tablet on her tongue, which has gone bright orange.

'That was a good night,' she says. Then she remembers something. 'All my emails yesterday were about you. The photos of Natasha are brilliant, apparently. The art director loves them, the agency loves them, and your new best friend Vera reckons you should launch your own label for pregnant women.'

'Really?' I try not to sound too excited.

'Yeeeee!' Suzanne squeals, and links her arm in mine. Honestly, there's no point in trying to be cool around her, because she's the least cool woman in London. 'Gave myself carpet burns being an ant last night,' she says dolefully, examining her arm.

We race towards the market in the cold, passing puddles, drunks, chuggers, pigeons and the occasional pool of sick.

'Lovely,' Suzanne jokes. 'I can't understand why you want to leave London behind, darling. You must be mad.'

She unlocks her stall – which is more like a shop – at the back of the market. She uses five keys and it takes fifteen minutes. As she does this, I remember something I read about how some parts of Australia are so safe, you can leave your back door unlocked – and your car. Nash and I were talking about it this morning, after we realised we'd both woken up from vaguely Australian dreams. Imagine what it'd be like to live in a country where you could leave your front door unlocked. If there's one thing I won't miss about London it's all the bloody keys we have to carry around. There are times when I feel like some seventeenth-century jailer.

Suzanne introduces me to various stallholders. There's Gary One, who sells Bob Marley T-shirts with giant cannabis leaf patterns on the sleeves, Gary Two, who sells vintage cigarette lighters, and a woman called Beryl who seems too disorganised to do anything except throw brown paper bags around.

I have always loved Suzanne's stall. It's like a cross between a gigantic rabbit hutch and the most glamorous jumble sale in the world. She buys and sells clothes from vintage Dior to 1990s trainers. The only rule is, she has to find it interesting. Apart from that, anything goes. Her stall is mentioned in all the London guidebooks, and loads of stylists shop here, looking for accessories for television programs or special-event clothes for their clients.

'Fake Pucci,' I say, spotting a scarf.

'Is it?'

'Bad print job.' I examine it more closely. 'They've snipped the label out, to make you think it's a sample. It's a copy.'

'Hmm. I'm not so good on my Pucci. What about this bag?' Suzanne waves a filthy patchwork handbag at me. 'I've got a funny feeling about it, but I don't know why.'

'Could you bear to rip off the patchwork to see what's underneath?'

'You do it.'

'Okay.'

I rip – and keep on ripping.

'Incredible,' Suzanne says, when I show her the beautiful late-1960s green leather bag underneath. It has a zippered secret compartment in the bottom, and a tiny vanity mirror on a chain sewn on the inside.

'Those posh Hermès copies were so unfashionable by the '70s that hippies just used to stitch patchwork all over them. And bits of carpet. Any old stuff. But what you really want is the bag that's underneath. You hardly ever see those false-bottomed bags around now.'

'Alice, you are bloody amazing. I mean that. You are really staggeringly amazing,' Suzanne says.

We keep sorting through piles of bags, and smelly silk scarves, and trunks full of ancient tweed coats. There are fox furs with beady glass eyes, and beautiful old paisley dressing-gowns, and red leather vanity cases that still have old theatre tickets in them. It feels like time-travelling. I'd forgotten how much fun her stall was. And, apparently, I'm bloody amazing. Someone has actually said something nice about me for a change.

The wind picks up, so Suzanne offers me an enormous tweed coat from her collection, and puts one on herself. Then she finds two big cashmere scarves and two flat caps. We put them on over our other clothes and point at each other. After that, Suzanne makes me put on a pair of gloves knitted in the shape of pink pigs. I'm now wearing so many heavy layers I'm worried my fold-up chair will tip over.

I eye off the gorgeous red Dior coat that she's been trying to sell forever. It's far too expensive for most people, even though it's worth every penny. It nips in at the waist, and the lining is so beautiful it's the kind of coat you want to hang on the back of your chair every chance you get. It fits me perfectly. I will never be able to afford it in a million years.

'So how is it with Nash now?' she asks.

'Alright. Good, actually.'

'Thought so. A relationship is like a shark, Alice. It has to keep moving to survive. You just needed to give the shark a bit of a shove.'

'Maybe.'

I tell her about my application to work at Bark's of Byron Bay.

'No!'

'Oh yes. I wrote to Danielle Coles, the woman who owns it, and she asked me to ring her. Anyway, once I got the time zones right, I did. She said I could start any time after we got there. On a trial basis.'

'Nash hates dogs!'

'Byron Bay is also about nine hours' drive from where Nash'll be working. He won't like that either. Or maybe he will. I don't know. Maybe we need a bit of space. I haven't told him.'

She introduces me to the stallholder on her left. His name's Alan and it turns out he sells second-hand self-help books. I look at his stall. He only has about . . . ooh, twenty-eight copies of *Should I Stay Or Should I Go?*.

'It's a very good book,' Suzanne says, shrugging her gigantic tweed shoulders. 'Then again, you have to wonder if all those people are getting rid of it because it didn't actually help, or because their relationships became so fantastic that no further advice was required.'

'Why did you buy it?' I ask her.

'I had to decide whether to get rid of Sam or not. And now look at me – I'm off to New York to stay with him. Didn't tell you that, did I? I had a last-minute change of plan. Vera offered me her apartment, and so I poked Sam on Facebook, and the next thing I know he's poking me back.' She smirks and tries not to look too pleased.

'Lucky you, going to New York.'

'Even luckier you, going to Sydney,' she contradicts me. 'Apparently they've got it all sorted in Australia so you can just drive up the coast from Melbourne to Brisbane and go from one market to another. People actually live like that. They do the whole boho caravan thing.'

'Sounds amazing.'

She nudges me. 'Could be good for you. Personally I think you should have a go at vintage. You're bloody good at it. Or set up your own label, sweetheart.'

I make a horse-snorting noise, because she's embarrassed me, but also because she's rumbled me. That's part of my Australia dream I haven't dared tell her: a hand-sewn label with 'Vintage Alice' embroidered in old-fashioned, cherry-red writing.

Suzanne starts fizzing about her trip to America again – until the first customer arrives.

As the day goes on, I realise I'm getting the hang of it again. Part of the trick is judging what people are wearing. Serious customers have serious vintage clothes already, even if it's just a pair of brogues or Terry de Havilland boots. They're not interested in markdowns, and they certainly don't want you to tell them about the labels because they know it all already. Casual customers are different. One peek under the trestle table at their trainers and jeans and you know they probably have no idea at all.

'For them,' says Suzanne, 'the £5 suitcase of scarves. Just tell them they make a fantastic substitute for a belt and everyone's doing it.'

When I peel off my borrowed vintage clothes at the end of the day and go home, I find that Nash has gone out – he's left a note saying he's with Richard – and so I run a hot bath. At last, I have hand cream. And a jar of bath salts. They're the two treats I allowed myself with Suzanne's money. I really should have got some Alka-Seltzer as well. My hangover is still dreadful.

I'm sitting in the bath with a packet of frozen peas on my head when the phone rings. It's Robyn. She wants to wish me Merry Christmas before she leaves for Bali. She won't be back till February, so she wants to double-check that I have all the keys to her flat and I understand the spa instructions.

'What are you up to?' she asks.

'I'm having a bath. We had our leaving party last night and I've got a terrible hangover.'

'Gross.'

'I'm trying this technique where you draw the pain away from your head by putting ice on your skull and sitting in hot water. We don't have any ice though, so I'm using frozen peas.'

Robyn laughs at me. 'So how was the party?'

'It wasn't a proper party. We just met some friends at the pub for drinks. It wasn't as bad as I thought it was going to be. I suppose some people are happy for us and some people aren't.'

'Really?'

'Some of Nash's friends are definitely feeling rejected. I think my friends understand it though. Everyone wants to move to Sydney, don't they?'

Robyn remembers why she's calling. 'Hey, I got some news. Joel's coming back from India. He actually used a phone to call me. He's in Kashmir at the moment, but he'll be back soon. He's got a cheap round-the-world ticket so he's going to see a few places on the way back.'

'Does he know I'm coming?'

'Yes. He's really excited.'

'I don't even know if I'd recognise him.'

'He's got a beard now.'

'Beards can be sort of funky though, can't they?'

'Trust me,' Robyn says, 'if my brother has a beard it will not be funky.'

'What will it be then?'

'Spiritual,' she says. 'Rilly serious.'

An image of my cousin – looking a bit like Uncle Roland, but with a beard and an Om symbol on his T-shirt – drifts into my mind.

Nash comes home, and bangs on the bathroom door to find out how long I'll be.

'I'm *frozen*!' he complains. 'And seriously hungover!'

I finish the call, thanking Robyn again for her amazing Bondi Beach breakfast DVD. Then I wrap myself in a towel and stagger out with the packet of peas. Nash shoots in like a speeding bullet, looking pale and ill and heading straight for the loo.

All I can think about for the rest of the night is that I almost have a real job again. Or even two real jobs.

'My designs have featured in several magazines,' I tell the bathroom mirror. 'When I arrive in Sydney, I'll probably be working with one of America's best-known stylists, Vera Van Der Meer. In the meantime, I'm placing vintage fashion with some of London's keenest collectors.'

It's funny how when you say things like that in the mirror, your mouth automatically goes all round and pouty.

The following week goes quickly. Nash and I have a million things to do. Lisa wants him to drop off copies of all their old band recordings to her flat, because she's still too ill to move and she wants one final chance to say goodbye. A group of friends who missed the party call us to try to organise a last-minute drink. Then there's all the hassle of packing up and leaving the hostel.

Nash also has extra work at school, and I've got my mother on the phone every single day. She wants me to come to Hove, but I can't. And she's desperate to get to London, but every train seat is booked solid and she's too frightened to drive. I suppose she means every *first-class* seat is booked solid. She won't travel any other way, despite me spending the last ten years trying to convince her.

The hostel owners still haven't found anyone to replace me as their live-in cleaner, which means worried-looking couples who don't speak English very well keep turning up wanting to see our two rooms. I don't have the heart to tell them how awful it is living here. Maybe they're all chasing a London dream, just as I'm chasing a Sydney dream.

Before I realise it, Friday swings around – with an excitable parting phone call from Suzanne at Heathrow Airport, who promises she'll keep up with me on Facebook, shortly before remembering I don't own a computer.

The next day, I wake up in Nash's arms again and breathe a huge sigh of relief. Gently, very gently, we seem to be thawing. It's still freezing in our room, but at least it feels as if *we're* turning a corner. Then I realise it's Saturday and I have to go to work. The shock is terrible.

When I arrive at Camden Market, small groups of people are already queuing outside the main entrance. The tourist traffic is unbelievable. A licence to print money, they always say.

Years ago, Suzanne bought a little row of Union Jack bunting at an auction and it's become her trademark. The first thing I do is pin it up from one end of the stall to the other. Next to go up are the fairy lights, which I'm always terrified will electrocute me (or a customer) as they're connected to an overloaded power point hooked up to a generator that seems to be built on top of a puddle.

Suzanne has her own way of laying out the stall and I'm under strict instructions to copy it. Cheap paste brooches at the front to draw people in, but nothing too valuable in case shoplifters are around. Show-stopping clothes high up at the back. Cardigans sorted by colour. Handbags strung up on a washing line from right to left; no rubbish, designer labels only.

As soon as the big main entrance is unlocked, people come rushing in. I sell three paste brooches in the first ten minutes – all Christmas presents, because the customers want them wrapped in tissue paper and tied with a ribbon.

My own Christmas presents are under the stall. I've made shortbread iced with people's names, their star signs or their favourite football team. My plan is that when business slows down I can start wrapping them, to keep me busy. I'll use some of my precious stall money to buy Nash a second-hand Bob Dylan book that I know he doesn't have. I saw it in one of the stalls last week. So that's it – shortbread and Bob Dylan means Christmas is officially sorted.

I am determined that the bulk of the money Suzanne gave me will be spent on my debts. There are four jam jars under the bed stuffed with notes and covered up with a blanket. If I'm very, very careful over the next few weeks, I will be able to put a big cheque inside the cover of Nash's book, and another one into Mum's shortbread tin. Then I can sort out my overdraft and my credit card. The feeling of relief is incredible.

A tall woman with tufty orange hair and a black Beatles cap starts sorting through a box of cheap nylon scarves on the ground. Oh my God. It's Vera Van Der Meer.

'Hello, stranger,' she honks in her ridiculously loud voice, and gives me a bucky beaver smile. She says Suzanne just Facebooked her and told her to visit the stall before she flew back to New York, because of the Vuitton.

I instantly know what she means. The small Louis Vuitton trunk is one of the objects that Suzanne padlocks to the leg of her trestle table.

Vera inspects it – strangely enough, sniffing the interior – then nods. 'Done.' Then she rifles through Suzanne's cheap scarf collection. 'I'll tell you something wonderful you can do with these,' she says. 'You use them as Christmas wrapping. Look – I'll show you.'

She turns the scarf into a kind of origami box, then picks up a silver cigarette case from the table and puts it inside.

'That's amazing.'

'You just need a few pins here and there, but it looks fabulous. So I'll have a few of these, thank you, Alice.'

'Oy!' Alan, the self-help book man, calls from across the market. 'Do you want a cup of tea?'

'Yes, please!' I shout back.

Vera asks me to take down a crocodile suitcase from the back wall so she can have a closer look.

She inspects the tag. 'Good price. Bit of water damage. It might have been on the *Titanic* though. So we can forgive a few drips, can't we?'

Various women inspect a row of 1950s jackets – most of them separated from suits – then tut and move on.

'Sometimes I'm worried Suzanne's charging too much,' I confide in Vera.

'Right price, wrong size,' she informs me, and pulls a boxy velvet evening jacket off the rack. 'Women were smaller then. The food was crapola, it was after the war.

Every woman who's just come past this stall is at least two sizes bigger, maybe three.'

'I often think that. The clothes are lovely, but they're too small.'

'I look forward to seeing your summer collection.' Vera raises an eyebrow at me.

Yes. Right. My summer collection.

'Anyway,' she says, 'may your yak butter never go rancid, as they say in Tibet. Happy Christmas. Twenty quid for these four alright?'

I notice she loves saying the word 'quid', as all Americans do. I go to wrap the scarves, but they're already in her Vuitton trunk – now unpadlocked – before I can find the tissue paper.

'I'm such an eco-warrior, darling, I never take wrapping these days. Think about those jackets, alright? You know the Achilles heel of most designers? They're lazy. So . . . do the work. Measure the women. Make the clothes. Oy!'

Then she asks me to keep in touch on Facebook and I go bright red, because if Vera Van Der Meer knew that I use the computer at the Indian corner shop, she might never speak to me again.

Vera waves and departs. She stops at Alan's stall and picks up *Should I Stay Or Should I Go?*. I wonder what her love life's like. Probably not great, with that hamster hair and constant chain-smoking.

Customers who were too frightened to shop when Vera was waving her silk scarves around now return. Soon, all Suzanne's paste brooches are gone, so I'm forced to put out what she calls Plan B – badges showing New Romantic groups from the 1980s.

A woman whose problem is probably Christmas (and life) decides to take her anger out on me.

'Do you have anything at all here that's a large?' she challenges me.

I can tell she hates using the word 'large' to describe herself. She's about my age, shortish, roundish – and fed up.

'It's vintage, I'm sorry. They didn't size things that way.'

She picks up one of the 1980s badges, puts it down again, then storms off.

There's a shirtwaister dress in crisp, dark-grey cotton that would really suit her if it was cut bigger. She has the kind of pale skin and dark hair that can look great against dark grey. I kick myself for not talking to her properly. I could have had a client there. Then again, how am I going to afford the material to make clothes, never mind the time? We'll be in Australia in a few weeks. And after that, it'll be difficult enough just finding a place to live. We can't stay at Robyn's flat forever.

I pick up one of the New Romantic badges – Adam and the Ants. I'm surprised Suzanne hasn't saved that one for herself, after the other night. Now all the cheap stuff at the front of the stall has gone, I notice people are more reluctant to stop. I suppose everyone's looking for a bargain. The women crouching on the ground to rifle through Suzanne's bargain hatbox are just like me. All skint, all hoping to find something second-hand, cool and fabulous for those friends who'll be mortified if they resort to bath bombs this Christmas.

The wind picks up and suddenly all the customers vanish. I start daydreaming about Australia again, and imagine Nash and I kissing waist-deep in the blue, blue water on Bondi Beach. I practise my Australian accent out of the corner of my mouth as quietly as I can, like a gangster.

'Gerday.'

Nope. I can't do it.

'Heer ya gawn?'

Nope – I definitely can't do it. But imagine if I could.

I'm definitely, positively, not going to get excited about Vera's business card. Or becoming a fashion designer for pregnant women. Or becoming a designer for women full stop. No, I'm just going to sit here on Suzanne's fold-up chair and extend the Bondi Beach daydream, that's all.

Imagine if I moved to Australia and had my own shop. And my own website. And hot pink engraved business cards. I would never have to work as a cleaner, or buy my tights from a charity shop, for the rest of my life. It's a mad idea, but now that both Suzanne and Vera have put it in my head, it won't leave me.

I keep wrapping my shortbread under the trestle table until lunchtime, when there's another rush. I eat the broken bits of shortbread I've put aside, and a salad sandwich, and say no to another cup of tea from Alan. Every piece of spare change counts at the moment.

Eventually, it's time to go home. The day has been a blur, which is the way it should be. Not too much sitting around and just enough panic. I have made much more money than Suzanne anticipated, and I text her to let her know.

I can't wait to go back to the flat and tell Nash about Vera. When I arrive home though, Nash stops me from talking before I can even open my mouth.

'Bailiffs came round,' he says.

'What?'

'Two blokes from a debt-collection agency in Wolverhampton. They've sent you six letters apparently.'

'I've got the money,' I say, feeling panicked.

'I paid them. They've gone.'

'Shit.' Suddenly I feel trembly, as if I need a big cup of tea with sugar.

'Sit down.' Nash pats the sofa and moves a cushion aside.

'I'm so sorry,' I tell him. 'Why did they come? Was it the credit card? Or the overdraft? Seriously, I've been saving up my money in jam jars. Look!' I scramble under the bed and pull them out, spilling coins and notes all over the floor.

Nash laughs at me. And then the laugh turns into a smile. 'Sit *down*, for God's sake,' he repeats.

I sit. He's still smiling – grinning, even. Why is he grinning like that?

'I have news,' he says.

'Really?'

'Good news.' He hugs me.

It must be good news. He only usually hugs me like that if we're making up after an argument.

'I've been offered the best job in England,' he whispers, cuddling me.

'Say that again?'

'The best job in England is mine. Romney College want me to take Lisa's job as head of music.'

I wriggle free and sit down at the end of the sofa where I can talk to him properly. 'But we're going to Australia.'

'Ah. But do we really need to go to Australia?'

'*What*?'

'Why do we need to go to Australia now, Alice? I went to see them this morning and the head offered me almost one-and-a-half times what I'm earning now. And that's before private tutoring. Do you know what these people pay for flute and clarinet tutoring by the hour on the weekends?'

'It's always money with us, isn't it?' I look at my sad little jam jars under the bed.

'What do you mean?'

'I thought we were going to Australia.' I want to cry.

'And there's a job for you there as well.'

'Is there?'

'I told them you could cook. You know it's a boarding school – huge, posh boarding school. Well, they need someone in the kitchen.'

'School dinner lady. Yeah. Fantastic, Nash.'

'We've been offered a self-contained flat in the grounds. Incredibly low rent. And, well – you saw the college that time. It's huge. Gym, pool, tennis court, drama theatre, music studio . . . You can use the library.'

'Do you really think my life revolves around bloody libraries? I only go there because they're free, Nash, and because there are heaters.'

'Can you stop being so uptight about this?'

'But it's a fait accompli. And you didn't even tell me you were going for an interview. What about our plane tickets? We paid for them ages ago. That's why I've got this thing from the bailiffs. It was on my credit card.'

'It's nothing, Alice. We'll get some of the ticket price back, and I'll make up the rest in the first month of tutoring. This is serious money. Much more than I was going to be paid in Australia.'

'What about Robyn?'

'She won't mind. She can come and stay with us in England sometimes. You should see the flat, Alice, it's extraordinary.'

'And what does Lisa think?'

'She'll be fine.'

'She doesn't know?'

'I'm going to clear it with her later.' He waves the subject away, as if Lisa suddenly doesn't matter.

'Nash. Did you ring them up first?'

'Yup.'

'You rang up the college behind Lisa's back, after they'd sacked her? While she had the flu?'

'Come on, Alice. Be fair. It's just common sense. It's the way these jobs go. The head remembered me from that charity swimathon thing last year. We got on well then so I assumed we'd get on well now. And we did. He was grateful he didn't have to advertise the position. Instant offer.'

'And what if I don't want to be a school dinner lady? Was this what you wanted to tell me about in the taxi the other night? Your cunning plan? How long did it take after Lisa told you she'd been sacked for you to work all this out?'

I realise that when Nash visited Lisa in the flat to say goodbye, he was probably just checking it out to see how many rooms there were. Yuck.

I walk out of the room, up the corridor, past the communal hat-stand at the front door of the hostel – where I grab everything I own that will keep me warm – and slam the front door so hard when I leave that the broken brass bell at the top pings. Oh Dr Ray Stein, where are you when I need you?

If my family and friends staged an intervention right now and said it was alright to walk out on Nash, would I pack my bags and go?

What about if Buddha said it was alright? If the sky opened in the next ten seconds and thousands of pink lotus blossoms dropped on my head as some kind of cosmic blessing, would I finally feel that I was justified in leaving?

I need to be somewhere else, immediately, so I can think about everything. I have no idea where – but I think I need a park, a bench and a big sheltering tree.

Right now, on the pavement outside the Swiss Cottage laundrette, it is freezing, cold and dark. The pigeons – our English war heroes – are eating cigarette butts as usual, and there are tracksuit hoods pulled up everywhere you look. I don't want to do my thinking here.

Trafalgar Square? Maybe. It was strangely comforting there the other night.

I catch the train to Charing Cross, along with all the other Swiss Cottage escapees who are on their way to parties, nightclubs and films. It is Saturday night. The tube is packed with couples holding hands. I wish they wouldn't. I can remember the last time Nash held my hand. It was on my birthday and he only did it because I asked him to.

In the beginning, most of the Saturday nights that Nash and I spent together involved The Believers and, occasionally, a band I liked. These days, because of his own passion for *serious* guitar, as he calls it, Nash will only go to watch other musicians if they're a) not English, and b) much older than him. Someone more cynical than me would say he just doesn't like competition. I'm sure he's secretly threatened by other men. That's why he's so aloof all the time. And . . . alright, I know I'm inventing excuses to leave him now. But part of me no longer cares.

The train stops at Leicester Square, and I get off and walk. I now have a hole in each of my tartan wellies. I may have to spend more of my vast fortune from the markets to buy replacements, before –

Before what? Before I go to Australia? Or before we move to Romney College? Or before I'm forced to move to Hove and live with my mother?

Nash has often been right about my life. He was right about fashion college – it turned out to be a dead loss – and about things like booking the dentist six months ahead and talking to the bank about weekly repayments. He was right about the Swiss Cottage International Travellers Hostel too. If we'd moved out of there last year, when I wanted to, and rented a flat, we'd both be utterly broke by now. Still. He's not right about this. Or is he? Round and round my stomach goes, like the coin-operated washing machines at the laundrette that turn everything grey as you watch.

I walk to Trafalgar Square as quickly as I can, and jam my hat down on my head to stop my ears from stinging with cold. I can see the lights and the lions in the distance, and the front doors of St-Martin-in-the-Fields, although it's closed for the evening. Nobody wants to go to church on a Saturday night, except mad people like me. Teenagers are texting each other, and screaming children are running in huge circles around Nelson's Column.

If Nash becomes head of music at the college, and I become a school dinner lady, and we live in their flat, and hang around their swimming pool, and use their lovely tennis courts, will everything be alright then?

I'm not surprised that Nash has been snapped up. Even I know that he's a kind of superstar in the world of London music teachers. Plus, he can speak three languages and teach the girls how to play football. What more could they possibly want? He even owns his own trombone. It's in storage at his parents' place.

What will his parents say if I walk out on him now? What will my mother say?

I look around me and realise how much I love this part of London. I just love, love, love it. If I go to Australia, though, I will lose, lose, lose it.

I feel panicky and weird, so I try to make a list in my head and get things straight.

If Nash takes the job, and I go with him, then I will have some of the things we would also gain by moving to Sydney. I will have a swimming pool, and far more money. I will probably be able to afford a pedicure. And a manicure. (It's amazing how my immediate life plans at the moment seem to revolve around my stupid nails.)

Nash will be much happier if he takes Lisa's job, so our relationship will probably become happier too. Maybe we'll even get married one day. We could even have a baby, and maybe the baby will be a girl, and she can go to the college and end up being a musical genius, like her father.

I suppose I could be a school dinner lady for a while, at least until I've paid Nash back. Then I could look at other options. Suzanne thinks I can do anything. Perhaps I should give her the benefit of the doubt. Maybe I can make jackets for her stall.

It's raining now, and I didn't bring the tartan umbrella. There's only one thing for it – I'm going to have to stand underneath a lion.

The phone rings in my pocket. It's Nash.

'Look, I know you're probably feeling anti me at the moment, and anti everything.'

'Yes.'

'Where are you?'

'Doesn't matter.'

'Think about it though, Alice. And think about this – if I take the job at the college and make that kind of money, I can become the kind of man who doesn't have to lend his girlfriend anything.'

'What do you mean?'

'If I'm earning that sort of money, then you can forget about debts and all that kind of stuff. We can just walk away from all that.'

'Is this a bribe?'

'*Listen* for once. If I take this job, we can have *holidays* in Australia. We don't have to move there. We don't have to leave your friends, and Lady Penelope, and everything here. Alice, on this kind of salary package, we can save up so much money that we can afford to go to Bondi Beach every bloody Christmas!'

'Alright then, I'll think about it.'

I snap my phone shut and pull back under the lion's enormous stone ears as the rain comes down. I want to stay here as long as I possibly can, so Nash will be asleep when I go home and I can quietly make a bed on the couch. I don't want to have to lie next to him tonight.

six

Nash and I usually spend Christmas Day with my mother and Boxing Day with his parents, or the other way around. This year, though, he has decided to go to Cambridge and leave the rest up to me. According to his email to me this week (with the very sensible subject header PLANS) this time the Christmas and January break is very much up to me. He will be in Cambridge with his parents, and that's that. I can either join them – or not. It takes me about five seconds to decide *not*.

Between Christmas and New Year, I go into a shortbread frenzy, and bake – and eat – about eight tins of the stuff that I made for other people. Apart from that – after I queue at the post office for half an hour to send the shortbread (Nice Heidi was right to tear her hair out, that day that she banged on and on about British post offices) – I do nothing and see nobody.

I spend Christmas in bed with my woolly hat on, with both bars blazing on the radiator I have nicked from the breakfast room, reading *Should I Stay Or Should I Go?* (now two weeks overdue) and picking shortbread crumbs out of the sheets. I listen to the Shipping Forecast because it's the only thing on the radio that isn't Christmassy. There are warnings of gales in Rockall, Hebrides, Bailey, Faeroes and Southeast Iceland, and a low Denmark Strait. Plus there's a low Trafalgar 1011 and a low Irish Sea losing its identity.

That was me, a few nights ago. A low at Trafalgar losing my identity.

Even my favourite second-hand tights couldn't help.

I ring my mother and tell her I have a cold and can't talk. Half true. Depression isn't a word we have ever used in our family.

Occasionally I check the answering machine to see if there are any real emergencies, but it's mainly people wondering where I am, and saying Merry Christmas, and Good Luck In Australia, and sometimes just getting the wrong number, so I am free to stay in bed.

When I finally make it outside, to the corner shop to check my email, there's a message from Suzanne saying she's having a fabulous time with Sam and she's sorry the stupid Twad editor held the pregnant fashion story over. She's sure though – absolutely sure – they'll run it soon. I email back using a smiley face that's wholly unrepresentative of my mood.

It's well and truly past New Year, and I'm about to take another tin of shortbread to bed, when the phone rings. It sounds like someone pretending to be a dog, so I hang up. Bloody kids. A few minutes later, it rings again. More demented barking.

'Bugger off.'

I put the phone down, and decide to put on a second woolly hat because the top of my head is going numb with cold. If they ring again, I decide, I'm going to bark back.

Ten minutes later they do, so I yap loudly like our old Labrador Charlie before slamming the phone down.

Five minutes later, another call. No barking this time – just a worried Australian woman wondering if she's got the right number.

'Alice?'

'Yes?'

'It's Danielle Coles. I have to apologise to you.'

'Oh God. The *dogs*! No, I'm sorry. I thought you were kids having a joke. Or I thought your dogs were kids having a joke.'

'No, no. I just had you on speakerphone while I was washing Mr Chang.'

'Who's he?'

'This ratty little Pekinese who's got himself covered in sheep poo. Get back in the bath, Mr Chang!'

More barking. It seems I have been receiving prank phone calls from a dog.

'I just need to find out when you're coming over, Alice. Heidi said she thought it was quite soon.'

'Yes.' (Just keep saying yes to everything, I think, then you can crawl back to bed.)

'I'm in a bit of a spot up here and I was wondering if we could try you out sooner rather than later.'

'Yes?'

'My usual guy's got to go up north, his dad's crook.'

'Yes.'

'Mr Chang, you are not to go near King Tut or I will smack your bottom!'

Suddenly, I feel exhausted. The strain of trying to hear someone from the other side of the world shouting over what sounds like the combined racket of 101 Dalmatians is just too much.

'Danielle, do you just want to send me an email about all this? I have to use an internet café at the moment, but I pick them up every few days.'

'Yeah, sure, Alice. I apologise again for these naughty little boys. I'll send you an email!' she yells, followed by a gurgling sound which may or may not be Mr Chang being drowned in the bath.

I put the phone down and go back to bed.

I must take Dr Ray's advice. I must be positive about my life. I must see my options from every angle. I must take time to ground, balance and restore my centre.

I must not go into a trance, like Goggles the fox terrier, every time I attempt to work out my future career path, my future love life – my future life.

I am not going to Australia, of course. I can keep on trying to debate with myself about it – but it just doesn't make sense. Some dreams deserve to go down the drain, and perhaps this is one of them. It's like becoming a fashion designer. It's madness.

Nash is right as usual: Romney College is the only sensible future we have. I did the sums after he emailed me a copy of their offer. If he takes this job, and all the private tutoring as well, we'll be well and truly in the clear. My new salary as a dinner lady (if I back it up with a bit of tailoring) means I will be debt-free, eventually. I try to get myself excited about the prospect. Cooking school dinners, plus not paying any rent, plus lots of saving in the jam jars, equals freedom.

Well – a certain kind of freedom. I'll never be able to go out again. My social life will consist of listening to Nash playing the guitar, and ducking when the posh Romney College children throw quoits at my head.

I try to concentrate on Mum and what it will mean to her if I stay. For a start, if I pay her back, she can stop dyeing her own hair. I was terrified by the idea of being so far away from her, and now look. If anything happens to her, I'm just a train trip away. A mere motorbike ride. (The last polite communication I had with Nash included the news that he's already seen the new bike he wants to buy once he has his new salary.)

The phone rings again and I listen to the answering machine click on. It's Lisa.

'I've got to talk to you, Alice. Are you there? I can't get you on your mobile. It's urgent.'

I pick up the phone.

'Hello Lisa.'

She gives a floaty little pant. 'Phew!'

'Nash's in Cambridge with his parents. Have you tried his mobile?'

'I know where he is. I need to speak to you. I need to apologise to you actually.'

'Really?'

'Yass.'

That strange, polite little voice. *Yass.* This conversation is probably the longest we've ever had.

'Why do you need to apologise to me?'

'I've sort of been lying for Nash.'

'What?'

'I've been covering up for Nash. He's not really over Sarah, you see.'

Oh my God.

'Anyway. I just needed to ring and let you know. Now that we're all saying goodbye to you. It wasn't an affair or anything like that, Alice, so please don't worry. But last year, when we all did that sponsored swimathon, he slept with her.'

'Are you saying Nash had sex with Sarah?'

'Well, I caught them. In the big jacuzzi next to the pool. It was dark and everyone had gone home, so I suppose they thought it would be fine . . .'

Her tinkling, frail little voice trails off. Suzanne says she sounds like the top notes of a posh school recorder.

I hang up on her, then I go back to bed and shake out all the shortbread crumbs until the horrible hostel carpet is covered in them. I suppose Lisa's just found out that Nash's got her old job. I had no idea she was so vindictive. I always had her pinned as some kind of wafty, straw-hatted twit.

I wondered why they were all so late coming home that night, when the three of them went off on their swimathon. Suzanne told me I was being stupid, but I knew something was up, even then.

I have never been in a jacuzzi with Nash. I've never even had a bath with him. The jealousy is awful and instant. *Sarah.* How much of an idiot have I been all this time to believe that she'd just disappeared?

I leave Nash a message on his mobile telling him to come home because I need to talk to him. Then I offload my shock into all the housework I can find.

There are three vacant rooms in the hostel tonight, and I blast each of them in turn, taking down nylon curtains and shaking them out of windows, scrubbing at ancient stains on the mattresses and cigarette burns on all the sad little Formica-topped tables. If I'm going to leave this hostel – one way or another – then I'm going to leave it clean.

It's what I did when I heard Dad was dying. I vacuumed my parents' house from top to bottom, then washed and ironed every piece of linen they owned, polished the silver, and even got the hair out of Dad's old hairbrush. I went mad.

I go back to our rooms and sweep the lino in the bathroom, then get down on my hands and knees and scrub it like a proper maid, with a bucket of hot, soapy water. If I scrub hard enough, maybe I can scrub Lisa away too. I never want to hear that faint, wobbly, smug little school recorder voice again as long as I live.

Some stupid line from one of Nash's songs comes into my head. *What is to become of me?*

Or maybe it's on that compilation tape one of the Pauls made for me. Anyway, it's from a song. And now I can't get it out of my mind.

I keep on cleaning the bathroom. This has been my job for the last year and I hated it. How strange that it should be so comforting now.

Nash rings back and tells me he's at Kings Cross and will be home soon.

'See you then,' I tell him, as chirpily as I can – I sound like a deranged chipmunk.

What is to become of me? I can't think about that now. I need to think about the state of the hostel instead. I had no idea it had become so filthy over autumn and winter, but at the moment, I have to say – at least in our two rooms – it has never looked so good.

I curl up on the sofa and flick through every page of *Should I Stay Or Should I Go?* at breakneck speed, writing my answers in red pen in the margins.

Do Nash and I have anything in common, other than a long-forgotten, vaguely expressed desire to have kids? Not any more, no. I suppose we both used to have *him* in common, back in the days when I was content to sit at his feet while he strummed his guitar. But I know better now.

Does Nash stop me from pursuing my dreams? Yes.

Does Nash make me feel like I don't matter, or don't exist? Yes, yes, yes, yes, yes.

My God. That's it!

I close the book and feel myself gently passing out on the sofa. I don't care what the rest of the questions are. I just want to sleep.

When I wake up, Nash is pulling the book out from under me.

'What's this?' He inspects the jacket. 'Oh yes. *Should I Stay Or Should I Go?*. Good old Dr Ray. So have you worked it out yet?'

'Go.'

'What?'

'Go, go, go. Lisa rang up and told me you had sex with Sarah. On that day you all did the sponsored swim. You shagged her.'

Big silence. Huge silence. Nash wasn't expecting that.

'Wow.' He sits down on the floor cross-legged, looking exactly like one of the boys in his music class.

'But it's not really about that. Because I sort of vaguely knew something like that might have happened, and the thing is, I never really cared.'

'What do you mean?'

'I mean I never felt jealous. And I don't feel jealous now. I just feel . . . let down. Sad. Fed up, I suppose.'

'Right.'

'Because it's so lame, basically. Your bloody ex-*wife*, for God's sake, Nash! And Lisa's only telling me now because you went behind her back and wangled your way into her old job. She's pathetic too.'

Nash looks down at his feet.

'If I ever had any doubts about how self-centred you actually are, you prick, I don't have any now. You've done everyone over, haven't you?'

He shakes his head slowly from side to side, smiling to himself as if he's in possession of some precious information that I'm not privy to, which makes me a very, very stupid woman.

'So was it just the once with your ex-wife or has it been going on all year?' I shout at him.

'Anything in your book about that?' Nash jerks his thumb at it. 'Because if I was to leave now – and I have been thinking about it, very seriously – it would be because your commitment to me is so pathetic that you base your decisions about our relationship on some self-help book you found at Oxfam.'

'Don't make this out to be my fault. And I didn't find it at Oxfam. I borrowed it from the library.'

'Whatever. You've been reading it in front of me for the last two months and you expect me to believe you're committed to this relationship?'

'Don't talk to me about commitment. You've just changed your mind about Australia.'

'We've already talked about that.'

'No, we haven't. Not properly. The book's great, Nash. Really, really great. I love Dr Ray, I think he's completely on the money. There's this question that goes, "Does your partner make you feel as if you don't matter, or don't exist?"'

'Alice. Come on.'

'But it's such a great question! And it was so amazing to read it. I felt as if my problem had suddenly appeared in someone else's book. All this time I've never been able to put it into words – but there it is, in black and white.'

Nash stands, sighs as if he's given up, and stares at the ceiling.

'How much of your life have I bankrolled?' he asks.

'Here we go.'

'You're saying cra-zee thangs.' He puts on a bad American accent and taps the cover of the book. Then he pulls a crazy face, which I suppose is meant to be me, or Dr Ray Stein.

'You're just shit, Nash. I'm going.'

'To Lady Penelope, I suppose. I don't know why you ever left home in the first place. You can't look after yourself.'

'You won't know where I am, wherever I go.'

He turns away and stares out of the window. When he turns back, I see he has tears in his eyes.

'Nash. For God's sake.'

He stands there for ages, like a statue, until I see him relaxing again into his familiar cool.

'Alice, we should both calm down and think about this. I'm sorry about Lisa. For what it's worth, we were stoned immaculate in that jacuzzi – me and Sarah. And . . . I'm genuinely sorry that I succumbed. For all kinds of reasons. I am also unbelievably sorry you had to find out like that.'

'Don't. How bloody *dare* you have done that behind my back. Did you tell Michael and Richard as well? Does everyone else know about this except me?'

'Nobody knows, Alice. I promise. It was a mad thing to do. And Lisa should never have rung you like that. I'm sorry.'

I start picking up my things from around the room – cushions and books, blankets and rugs – and throwing them on the sofa in a pile. As I do, I realise I'm scaring myself as much as I'm scaring him. I know other couples do this all the time – this angry moving-out thing. And then they change their minds, and kiss and make up, and everything's okay again.

We're not like that though.

This isn't a dress rehearsal. And I know we're both terrified, but . . .

Nash watches me in silence while I try to take big, deep breaths and gather sunglasses, and old magazines from when I had money, and albums, and socks, and soap. I know at a glance what's mine and what's his because I did the big inventory in my head last year. That's another of Dr Ray's tests, incidentally. *Have you ever seriously thought about leaving, to the point where you calculate what belongs to you and what belongs to your partner?*

I own a chest of drawers, some hatboxes, an old Augustus John drawing of my grandmother's, a dressing table, and numerous other objects that I can live without for the moment. I'll find a way to get them later. I'm very grateful to these material objects for making these shitty hostel rooms feel like a home. But at the moment, the last thing I can imagine is asking Nash to help me lug them down the stairs. I silently thank my mother for her old spare suitcases. I use two of hers, and two of mine, packing everything in as tightly as I can. Thank God for Suzanne's expert training at packing – I know how to roll towels so they won't take up too much room, and how to get eight pairs of socks inside a pair of shoes.

Eventually Nash gets up and leaves, clicking the door shut softly behind him. I suppose he's gone to ring up Lisa in a park somewhere, so he can shout at her. Or is he ringing Sarah, to warn her off in case I pick up the phone?

I have no idea where he's gone. I just know I have to pack my stuff as quickly as I can, before he comes back.

I go into the bathroom and pick up Ducky, an oversized rubber duck that Nash won for me at the Hampstead funfair when we first got together. I put him down. Then

I pick him up again. Should I pack Ducky in my luggage or not? Oh my God. I put him down. An inanimate object is doing my head in.

Shock is an interesting thing. I feel exactly the same as I did when my mother told me about Dad. I feel as if I've left my body – the same way that Elvis once left the building. The only bits of my physical self that are currently in this room are my heart, which is banging away non-stop, and my sweat, which is pouring off me.

When I finish packing, I have four bulging suitcases on wheels. If I tie them in pairs with scarves I should be able to drag two on each side – at least until I find a taxi to get me to Victoria Station. Then Mum can pick me up in Hove and we can take two each.

Suzanne's money has just become my running-away fund. At the moment I don't give a stuff about the debts. As I empty the jam jars into an old handbag, I bless her again, all the way from Swiss Cottage to New York City. Then I drag my suitcases out of the room, look at the stinking hostel hallway for the last time, and slam the front door so hard that the old brass bell falls off.

It is only when I am in the back of the taxi on the way to the station that I realise Joel Templeton has texted me.

He has just arrived from Moscow on his long trip back to Australia and wonders if I'm free to meet up. He has a few more nights in England before he finishes the rest of his journey.

Joel writes one of the longest text messages I have ever seen. It is the kind of message you imagine someone would write, if they hadn't actually seen a mobile phone before. He says he's going back to Australia the long way round, and also the wrong way round, because it makes the journey more interesting.

'How wonderful' my mother says, when I show her his message – much, much later – when we are drowning ourselves in brandy in Hove. 'Wrong way round and long way round. That's exactly the kind of thing I'd like to have engraved on my tombstone.'

I held back the tears all the way to Victoria Station in the taxi, then all the way to Hove on the train. It's only when I got into my mother's car that I started to cry.

'I'm not going to Australia any more,' I tell her, as I unpack my things.

'Not to worry, darling.'

'I've got some of the money I owe you too.'

She looks at my collection of notes and coins. 'Alice. For goodness sake. There's no need to worry about money ever again. I don't want it back, not for all the tea in China. Do you hear me?'

'The bailiffs came round to the hostel,' I say, still a bit teary. 'Nash paid them off.'

'I'm sure he did, and let that be an albatross around his neck.' She coughs, and lights a cigarette. 'Now, shall we talk about something else?'

She leads me to an enormous leather trunk in the hall – the kind that boys used to take away to boarding school with them – and flips open the lid.

'Look, Alice. All your Aunt Helena's clothes. Well – all the things she left behind, when they went travelling, anyway. Joel's organised it. When I told him you'd been working on Suzanne's stall at the market, he said I had to collect them, and give them to you. They've been in storage all this time, with your Auntie Bat.'

Auntie Bat's been called that for years, because both Roland and my father (her brothers) maintained she had bats in her belfry.

'Bat has had the trunk in the attic for over twenty years. Joel rang Helena in Jamaica to check – anyway, she said you could have the lot. She's never going to come back for them now. She said they were all her best clothes, and her mother's and grandmother's too.'

Oh my God. Hippy Helena's wardrobe. I've seen those photographs of her from the '70s. She had *everything*.

I get down on my hands and knees and rifle through the trunk like a madwoman. There are monogrammed silk dressing-gowns and houndstooth check suits with velvet collars. There are tapestry slippers and pink satin dancing shoes and velvet capes. Then there's the fabric. Yards and yards of the stuff, pre-war and 1950s. This must be her mother's stuff, and her grandmother's. Some of it's still in carrier bags from Harrods with the old royal warrants in both corners.

'A few Mary Quants in there, I noticed.' Mum puffs away on her cigarette. 'And Ossie Clarks. Helena wasn't frightened of a mini, or a maxi.'

The trunk has three layers, each separated by a wooden shelf. I take down the first shelf and see a sleeveless Mary Quant summer dress with the original daisy label sewn next to the zip. I kiss it.

'Who knew that fashion could inspire so much passion?' my mother muses. 'One thing that might bother you though – this little stoat fur collar.' She finds what looks like a recently deceased weasel and pulls it out. 'Do you remember that television program?' She shudders. 'Stoats must be the most charmless creatures in the country with their horrible glands. Chuck it out, Alice, as soon as you can.'

'I can't possibly take all this stuff,' I say, putting the stoat to one side and pulling out a pristine Yves St Laurent tuxedo jacket. 'It's worth a fortune. Helena should have it. Or Robyn.'

'Oh no,' my mother shakes her head, and then shakes her cigarette as well. 'Joel said his mother was quite insistent. Nobody else has ever wanted it in the family, and she said it must go to you. I'm only sorry I've been so dopey I didn't think of it before. But then, Auntie Bat never mentioned it. Too interested in her pipe.'

I had forgotten Auntie smoked a clay pipe. No wonder both my father and my uncle used to avoid her.

Later (much later) when I have tried on the Mary Quant dress (which doesn't fit) and the beautiful Yves St Laurent tuxedo (which does), I tell Mum the whole horrible story about Sarah and Nash at the swimming pool.

'Aha!' she cries. 'The floozy in the jacuzzi! Well, the sooner you put that behind you, Alice, the better. Just think about how your fingers go all wrinkly when you've been in the bath too long. That's probably exactly what it was like for them. It can't have been much fun for *her*, having to look down at *that* bobbing around in the water . . .'

seven

Nash wants to put me on a regular repayment system, which he calculates should have me free of my debt to him by the end of this year. This, of course, depends on me working almost constantly, but he's fairly sure I can find a job as a cleaner again.

'Happy New Year to you as well,' my mother says when she reads his email over my shoulder.

We are in Brighton for the day, and every shop, café and business is crammed with people after the Christmas break, including this tiny internet and photocopying place.

'I suppose Nash is putting all this in writing so he has some kind of record about the money,' she goes on. 'How sad.'

'It's not that, Mum. It's just that he doesn't want to talk to me. And I don't want to talk to him.'

Nash and I have exchanged more emails since I left than we ever did the whole time we were together. This morning we seem to be typing them at the same time so they cross in mid-air. I suppose he's using the computer at his school. At the moment, we're competing to see who can create the most mature, sensible and practical subject header. *Immediate Priorities* (Nash) is followed by *Finances* (me), then *Options* (Nash), then *Important Issues* (me).

Nash writes that he feels the harmony in our relationship has been damaged by my financial dependency on him, that this constant looming debt has upset the balance of our partnership. He says he thinks we need some time out from each other, but he also thinks it's time I paid him back in some structured way. He also says that, overall, we've had a good time together.

'A good time?' my mother says. 'He makes it sound as if you've been playing tiddlywinks.'

'Listen to this,' I tell her. 'He says my decision not to go to Romney College with him put his position there in jeopardy, as his application was accepted on the basis that I'd be joining him in the flat. The school prefers couples.'

'Hang on, I want to read that myself, just let me find my glasses,' my mother says, peering over my shoulder again.

This is her first encounter with computers for years. The last time was when Dad made her go on a Microsoft Word Silver Surfers' weekend with him in Dorset. Dad took to computers immediately, of course, but Mum spent the whole time smoking in the garden and listening to the racing results on her transistor radio. Now that she's seen the internet for the first time though, she's begging me to help her sign up for The Google. She calls everything connected with the internet – email, websites, spam, blogs and all the rest of it – The Google.

'What else does Nash say on The Google, Alice?'

'I'm paraphrasing, obviously, but it seems that, luckily, he's so brilliant and charismatic that the head at Romney is prepared to overlook the fact that I'm such a hopelessly feckless and unreliable cow and so Nash is still being offered the flat and the job on the condition that he signs up for two years. Oh, yeah. And he hopes we can work our issues out.'

'Why don't you google him back,' my mother says, 'and tell him you'll pay him his loan back, with interest, when you marry a rich man.'

'Mum, I'm never going to marry a rich man. I don't know where you get this rich man thing from. They don't exist. Maybe in your day, but not now.'

'He's quite mad to talk to you about money like this,' she whispers, presumably to keep my private life private from the people tapping on keyboards all around us. 'Especially after everything he's done. What about his ex-wife? What about her chap? Does she have a chap? Imagine what he's going to say about all this business in the jacuzzi!'

'Mum!' I hiss, and nod towards a man obviously listening in on our conversation.

'Okay, darling,' she says. 'Sorry.'

We pick up our bags and leave. My mother wants to go to Brighton Pavilion because she says it's good for the soul. I haven't been there since I was a teenager, but she thinks it will take our minds off everything.

'So funny how everyone wears these American hats now,' she says, as we pass one couple after another wearing baseball caps. 'I always think they make everyone look like big geese from the side.'

We take a shortcut to the Pavilion across the park, and I gaze up at the domes and minarets above the trees. I wonder if George IV built the Pavilion because he thought it would make his love life better? It was never very happy. Perhaps he thought the solution to his marital problems lay in grand gestures – just as Nash and I did.

The last thing either of us feels like doing at the moment is sorting out the Australia mess. We've agreed to sort it tomorrow, instead. He'll call Australia House and I'm going to call the airline. Then that's it. Everything cancelled. Over.

My mother and I pick up our free leaflets and wander through the Pavilion's entrance hall. I want to ooh and aah at the hand-painted wallpaper and the beautiful bamboo stairs, but it's completely silent in here because everyone's overwhelmed by all the velvet, dragons and carved palm trees. I wonder if even George IV was intimidated. It's not just a palace. It's like walking into heaven. There's a rumour that Hitler wanted the Royal Pavilion as his seaside home after the war, which was why the Nazis never bombed it.

I find myself automatically worrying about all the cleaning the servants had to do back in George IV's time. And, of course, the cleaning some poor people must still do now. In contrast, my mother says that every time she comes to the Pavilion it makes her want to redecorate.

'I do need new curtains,' she says, eyeing the vast drapes in the Banqueting Room.

'I love it. But imagine the work.'

'Don't think about the work. It's too beautiful for that. I thought you'd like this place more now you're older. I don't think we've been here for years, have we? And when you're *here*, you can't think about anything else.'

I try to succumb. After months of baked beans on toast, wellies with holes, pouring rain and £1 shampoo, perhaps a dose of the Royal Pavilion is exactly what I need. It doesn't take long to give in – the palace was built for seduction after all. After an hour, I find myself wanting to bounce up and down on Queen Victoria's lush four-poster bed.

'I've invited Joel for supper,' my mother says. 'Did I tell you?'

'You did, last night.'

'Oh, sorry. Senior moment.'

'He's coming up here to see Brighton, remember? Then going back to London to catch his next flight.'

'Could you repeat what he wrote on your phone message again?' my mother asks. 'I liked it so much.'

'He said he's going back to Australia the long way round and also the wrong way round, because it makes the journey more interesting.'

'That's it.'

'Apparently he's grown a beard,' I tell her. 'Robyn said he's a bit serious.'

'Uncle Roland was like that too,' my mother says. 'I think it's sad that they moved away when Joel and Robyn were so young. He was a lovely boy. Your father was very disappointed when they all left.'

'Did they just want to travel, or was it something else?'

'Oh, Mrs Thatcher.' My mother shrugs. 'Roland had a vendetta against her. He used to throw jaffa cakes at the television.'

'Shall I go and buy some wine for supper?' I ask.

'Oh no. Don't waste your money on wine.'

'It's fine. Please stop thinking about Nash's email, Mum.'

'Your father always said relationships weren't about money, and I believe he was right,' she says. 'But now that you have to paddle your own canoe again, Alice, I do think you have to stop other people taking advantage of you. If you hadn't scrubbed all those floors at the hostel, Nash would have been homeless. You lived there purely because it was close to his school. His choice. Not yours.'

She goes to the loo, and I think about the money I owe Nash and if there's any way around it. Our relationship – or what's left of it – has suddenly become about additions and subtractions. Giving and taking away. Dividing and bean-counting. It's not just about pounds and pence, either. It's about time, energy, and hopes and dreams. If Nash wants me to pay him back every week for a year, I will, but I want him to know it's because I choose to do it – not because he's demanded it.

'I need to get a job in Brighton,' I tell my mother when she comes back.

'Perhaps you could do his job,' she whispers, looking at a security guard.

We find our way to the café upstairs, and halfway up, my mother trips and nearly falls over. 'Crivens!' She inspects her foot and sees the sole of her shoe has come away. It's the same pair of Gucci loafers she's been wearing for years.

'Ruddy things,' she complains, and rubs her ankle.

I wonder what would have happened if I hadn't been here to catch her. Maybe it's best that I'm staying here with her after all.

We sit down at a table overlooking the gardens and the waitress talks us through the specials. I'm having incredible flashbacks about this place now – the egg and watercress sandwiches, the pots of Darjeeling, the prints of fat old George IV on the walls . . . I don't think it's changed since I was a teenager.

'What do you think you'll do, Alice?'

My mother's question is so casual and so easy that it takes me by surprise, and I find myself telling her the truth.

'I want to make clothes with vintage fabric. I know it's ridiculous.'

'No, not ridiculous at all.' She waves her red gloves at the portrait of George IV. 'He would have been a good customer – he loved clothes. Do you know, after he died, they found he owed his tailors nearly £2 million?'

'He did have a big bottom. That takes a lot of tailoring,' I tell her.

'Well, if you need to get to work on your clothes, you know you can stay here as long as you like,' my mother reminds me.

'I know. Thank you. I thought I'd get into a share house though, on the other side of London for a change. I might go south or east. I've had enough of North London. Once I've saved up enough money, anyway.'

I'm trying not to think about that bit.

Our tea arrives, along with shortbread. I know one day I'll never be able to eat shortbread again, because it'll remind me of this depressing, scary time, but for the moment I am making the most of it.

'Not as nice as your shortbread, darling,' my mother whispers after she's taken a bite. 'Thank you for putting my star sign on it, by the way. Although I'm never quite sure if I'm Leo the Lion or . . . what's the other one? Is it the python?'

I laugh at her.

Mum changes the subject back to clothes. 'I don't often go into the shops now,' she explains, 'but when I do, I notice that people seem to be making the skirts out of tights.'

'Cheap nylon,' I explain. 'Manufacturers love it because it stretches, so they can churn it out in three sizes – small, medium or large.'

'It's funny,' Mum says. 'We used to make our tailors fit the clothes around us. Now it seems to be the other way around – we have to make ourselves fit into the garments they provide. Do you know, I tried on a tweed skirt in the sales last year and the label said Made in Turkey.'

'Made in Turkey by fifteen-year-old girls on 50p an hour, probably.'

I look outside at the wind shaking the trees and wonder what the weather's like at Bondi Beach today. I suppose I'll have to ring Robyn at some point and tell her we're not coming after all. It's not a conversation I particularly want to have.

We finish our tea, and my mother returns home for *The Archers* – she never misses it – and I go for a walk along the seafront. Brighton on a windy day is like seeing a film running backwards. Seagulls fly in the wrong direction. Umbrellas blow inside out and drag their owners back along the streets. Even the waves on the beach seem to travel in the wrong direction.

I feel as if everything in my life is going backwards as well. I'm back from Australia before I've even caught the train to Heathrow. Nash has gone back on all his promises to me. And suddenly I've gone from loving him to feeling repulsed by him. He's turned from giving to taking – even grasping. I didn't show my mother the last paragraph in his email this morning where he suggests buying everything I left behind and giving me half the price I paid for it – which will then, he suggests, come off my debt. I told him I'd rather he gave it to the donkey charity shop in Finsbury Park, which is where half of it came from anyway.

I have been replaying my last horrible conversation with Nash in my head since the moment I got on the train to Hove. I wonder if he's called Lisa yet. Or Sarah.

Lisa in particular must also know what it feels like to be nonexistent now. She thought she loomed large in Nash World, but she reckoned without his ability to wave a magic wand and make the women in his life become invisible. Lisa's now inhabiting the same thin air as me – we're nowhere girls, utterly irrelevant to the main action, which is always about Nash.

I think about the way Nash never mentions his mother. Maybe he's just got a problem with women. I'm sure that's what Suzanne will say when I finally steel myself to tell her the news. Part of me longs to call her now, just for the bliss of being able to moan – finally – about all the awful things about Nash I have put up with, and covered up, for so long. Then again, another part of me just wants to lie in bed and eat more shortbread. And have some space.

I don't care if it's a silly American word and people make quotation marks with their fingers whenever they say it. Space is good. Space is oxygen, blue skies, air, stars, clouds, freedom – and all the things I have lacked in my life in Swiss Cottage.

Brighton has a lot of space – especially here, on the edge of the sea, with the sky above you. You can gulp it in, wave your arms around in it, even throw your hat into it. Apart from the occasional old man with binoculars and a raincoat, or the odd waddling teenager with a pram, I am the only person on the pier. The sensation of being here without Nash – and not really having to worry about Nash – is incredible. It's so lovely to be here for once without his voice in my ear – drawling, cynical, smug. Instead, all I can hear are the seagulls crying for chips.

I suppose I am technically single now. A state both terrible and wonderful.

eight

I haven't talked about this bit with Nash, but I'm sure, dear Dr Ray Stein, that if my friends and family staged an intervention right now and told me it was okay to sleep with other people, I would go right ahead. The last time I had sex with Nash, just before Lisa's phone call, it was so try-hard that I wished we hadn't bothered. My old teddy was watching from the top of the chest of drawers and even he looked comatose with boredom.

But would anyone have me now, this afternoon, with my woolly hat, and my charity shop tights? I haven't looked in a mirror properly for months – mainly because Nash has ignored me for so long that I've convinced myself there's nothing much worth looking at.

Poor me. I should get out an invisible violin, make a sad face and play Brahms' Tragic Overture.

Instead, I play a game with myself from the days before I met Nash. I pick out ten men in the street and analyse whether I could sleep with any of them. If you find one, it cheers you up, and you feel it's worth putting on make-up again.

On my way to the station, my man-count goes like this:

1. Man with long woolly jumper, crocs, socks, yoga leggings and no underpants – no.
2. Man with Liverpool tracksuit top and fat girlfriend panting along behind him – no.
3. Respectable fifty-ish bloke whose hair is blowing sideways – no.
4. Bearded construction worker with sexually aroused pigeon following him – no.
5. Man with interesting glasses and suede shoes – yes if not gay.
6. Man looking at his own reflection in window – absolutely not.
7. Possibly gay man with shaved head and tiny dog with bondage-style black halter – nope.
8. Vaguely alright bloke with shaved head, denim jacket and iPod – yes, depending on contents of iPod.
9. Tall bloke in jeans with scruffy dark hair, sideburns, old tennis shoes and amazingly sexy, sincere, serious expression – yes, yes, yes!
10. Potential flasher in raincoat with (possible) wee stains looking like Peter Cook and Dudley Moore circa 1966 – no.

I cannot quite believe Number Nine. Surely he must have a ring on his finger – but he doesn't. Gay? Possibly. But I'll claim him as heterosexual because I've counted enough members of the other team for one day and statistically I feel I should be on the winning side.

Whoops. Number Nine has seen me staring at his hand. Oh bloody hell, he's definitely seen me staring at his hand, not to mention the rest of him, and now he's coming over to tell me to go away. I watch while he walks towards me. Suzanne would love those old tennis shoes he's wearing.

'Hi,' he says, with a funny, shy smile. He looks almost as embarrassed as I am.

'Oh. Hello.'

'I'm Joel. You must be Alice. I spotted your tartan umbrella. And the boots. I got in early, so I rang and your mum told me to look out for you.'

Oh my God. I thought Joel Templeton had a beard. I thought he was supposed to be spiritual. Most of all, I'm disappointed by the sudden transformation of the extremely promising Number Nine to a member of my family. Suddenly I tune in to what my cousin's saying.

'Your heart is breaking.'

What?

'Your heart is breaking,' he repeats. 'My mother had to leave my father too, so I know all about it. Do you want to go for a walk?'

'A walk?' I feel like a stunned mullet.

'A cup of tea then.'

'Oh yes.'

Joel grins. 'I knew the cup of tea thing would work!' He looks sideways at me. 'I remember that from when we lived in England. It doesn't matter what happens, if you put the kettle on then everything will be okay.'

We walk up Ship Street and find our way to the Lanes. I spot a newsagent.

'Can we just go in here for a minute?' I say.

I know Suzanne has banned me from endlessly checking for my story in Twad, but I can't help myself. While Joel stands over a pile of *Guardians* and tries to read them upside down, I flick quickly through the latest issue of Twad from back to front.

It's there! My God. Natasha looks fantastic. Like a beautiful, pregnant green tree. The old tweed Biba coat has become a sharp, chic, angular jacket – just as I imagined. I had no idea it would look this good in the photographs.

'Joel!' I squeak, and jab him in the ribs. 'It's me, this is me, this is mine!'

I realise I'm not making any sense, but Joel flips the magazine sideways and reads the credits in the margin. 'Dress and jacket by Vintage Alice. Alice Templeton.'

It's the first time I've seen my name in print. It looks so serious. So grown-up. So . . . not like me at all.

Joel makes me buy extra copies for Robyn, Helena and Mum and kisses me on the cheek. 'Congratulations, Alice.'

The kiss stays in my mind for the next hour – like a forgotten chocolate bar in your coat pocket that you keep coming back to.

We walk through the Lanes and it takes all the willpower I have not to keep checking my photo shoot in the magazine. It's not *my* shoot, of course. It's everybody's. But the clothes are mine, and that's all that matters.

'I think your phone's making a noise,' Joel says, once we're inside a café having a cup of tea.

I check it. It is a message from someone at the magazine wanting to know what she should do about all the phone calls and emails they've been receiving from pregnant women asking where they can buy my clothes.

'Look!'

I show Joel, who smiles in his nice, warm, crinkly way. He looks nothing like any of us – not remotely like a Templeton at all.

'Fantastic. You're in business.'

'I'm scared.'

'No, you're not. Come on, Alice.'

'But how am I going to do it?'

He grins at me. 'Move to Australia. Big fish, small pond. That's what Robyn said on the phone last night. "If she wants to make it in fashion, forget London – she should start in Sydney." You know, there's a fantastic view from Robyn's spare bedroom. That could be your sewing room.'

I blink at him. It's all too much, suddenly. Him, Australia, the pregnant women calling the magazine.

'I'll be in Sydney soon,' Joel reassures me. 'I'll help you.'

nine

I am moving to Australia next week. I have been for many walks with Joel in that time, and things that made no sense at all before suddenly add up.

Our favourite walk is an epic three-hour journey along the seafront to Rottingdean and up across the South Downs as far as Saltdean. There are sweeping views of both Sussex and the English Channel from the Downs and somehow it's been helping me think clearly for a change.

Joel and I have been rained on and confronted by stray sheep, but I've become like Goggles the fox terrier – I can't wait for my walks. Along the way, we've talked about men, women, commitment, marriage, love, hearts and space. I've never heard a man talk about hearts as much as my cousin Joel, but once he started me off, I found myself doing it too. After all this time it's a relief.

Joel is a bit mad, like my Uncle Roland, but sitting with him on a hill high above the English Channel has helped the stuck wheels in my brain start going round again. At last I know what I'm doing – and what I'm doing is gambling.

'It sounds like you've been living that way anyway,' Joel says. 'You took a punt on all those jobs. Even on living with Nash.'

'Yes.'

'So if you've been having small bets, why not switch to big bets for a change? What scares you more – going back to your old life or risking the lot?'

'I don't even have to think about that. Going back.'

'So there you are.' Joel smiles. 'You're better than me. I was with the same woman for five years, and I couldn't take any kind of gamble.'

'You broke up?'

'She left me. She said I was incapable of making a commitment and she was right. Just like my mum.'

In all the talks that Joel and I have had about life and love, it is his mother who comes up most of all. My parents never told me this, but Helena was already pregnant when she married Uncle Roland – with someone else's child. The child grew up to be Joel, but even now nobody knows who the father is. So, Joel's not my cousin. And yet he's *still* my cousin, which is the most confusing feeling in the world.

'So what now?' I prompt him.

He looks thoughtful. 'It's been a long time since I've been with anyone. I'm still open to it. But that's all.'

In India, Joel taught English to Tibetan refugees who had to leave their homes and families behind. He says he knows a lot about sitting with people who are in trouble. Right now, I want to sit with him on this hill forever. He has a low, quiet voice, and a steady, patient way of listening. It's such a novelty to be listened to, and looked at, properly. Two years with Nash has taught me to gabble everything quickly so I won't bore him; so I won't be interrupted. There's none of that with Joel. I feel as if I've known him for years, even though he left when I was a kid. I feel ridiculously at home with him.

The plan I have hatched with Joel is this: I am going to ring up Heidi and ask her about moving to Australia without Nash. I am also going to text Robyn in Bali to let her know what's going on. Then, if everything goes according to plan, I will get on the plane and go to Robyn's flat and stay in Bondi Beach until she gets back. After that I'll catch the train to Byron Bay and start work at Bark's with Danielle Coles. And *then* I'll have enough money to start Vintage Alice and make tweed jackets for pregnant women.

Joel runs me through the plan again and again, until it seems manageable.

'You're forgetting to breathe, Alice.'

'Sorry.'

He makes me do a yoga pose called the Child. He says it immediately makes you feel safer, no matter what's going on. The Tibetans do the Child pose all the time. You curl up in a ball like a hedgehog, with only your back showing. Joel does it first, right there on the hill, and I follow. If Nash could see me now he'd just walk away. I feel ridiculous at first, but after ten minutes of hedgehog, I have to admit that it's working.

'Good?' Joel asks.

'Alright. Actually, better than alright. Although I won't do it in sheep droppings next time.'

* * *

After our walk, we go to some tearooms in Brighton, eat cinnamon toast, because Joel is a vegetarian, and look at his old photos. We also talk about what might happen if I get to Australia and realise I hate it. I know I can always come back to England and live with my mother, but Joel doesn't think I'll hate Australia at all. He thinks I'll fall in love with it, because now that there's a big space in my heart, there is also room for something new to get in. I have honestly never heard any male in England talking like this.

My cousin is a funny combination of rules and no rules. He makes me feel free, because he makes me feel that everything is possible and nothing is off limits. I have also received several lectures on the evils of meat, however.

'Joel's just like Roland,' my mother said, after he told her off for hoarding plastic bags. 'They may not be blood relations, but he certainly inherited all that change-the-world thingy.'

Joel pushes photographs of places like Bega and Merimbula, Bunbury and Mole Creek across the table to show me how different Australia can be. Nash would put on a silly voice to pronounce all these place names, of course. Before he went to India to work for Tibetaid, Joel spent a year in a campervan driving all around Australia. There are numerous shots of him looking Number Nine-ish in shorts and little else, but as he is my cousin, I have naturally moved beyond all that.

Suzanne told me about a dating website called Single Sydney and I can't wait to try it, now that Joel's laptop is on Mum's dining-room table.

I try to stop thinking about men and concentrate on drinking my tea.

'If you get a chance to do the big Australian odyssey, then you have to go,' Joel says. 'I should have done it years ago. Maybe I'll do it again when I'm back. But I really just want to get back to Bellingen. Grow some strawberries. Get a cow again.' Before he left for India, he bought five acres of land on the Bellinger River, which is between Sydney and Brisbane. He says the river is beautiful. 'You can swim in it and drink it. You should go up there and pitch a tent on my property,' he encourages me.

'What do you think of England?' I ask him.

'Well, I was born here.' He laughs at me. 'I really like it. Why?'

'Australians seem not to like it. They come here to work, but once they arrive in London, they just moan about it.'

'That's because they haven't tried the cinnamon toast in Brighton,' Joel says. 'What do you think of England?'

'It's a bit like my boyfriend. I tried and tried to make it work, but it was no good.'

'Are you over it?'

'Nash? I think so.'

'Are you over England is what I meant.'

'Oh, yes. That bit's easy. I went backwards and forwards and now I've gone back to the start. Back to the way I felt before, when I really *knew* I was ready to go.'

My mother rings. She has finished listening to *The Archers* and is worried that we've got lost.

'It's fine,' I tell her. 'Joel and I went for a walk along the South Downs. We're just having a cup of tea.'

'Isn't he nice?' she says, not waiting for an answer. 'He told me the first thing he did when he landed at Heathrow was to shave his beard off in the loo. He reminds me of you, Alice, doing a thing like that – although I couldn't say why.'

'We'll be home in time for supper,' I tell her. 'We walked for miles. We're having something to eat now but I'm sure we'll be hungry.'

Joel and I work our way through the cinnamon toast, and he admires the low plastered ceilings in the tearooms. 'Like the ceilings you see in Beatrix Potter drawings,' he says, and shows me his own notebook, which is full of pencil drawings of Indian birds and rough sketches of Hindu goddesses.

The back of the notebook has become his address book, because he says that since he's been travelling he's run out of space. He shows me his parents' addresses in America and Jamaica, so I can write them down, and as he flicks through the book I realise there are hundreds of names in there. Joel seems to be friends with the whole world. And his friends seem to move around – like him. Their addresses are repeatedly scratched out, as they change from Australia, to India, New Zealand, Thailand and back again.

He shakes out his bag to find photographs of his parents, so he can show my mother later.

'Your mother's cut her hair,' I say.

'Yeah, it's really short now. It used to be down to her waist.'

'Your dad still looks so much like my dad.'

'That's his old house in San Francisco. He's moved into this great apartment now.'

After the photographs, out come more tennis shoes, seagull feathers, little velvet pouch bags and a plastic bag full of tiny orange seeds.

'What are they?' I ask.

'Invisibility seeds. The Tibetans use them to become invisible when they escape from China across the border. They've been blessed in a special ceremony. You carry them with you and the guards don't see you. They were given to me before I left. I thought they might come in useful.'

I realise how relieved I am that Nash isn't here right now. There are some conversations that can never happen in his presence, and this is one of them.

'What do you mean, invisible?'

'Well, it's an interesting thing,' Joel says. 'Think about the people here now – in this tearoom. How many of them can you actually say you've seen?'

'About one,' I tell him – a curly-haired child in the corner who looks a bit like Nash.

'Technically speaking then, everybody else in here is invisible to you. That's what the seeds do. The Chinese guards see the Tibetans, but they don't. It's a very strange phenomenon, unique to their culture.'

'Why would *you* need to become invisible?' I ask him.

'Well . . .' He gives me an embarrassed half-smile. 'I like being alone.'

Joel makes a quick sketch of the ceilings in the tearooms, then we walk back to my mother's house. We try to ring Robyn on the way, because Joel has promised me he'll be there for moral support when I tell her about my mad new plan. When we get through to her hotel in Bali though, she's out.

'Probably clubbing,' Joel says.

I wonder what Nash is doing, in Swiss Cottage. Maybe he's at the pub with The Believers – and Lisa. I'm trying not to think about Sarah.

Joel taps the side of my head. 'Stop thinking.'

'All I ever do is imagine what could go wrong.'

'Imagine what might go right for you, Alice. Come on. You're at the beginning of the biggest trip of your life. Don't weigh yourself down by packing all your old head baggage.'

My cousin has a strange accent – half Australian, half something else. He also has a funny, rhythmic way of speaking. When he talks to me, he looks straight at me, as if he's trying to read me – as if I'm a book.

'It's funny that you've got invisibility seeds,' I say, as we begin the long walk up the hill, past a row of doctors' surgeries, to my mother's house.

'Why's that?'

'I want the opposite of them. Visibility seeds. I suppose the Tibetans don't really need those.'

'They have something that performs a similar function. Why? Do you feel invisible?'

'It was when I was reading that book I was telling you about – *Should I Stay Or Should I Go?*. I found this question about *mattering* – about being seen, being important. And I realised Nash hardly ever saw me at all, except in relation to him. It was like this bell going off in my head. So now I want to be visible again. That's all.'

'You don't need any seeds,' Joel says. 'Here . . .'

He snaps a photograph of me with his mad old-fashioned 1970s Polaroid camera. He picked it up from a stall in Mumbai, along with a shoebox full of old film. It must be over a year since anyone took a photo of me.

'Instant gratification,' I say, watching the developing photograph slide out of the bottom of the camera. 'I used to love these.'

'So did my dad. I always promised myself I'd have one of my own when I grew up. The white border's the great thing,' Joel says. 'And these Polaroids have a way of capturing light that you don't see in other cameras.'

I sit on someone's wall to get my breath back – the hill is impossible – and wait while the photograph dries.

'There.' Joel hands it to me. 'You're a very long way from invisible.'

He has made me look wonderful. My hair is golden-white and my face looks pure and demure. It's a lovely photograph. He takes it back and puts it in his pocket.

'Nearly there,' he says, and swings his bag over his back again and strides off. He is much fitter than me. My legs are beginning to ache from the three-hour walk.

We get home to find my mother has also been looking through old Templeton family photographs. She is surrounded by them, all over the sitting-room floor.

'I'm looking for pictures of you and Robyn when you were children,' she tells Joel, getting up to kiss him on the cheek. 'You probably haven't seen them before. They're all Polaroids. Roland and Helena used to post them to us.'

'Fantastic. I'd love to see them. I keep my photos in scrapbooks,' Joel says. 'Then you can put other stuff in – like letters, or tickets, or pressed flowers.' He shows her the large notebook in his bag, with the torn-off maps and scraps of Indian sari fabric he's glued in, along with some handwritten diary entries.

'I do like a scrapbook,' my mother says. 'Oh Alice, would you mind helping me with supper?'

I follow her into the kitchen and she closes the door.

'Do you think Joel may be gay?' she asks, looking worried.

I laugh at her. 'Because of the scrapbook? Mum! He had a girlfriend for years.'

'Oh, thank goodness.'

'I've sorted things out, by the way.'

'How?' My mother looks as if she is about to burst. 'How did you sort things out?'

'I'm going to Australia. I'm leaving when I was supposed to leave – next week.'

There. It's out.

'Oh, dear. I have lip wobble,' Mum says, trying to keep her mouth in place with her finger. She sits down on the kitchen chair and allows herself a few seconds of crying time, then she sniffs and wipes her eyes on an oven glove.

'I'm glad you're going to Sydney after all,' she says, jutting out her jaw. 'Joel is absolutely right. Now, let me tell you what I've done about Nash.'

'What?'

'I've paid him off,' she says quickly. 'I used your father's emergency money, and now you need never hear from him again. Unless you want to, of course.'

'Mum!'

'It's all done, and the rest of Dad's money has gone into one of those accounts where they forbid you to touch it. So that's that.'

'*Mum!*'

'And you are not to waste any more time putting money in jam jars for me. It's forgotten.'

She turns her back, bends down and checks the roast duck in the oven.

I know there's no point in arguing. When my mother's mind is made up, it's impossible to persuade her otherwise. She's wrong about the jam jars though. For every week that I work at Bark's of Byron Bay, I'll put half the money aside for her. She desperately needs new shoes.

'I hope Joel likes his meat well done,' she says, prodding the duck with a skewer.

'He's vegetarian. Remember?'

She nearly drops the duck. 'Oh my giddy aunt!' I scoop the roast potatoes out and put them in a bowl with some salad leaves.

I go back to Joel and find him sitting cross-legged on the floor in the sitting room, sorting my parents' old photographs into something resembling chronological order. They begin with my grandmother in the 1930s as a child, and go right up to my first Christmas with Nash.

I made our Christmas cake that day. It was chocolate, and I made the snow out of real coconut. Other than that, I can't remember what I was thinking or feeling in that photograph. I look nauseatingly smug to have Nash by my side. I also look as if I'm waiting for my future self to tap me on the shoulder and tell me everything I couldn't possibly have known then.

'I'm daydreaming in that one,' I tell Joel. 'I'm not even there.'

'Look at this.' He points to a photo of him dressed up as a Goth. 'That was my birthday party in Sydney. I thought I was Nick Cave and all the members of The Cure at the same time.'

'The black lipstick is good.'

'Here's one from America, a couple of years later. See the difference? Before deep-fried doughnuts and after deep-fried doughnuts.'

'You have a lovely mullet too. Is that Robyn standing behind you?'

'Oh yeah. She had the pink fringe happening then.'

'Your parents let you try everything.'

'Yeah.' Joel raises his eyebrows.

I wonder if that's one of the reasons he has so many rules. Not only does he refuse to eat meat, he also boycotts television news, credit cards and deodorant.

I've seen what he uses for deodorant. It's a crystal rock. Despite this, he always smells fantastic. He chews on Indian cardamom seeds, which he keeps in a little bag in his pocket, and uses some kind of soap that makes him smell of lemons.

My mother brings in supper, and then she and I spend the rest of the night looking for photographs of all the other Templetons in the family to show Joel. We discover an ancient picture of Roland and Hippy Helena at their barefoot wedding in a park in London, then one of Robyn as a baby.

Joel asks if he can organise some copies before he flies to Bangkok – his last stop before Sydney – and then says his jetlag is beginning to kick in, so we let him go to bed.

When my mother's gone to bed too, I borrow Joel's laptop and look at the Australian dating website Suzanne told me about, Single Sydney. What are Australian men really like? I've heard so many differing opinions that it's hard to know what to believe. The site promises there are over a million single people waiting to meet me.

Hurrah! Then I look at the first four men and change my mind.

One calls himself Mr Paradox. In actual fact, his name should be Mr Dickhead.

One has a full and varied life – except he doesn't.

One says his mother-in-law put a curse on him.

One has gum-diseased teeth.

Oh God. It's like hurtling back to the late 1990s all over again. Single life on the internet. Bad photos. Dreadful fake names. Boring hobbies. I knew it would be like this if I left Nash.

Interesting things happen when you go down an age bracket though. Australian men in their twenties are a completely different proposition. There's a Piscean who likes Robert de Niro and parachuting. He is inarguably gorgeous. There's a 177-centimetre tall surfboard-maker who has no baggage and likes crap jokes and red wine. There's another 177-centimetre tall person – a twenty-five-year-old art teacher who hates Quentin Tarantino films (yes!) and loves giving massages (yes! yes!).

The photographs all seem to be taken on the brightest of sunny days, and in two of them I can see spectacular beaches in the background. When I go to bed, I catch myself humming.

ten

The next morning, Joel turns on his laptop and finds the dating site bookmarked in the margin. I go pink and pretend I was looking for Suzanne.

He grins. 'Oh, she'll love Australian men.'

I farewell my mother for the second-last time. The next time I see her, I will – hopefully – be at Heathrow with my luggage, my sewing machine, my passport and my Australian visa.

'Bye, darling.' She kisses me on the cheek.

Then she puts a bar of chocolate in both Joel's coat pockets and makes him promise to write when he gets to Bangkok. 'I'm going to get on The Google,' she warns him. 'So you'll be hearing from me.'

On the way to the station, Joel gives me one final pep talk about Australia. Even though we're both going to London, we'll be on different trains – me on the fast train to Victoria, and him on the next train to Bedford, where he's going to see some old friends from India.

'What you're about to do would scare a lot of other people,' he tells me, 'but you're going to have the trip of your life. Just go into Australia House, look like you mean it, and get every single thing you need to do this journey.'

'Every single thing I need,' I echo.

'I'm going to see you in Sydney,' he promises me, kissing me on the cheek. 'I may be off the air for a while, but I'll be there.'

'Thank you. Thank you so much, Joel. You have no idea.'

'Don't change your mind or I'll blardy murda ya,' he says, suddenly sounding very Australian.

On the train from Brighton to Victoria, I feel as if I have already left forever. I am detaching myself from England even as it disappears behind me through the train window.

My handbag is full of scribbled notes and sketches from my cousin, and the names of people he wants me to get in contact with once I reach Australia. Many of the names are male, and I can't help but wonder if somewhere on this rollcall of Joel's most trusted and long-established friends, there may be someone who is right for me. It was nice seeing Mr Pisces and Mr 177-centimetres Tall on the website last night – it gave me hope – but still. Once I've begun my new single life in Sydney I'm going to need all the help I can get.

I check my texts. Heidi Coles is expecting to see me for lunch at the same café near the Strand where Nash and I met all those weeks ago. She says she's going to tell me more about Bark's of Byron Bay, because Danielle gave her a briefing session over the weekend. After that, she says, we can whip through all my last questions about the big move.

I feel guilty because I haven't told her that Nash and I have broken up. I'm counting on her being Nice Heidi and coming to my rescue one last time.

We meet outside the café at one and I put an envelope with a cheque in her hand and give her the largest bottle of champagne I have been able to find at the train station.

'Oh, wow,' she says in her Australian accent.

'Nash and I didn't actually celebrate in the end,' I tell her, as we find a table. 'But thanks.'

'Thank *you*. But why didn't you celebrate?'

'We split up. I'm going to Australia by myself.'

'Faark!' Her cup of coffee stops halfway to her mouth.

'I left him. He slept with his ex-wife. And he wanted to stay here anyway. He got a new job in London at the last minute and changed his mind. Anyway, it was always bad with us – you know what we were like.'

'You poor girl!'

'It's okay. I'm okay. But I need to ask you – do you think I can still go? I've read the small print on the paperwork, and so has Mum, and my cousin Joel – but we need to check.'

'Oooh,' Heidi says. 'Hard one.'

'Please don't say that.'

'Hard one, but I think you'll be okay. You were fast-tracked anyway, right?'

'Yes.'

'Okay. What you need now is a fax from Danielle saying she'll go guarantor for you, as your employer. I'll talk to her. You can't be part-time though. You're going to have to be full-time. Full wage. All that stuff. Shit. You must be flying off soon. When are you going?'

'Friday.'

'What does Nash say?'

'He doesn't know. And I don't care anyway. He can't stop me, can he?'

'Not unless he physically throws himself under the wheels of the plane. No, they're not interested in him any more. They're only going to be interested in you.'

'Am I enough on my own?'

Heidi gives me her customary kind look and I immediately panic, because she has seen my file at Australia House and I know I am not enough – not by a long shot. I have made pottery, sold candles, cleaned houses, cooked toasted sandwiches, walked dogs, made soap, played a nun in an advert, sold vintage clothing and even been a woman with a key in my back, but I am still not enough for Australia – not even with my clothes in Suzanne's magazine and Vera Van Der Meer's business card in my purse.

'Shall I tell you something about Australia?' Heidi says, when she sees my face. 'Everything is upside down there. Nothing is the same as it is anywhere else. So just when you think you can predict what's going to happen in Australia, or what Australians are going to do about anything, you can't. Think of the impossible, and in Australia it's possible.'

'So you're saying that even though it makes sense that they'd turn me down, they might say yes?'

'Exactly. Life is the other way around over there. Like a platypus. It's a furry thing with a pouch that lays eggs and swims. What's that all about? So what I'm saying is, nothing will be what you expect. Expect the worst and you'll probably get the best.'

'Really?'

'Rilly.'

Heidi joins the queue at the counter for sandwiches and coffee, but I don't follow her because I'm feeling too sick with nerves to eat.

While I wait for her, I try to recapture the way I felt when I was sitting on the hill with Joel, looking over the South Downs towards the sea and talking about how everything was possible, and everything was meant to be, and everything would work.

I flick through an old newspaper covered in food stains. I see that we are expecting floods again and David Beckham's foot has not yet healed.

I remember Joel's photographs of those beautiful places in Australia – Merimbula and Mole Creek and Kakadu and Alice Springs. All that space. All that light, all that freedom.

If they won't have me in Australia, I'll go to Wales. Or Canada. But I know one thing – I am never again cramming myself into a London train full of sardine-humans the way I did this morning, so I can go all the way to a café where the only vacant table is one covered in other people's used tissues. I'm wearing my whitest of white shirts today, and just looking at the table makes me feel filthy.

The queue has come to a stop because there's a flap on behind the counter. The baristas are confused about something – and I'm fed up with that too. Everyone in this country seems to be confused about almost everything all the time – just like the post office at Christmas. No wonder I get headaches living here. Every question I ever need answered has to go through to a call centre. Nobody has a name. Nobody knows anything, and nobody takes responsibility. Everyone is on hold, and everything is on hold.

My God. I really do have to get out. I can't stay in this relationship with England any longer – she doesn't deserve to have me hanging around moaning about her. There are plenty of Australians here to do that.

Heidi pulls a 'What can you do?' face at me as some of the people behind her in the queue tut theatrically and walk out. I feel guilty. This is her lunch hour, she must be starving, and I've made her come to meet me in the worst café in the world.

My phone rings. It's an unlisted number. Lisa? I hope not. I'm not sure I could cope with her now. I take a deep breath and take the call – but it's not Lisa, it's Robyn. She's ringing me from Bali in the middle of the night because she can't sleep. She says she only just got the message I left at her hotel, because she's been on a surfing trip.

'I'm really sorry, Robyn,' I tell her, as I watch Heidi stand on one foot and then the other in the queue.

'What?'

'Nash and I have broken up. I want to come over there, but I'm not sure I can. I'm with Heidi Coles now – the woman from Australia House. We're trying to sort it all out.'

'Put her on,' Robyn snaps. Suddenly, she sounds like an Australian sergeant major.

I take the phone over to Heidi, bumping into all the people who are storming out. Whatever is taking place behind the counter has now assumed epic proportions – one barista is sitting on the floor with her head between her knees. Perhaps she's just been put on hold at a call centre in India and is now trying to suffocate herself.

'Crazy.' Heidi tuts. 'Hey, who's on your phone?'

'My cousin Robyn.'

A rapid conversation between them follows, spoken entirely in Australian.

'Yeah,' Heidi says. 'He's one thermos short of a picnic. Definitely. What? Bugger that. Well, why doesn't she get her arse into gear and just do it? Yeah, well, *he's* as mad as a cut snake. Rilly? That's rooted. Yeah, todarly.'

The remaining queue is now listening, trying to decode this strange new language spoken at great speed, but Heidi doesn't notice. She just talks faster, standing on one foot, and then the other. It's quite a different accent, and a different vocabulary, from the one she uses with English people.

'Yeah, well, Robyn,' she says. '*If* she bungs it on then it should be okay. Yeah. Well, it's a one-horse town, for sure. Yeah. Yeah. Up to my eyeballs. All right then. Not this little black duck. Well. No worries. Okay then. See ya later.'

She ends the call and smiles at me. 'I don't think you realised your cousin was a lesbian.'

The queue reels.

'What?' I say.

'Robyn's a lesbian and so is the woman who happens to be the director of Australian Immigration. And she's seriously got the hots for your cousin. So we both reckon –'

'Yes?'

'You're totally fine.'

'Really?'

'Rilly. It's just going to take one phone call. The only thing is, when you start the job at Byron Bay, my Auntie Danielle's got this bugger of a dog called Mr Chang. He's a Pekinese. Permanent weekend resident. Watch out for him. He comes with his own incontinence cushion.'

I smile at her. Then the smile turns into a laugh.

'I told you Australia wasn't like anywhere else,' Heidi says. 'Now are we going to get a proper lunch or *what*?'

Whenever my mother's forced to drive The Car to London up the M23, she gets so nervous that she has to take a herbal tranquilliser from the health food shop. Her parting gesture at Heathrow Airport was to put two in a plastic bag and slip them in my coat pocket. That was about eight hours ago. My coat is now rolled into a sausage shape behind my head and I am wide awake on Flight KA338 to Sydney, having been comatose – in a lovely, natural, herbal way, of course – for most of the trip.

The first thing I'm going to do in Sydney is ring Mum to find out what's in the pills. They must contain some kind of general anaesthetic because I have no memory of take-off beyond a recorded announcement (first in Korean, then in English) about storing my hand luggage underneath the seat in front of me or in the overhead locker. The flight attendant pronounced this as 'overhead rocker', which Nash would have laughed at – but I've really got to stop thinking about Nash.

I'm starving. When was dinner? The Korean woman in the window seat is asleep, her head pressed against the window. There's a spare seat between us – which I suppose should have been Nash's – and it's piled high with her magazines (all in Korean so there is no point in asking if I can borrow them), her moisturiser and her bottled water.

I summon up the courage to press the seat button with a cartoon on it showing a triangular woman and, amazingly enough, a non-triangular flight attendant appears three-quarters of an hour later.

Everyone else in the cabin is asleep. Most of them seem to be Korean. We are stopping at Seoul to refuel and then flying straight through to Sydney. The total journey time is twenty-five hours – the longest time I have ever spent sitting in a single seat. I suppose my four suitcases and my poor old sewing machine are down there somewhere in the hold. The excess baggage charge was enormous. It was London's last big cash extraction before I was finally able to say goodbye.

My mother was so zonked on herbal tranquillisers at the airport that she actually seemed to move like the real Lady Penelope. (Nash would have been very pleased.) When she waved goodbye, her arm jerked up and down as if it was on strings, and her little legs in their beige trousers seemed to jerk around, controlled by hidden wires. I hope she's alright now. I have to stop worrying about her. I suppose she just drove back to Hove and went straight to bed.

I look at the empty seat and wonder if Nash has found out about my Girl's Own Adventure yet.

While we were waiting for my flight, Mum forced me to go to an internet kiosk and sign her up to Hotmail, so she can enter the wonderful world of what she still insists is called The Google. I gave her Nash's email address as well as my own, so who knows – maybe he's already been informed of my great escape by my mother (email address: pennytempleton1945) on her first foray into cyberspace. She'd do it for the sheer thrill of shocking him.

The herbal tranquillisers have had a powerful effect on my central nervous system. I feel incredibly calm and detached about the events of the last two weeks – although I also have a cluster headache on the left side of my skull. Of course, that may be Suzanne's fault. Her parting gift to me was a bottle of vodka, which we consumed without the necessary twenty-five glasses of water and four vitamin B tablets to negate the alcohol content.

The flight attendant brings me some aspirin, and something that sounds like Bing Bang Yap with some extremely salty soup. I wolf it all down and try not to be annoyed about the man in front who has pushed his seat all the way back, into my knees.

If my mother hasn't told Nash about my trip by email, he'll find out for himself soon enough when he telephones Australia House. I love the fact that he never even contemplated the possibility I would use my ticket. If he has found out, I expect he'd already be predicting my imminent return to Richard and Michael. I can just hear him now, being smug about me:

'Alice'll be back by Easter.'

'My ex will probably be back when she runs out of money.'

'Alice doesn't know anyone over there. She won't like it.'

Lisa has left The Believers. I found out yesterday when I rang Richard to offer him my old chest of drawers. He asked me how I felt about it and I had to say that I had no idea. And that's when he told me Sarah was joining instead.

'We're two down, after losing you and Lisa, so Nash thought we should maybe get Sarah on board.'

'Of course he did.'

I try to forget about Sarah and Nash and get out my G'day Australia pack instead.

There's a scary back section with a list of dangerous spiders and snakes and a full inventory of sharks and jellyfish. Nash always said the spiders would put me off Australia more than anything else, and although I hate to admit it, he's right. The section's called 'Everything you wanted to know about biting, stinging things but were too paralysed with fear to ask'. At least, that's what Nash thought it should be called. The official title, of course, is: 'Everything Australian that can sneak up behind you and cause agonising death when you're on a picnic'.

The sneakiest creature of all seems to be a bluebottle. Not a character in my father's old *Goon Show* tapes, but a slimy jellyfish that is, in fact, blue and likes to travel in packs. It can be found all along the east coast of Australia. Pretty much where I'm going then. I think I'll stick to the swimming pool at Bondi Beach with the three old people in it. At least they're unlikely to have detachable blue tentacles.

I have a close look at the pointy-headed red-bellied black snake. It is the Morticia Addams of the snake world. After that, I look at the king brown. If it bites you, you will die. It can be aggressive, the chart says, and has been known to give chase. Bloody hell. *Where* does it give chase? Up the escalators at Sydney Airport?

The book has a full-colour wall chart of all these disgusting creatures. God knows why you'd want to stick that on the fridge. The chart says the redback spider hides underneath loo seats and has killed about a dozen people. I suppose once you've been bitten on the bottom, you're too embarrassed to call for help so death is inevitable.

The chart says that the funnel-web spider also likes bathrooms, but particularly bedrooms, and has achieved the same evil spider serial-killer tally. It also says that one of the symptoms of being bitten is 'visible signs of anxiety'. Funny about that. Surely, if you were bitten, you'd just kick back on the sofa with a large martini and *The Best of Olivia Newton-John*?

I wish Suzanne was here so I could show her the chart.

The woman next to me is snoring, but it's a comforting sound – a bit like those dolphin noises people sometimes play to send themselves to sleep.

Apparently, the Australian taipan snake's venom is so deadly that unless you're near a hospital, you may as well give up. It also turns out that everything Nash told me about snake bites is wrong. You don't wee on your skin to wash off the poison. No, no, you use your shirt as a tourniquet, then crawl off screaming in agony with a snake hanging off your leg and your best shirt from Top Shop ruined.

I think about Joel, who has been everywhere in Australia and is still perfectly healthy. He got away with it – so will I.

There is no option available to me now except mad optimism. If I allow my anxiety about Nash, Sarah, Mum, money, Bark's of Byron Bay, Mr Chang the incontinent

Pekinese, Robyn and high-powered lesbians in the Department of Australian Immigration to be channelled into a sudden panic about snakes, I will not sleep for the rest of the flight.

The flight attendant brings me a cut-up orange and an after-dinner mint humbug. Because the man in front of me has been mean enough to push his seat back into my knees, I do the same unkind thing to the woman behind me. Her mouth is open and she has on a free eye mask so I doubt she'll notice.

I check the time, and then I check my heart – the heart Joel spoke to me so much about – to see how it's faring. On a scale of one to ten, how much do I miss Nash at the moment and how jealous do I feel about Sarah now that she's replaced me on the quiz team?

I think about it long and hard. I probably miss Nash two out of ten and am jealous of Sarah one out of ten. Good. That may change at some point, but at least I can go back to sleep now.

I put on my free eye mask – the one that makes everyone who wears it look like the Lone Korean Ranger – and pass out.

eleven

When I wake up again, we are at Seoul Airport, and the cluster headache is back, with added heart palpitations. There are forms to fill in and complicated instructions in heavily accented Korean English to listen to. It seems we are to disembark through something, then get back on again at the other end of something, but I have no idea what it is.

On the form, I have to tell them what my job is. I only wish I knew. Fashion designer? Key woman? Potter? Candle-maker? International youth hostel cleaning supervisor? In the end, I put boarding kennel attendant, which is what Heidi told me to say.

It's nice to be somewhere that's not Swiss Cottage, although Seoul Airport is a herbal tranquilliser-induced blur. There seem to be lots of noodles, lots of bright lights, and lots of very short women, as both the sink and the mirror in the loos have been pitched at Toytown height. I can only see the bottom half of my face, which is pale, English, scared and spotty, and some of the Bing Bang Yap, which is decorating my T-shirt in hard brown lumps.

I change the last of my English pounds into Australian dollars. I hand over a tenner, wondering how long it will take before I forget what it looks like. I don't think I'll miss it. What's orange, brown and disappears as soon as you leave the house? The man behind the counter makes me fill in yet another Korean-English form, and gives me two Australian notes (two!), which have the Queen's head on one side (my mother would be pleased) but fail to feel truly like money because they are blue.

I now have $20 for my £10, and some gold coins. It's like the miracle of the loaves and fishes. I already know what I can buy with $20 in Australia. I've memorised the prices on their supermarket websites.

One tin of Milo, the strange national cocoa.

One pair of Razzamatazz black tights (no more donkey charity shop for me!).

One copy of the *Australian Women's Weekly*, which comes out monthly.

One steak.

If this was England, I could only get the steak and the tights. I already feel better. Or I would, if I wasn't stuffed full of Bing Bang Yap and my mother's herbal drugs.

I sleepwalk back onto the plane with everyone else, apart from the smokers, who are puffing away in a small glass room halfway down the corridor.

On the final leg to Sydney, I do my jam jar sums again. Each time, I slash more off my spending budget, to the point where I appear to be living on free muesli bar samples from the supermarket. Nevertheless, if I start work at Bark's at the end of this month, and stick with the dogs until Christmas (or similar – say, acting in a bad Australian soap opera, or making toasted sandwiches in rubber gloves), I will be fine. I can pay Mum back, she can buy new shoes, and the threat of poverty will go away. At least I don't have to worry about the debt collectors any longer. I've heard they can follow you anywhere, even to a mud hut in the Australian outback.

I miss Mum already. But if I start crying now, I'll never stop. I must remember Joel's final pep talk. I am about to do something that would scare a lot of other people. I have to summon up all the energy I have and use it.

I miss him already too. It's ridiculous. I've only known him properly for a couple of weeks. He's like one of those jackets you try on and can't forget.

One of the many things I liked about Joel was the way he took my World War II library book seriously. The one with instructions about creating your own kitchen garden and making spinach pie.

'I had some spinach growing on my land in Bellingen,' he said. 'I think it's a great idea.'

Joel used to own a house cow as well – although he doesn't actually have a house on his property, just a two-man tent, so she was more of a campsite cow. She was a Friesian called Sunny who gave eight gallons of milk a day, enough for him to make cheese, yoghurt and butter. Joel said that the neighbours' children used to ride Sunny around on the property in exchange for mooing duties.

House cows like you to moo at them apparently. They also like to have their heads rubbed and their backs scratched. I'm sure they would like it if you bought them a foot spa as well. At one point Joel was making thousands of dollars by buying calves from the saleyards, rearing them for six weeks on Sunny's milk, then selling them on. He said it's what turned him into a vegetarian though, so eventually he made sure the only cows he traded in were for milking, not eating.

I am so tired now, I can't possibly do any more provisional budgeting in my head. But – imagine if Joel let me camp on his property in Bellingen and keep a house cow. I think I'd be quite good at mooing duties. It couldn't be too different from arguing with Nash. Joel's already offered to buy me the cow as a late Christmas present. And I know it's ridiculous, but I can't stop getting excited about it. Perhaps all I will need, in the end, is a cow, a wartime recipe book and a garden full of spinach. That would be worth any amount of mooing.

I close my eyes. I can't wear my Korean Lone Ranger eye mask again, it makes my eyelids sweat. Then, suddenly, we are in Sydney and the flight attendant who was so nice and brought me the aspirins and the Bing Bang Yap is poking me with her sharpest middle fingernail.

'We are here,' she says.

I look around me. All the blinds in the plane are up, and there are blankets, old newspapers, abandoned eye masks, empty water bottles – the detritus of fed-up, bored passengers – over every seat. There are Korean chocolate wrappers on the floor and used ear plugs scattered in the aisles. Who'd be a flight attendant?

Because I am moving to Australia on a work permit, I have to answer more questions than anybody else in the arrivals hall. Have I been in a rural area with foot-and-mouth recently? No – unless you count the Swiss Cottage laundrette. What are my reasons for coming to Australia?

Oh my God, I can't answer that. It was hard enough when Richard and Michael were asking me about it in the pub.

I try to work out what is wrong with the world, and realise that everyone is speaking Australian.

'I'm flat out,' my taxi driver says, when I finally haul my suitcases off the conveyor belt and fall into the back of his cab. God, it's so bright outside. The sun seems to have been turned up since London.

'Why are you flat out?' I ask, trying to be polite.

'Ah, it's always like this, from Australia Day to Labour Day. Where are you from?'

'England.'

'Where in England?'

'Swiss Cottage.'

'Never heard of it. Is it somewhere near Switzerland?'

He turns the radio up so we can both listen to a talk show that consists of people ringing up and saying, 'I don't want to make a nuisance of myself', then proceeding to do so. They seem to be speaking a foreign language. Everyone is deeply concerned about the Shark's groin injury and what it will do to the Broncos next season. There's an ad for Carlton Draught, pronounced Caaaaaarldon Draaaaaught, as if someone's about to be sick. There's a lot of talk about something called Acker Dacker, which I eventually realise is AC/DC and people are voting for their favourite song.

The sun still hasn't been turned down. Joel said the light was dazzling in Sydney, but I had no idea. The buildings seem newer and cleaner, or just painted in paler colours, so the sunshine bounces off the walls and back onto the pavements, which have tiny glittery bits in them, like tinsel.

My taxi driver is deeply flatulent, as Nash would say. He must have been eating cabbage for breakfast. He turns the radio up even more, because another caller who doesn't want to make a nuisance of herself is talking about lesbian single mothers. I immediately think of Robyn, and am glad she's lying on a beach in Bali at the moment and not in the back of the taxi with me. I wonder if she wants to be a lesbian single mother.

'Yeah, well, if they want to get up the duff, that's no business of mine, but half the time they're drunk as a skunk when they make these decisions,' the caller says.

'Good on ya, mate,' the announcer says.

The taxi crawls through traffic and I watch the red numbers on the meter go up and up. So much for my two $10 notes.

'How much will it cost to get to Bondi?' I ask my driver.

'About three lobsters in this traffic.'

'Thank you.'

I suppose a lobster is a $20 note, which is orange. Either that or he wants me to pay him in luxury seafood.

I stare out of the windows and recognise bits and pieces of Australian life from the television and the internet. There's a giant poster for Milo. Good. I must be in the right country. The trees look familiar. They are definitely the kinds of trees you see on television. Flaky, patchy and brown with dusty green leaves. I look up, like the idiot I am, in the hope of seeing a koala. I hope the taxi driver didn't see me do that.

Is this a country I can stay in? Will this really be my new home forever and ever? It's like trying to decide about men. Within two hours of meeting Nash, I knew I wanted to be with him. But look where that got me. Maybe I should take a bit longer to decide about the rest of my life.

'How long are ya here for?' my driver asks.

'Not sure yet. I've got a job in Byron Bay.'

'Beautiful up there,' he says. 'Who ya gonna support in the cricket?'

'England. Australia. England.'

Oh God, I don't even like cricket.

'Better support Pakistan then,' he says, and makes himself laugh so much that another cabbagey emission drifts into the back seat.

At last, we reach Robyn's flat. She lives at 6/10 Cooper Street, North Bondi. I am disappointed that we don't pass Bondi Beach on the way, but I trust it's out there somewhere, with its packs of surfers and its avocado and scrambled egg breakfasts. I give the driver his lobsters and get a handful of change back. I already feel poor again.

The flat is on the third floor of the modern white building I remember from Robyn's DVD. The carpet is new. There are pot plants outside most of the doors. The staircase doesn't smell of wee. This is definitely not Swiss Cottage.

I have had Robyn's keys clenched in my hand since I got in the taxi. When I push open the door to her flat, I am dazzled by light all over again. Just when you think your eyes have got used to it, there's another blinding flash. No wonder everyone here wears sunglasses all the time. The old people wear sunglasses that wrap around at the sides, so they all look like villains in some science-fiction film.

The flat is completely white. There are white floorboards, white rugs, white bookshelves, white vases with white plastic flowers and even a gigantic white leather sofa. I don't remember it being quite this pristine in Robyn's DVD but I suppose she's tidied all her stuff away. Or maybe she doesn't have any stuff. I know Joel doesn't.

What do I do first? Drink? Eat? Go to the loo? Put the spa on? Make some phone calls? Watch Australian television? Fall in a heap on the bed and go into a prolonged withdrawal from herbal tranquillisers?

I trip over a pile of huge green plastic rubbish bags on the floor and find a note stapled to them. *Please help yourself to this and give the rest to St Vincent de Paul*, Robyn has written.

Who is St Vincent de Paul? I picture a friend of hers – Italian, bearded, pious – who has a secret interest in women's clothing. Oh, hang on. There's an address and a phone number. It appears to be a charity shop, on Oxford Street, in Paddington. That's two familiar names from London already – another thing that amused Nash about the big Australian wall map. When Australians aren't labelling everything twice, it appears they're pinching English place names.

I look through the bags. It's like Christmas all over again, although a lot better than the one I had in Swiss Cottage. Robyn is throwing out a travel hairdryer, an unopened electric toothbrush and a half-full bottle of expensive shampoo. No Arabic instructions for her. She is also chucking a pedometer, a shopping basket with a tiny hole in it, a tennis racket with Sydney Gay and Lesbian Mardi Gras stickers all over it and a black crepe Jigsaw skirt. I try it against me for size. No chance.

I suddenly realise that if I stand any longer I will fall over, so I sit down on Robyn's white floorboards and empty each bag out in turn. There must be hundreds of pounds – dollars – worth of stuff here. How much am I allowed to take, exactly, before I deprive the mysterious St Vincent de Paul of his Jigsaw skirt?

Robyn is throwing out a fake crocodile-skin mobile phone cover. Suddenly, I want it more than anything else in the world. I find my phone in my bag to see if it will fit. It has been switched off since London. I pick up a text from Suzanne and hit the call button – shortly before realising it's midnight in London.

'Alice!' she croaks. 'I'm in bed!'

'Guess where I am.'

'Swiss Cottage? Oh no. You're in bloody Australia. Did you? Are you?'

'I'm here. By myself. I just landed.'

'Eeeee!' she squeals.

'I can't talk much, sorry, my credit's a bit low. The main thing is, I've just let myself into Robyn's flat in Sydney and she's left me this treasure trove of her old stuff. There's a note saying I can keep what I want, as long as I give the rest to charity.'

'Good stuff?' She snaps awake.

'Really good.'

'Ooooh. Alice, I know you're probably jetlagged to the eyeballs and very little is making sense, but listen to me very, very carefully.'

'Okay.'

'First of all, you *are* a charity at the moment. So don't feel guilty. *Have the lot*. Secondly, I want you to go out tomorrow, buy a big packet of camera film, go back to Robyn's place and iron every piece of clothing in the bags. Then I want you to pin it all up, piece by piece, on a perfectly ironed large white sheet and photograph everything in turn. Then, darling, I want you to start an eBay account.'

'I can't do that.'

'Yes, you can. You can start an eBay account and sell Robyn's stuff, and then you can buy stuff to make pregnancy frocks, and have an eBay shop and start your own label – and then, hip, hip, hurray, as God is my witness, you'll never be hungry again!'

twelve

The time has come to find my way around. I have inherited a poor grasp of geography from Mum, so despite all Robyn's carefully hand-drawn maps, I have no idea where I am in relation to Bondi Beach, the nearest supermarket, a phone box, a bus stop or anywhere else. The heat in my head, combined with the intense heat of Australian summer, seems to have melted whichever brain cells are responsible for navigation. I spin around in the middle of Bondi like a Dalek in a tizzy, getting hotter and hotter.

If I had any money, I'd get Australian GPS put on my phone. Instead, I am still looking for an internet café by the end of the week. I give up, exhausted, and lie down on a bench for a rest. When I get up again, I see the internet café staring me in the face.

There's a spare computer inside, so I sit down next to two schoolboys playing a computer game in which flesh-eating mutants appear to be at war with American GIs. I thought Australian kids just rode bikes and made friends with kangaroos.

I check my email. Welcome to me: I have 142 new messages. Most of them seem to be from friends who are in shock because they have just heard about my Girl's Own Adventure.

I check the message from Nash's father first, to help me canvass general opinion. He's the person most likely to be offended by my decision to leave his son and run away to Australia, so if I can read his email, I can read anybody's. He says he is sorry to hear our news, sorry he didn't get a chance to see me at Christmas, and sorry that he and Nash's mother didn't get the opportunity to give me my present this year – a unique ceramic teapot from the gallery with a lid like a pumpkin.

I can't even be bothered writing back to tell him about Sarah and Lisa and all the rest of it. Part of me wants to set the record straight in the interests of truth and justice – but the other part just thinks, Go away, Mr Nash, with your cardigan and your big toggle buttons.

There's a picture of the teapot attached to the email. If I look very carefully I can see the marked-down sale sticker creeping over the base. Thank you very much. I hope you liked my crappy shortbread too.

I open an email from the person most likely to approve of my sudden departure from Nash and from England. It comes from Rosie, an old university friend from Huddersfield who came all the way to our leaving drinks in London. She's always been a free spirit. Whoops. She's sorry too. Sorry that I have just fled the country by myself without calling her first. Sorry that I have forgotten some of my oldest friends. Didn't I know that she was there for me?

Delete.

On balance, though, most of my friends are in favour and completely understand why I have run away. Almost everyone seems to have heard about Nash's affair with Sarah, and his new job.

There are messages from Heidi and Danielle Coles, checking that I've landed safely and letting me know that everything is in place at Bark's ready for me to begin. Danielle's email comes inside a special Bark's of Byron Bay design box, like a little note. There's a dachshund wearing a crown in one corner, and a golden retriever with an orbed sceptre in the other corner.

My mother has written me her first ever email, which has the following subject header: *Anthony Andrews, Pears Soap, Dad's Bicycle, Overdue Library Books, Nanny and Mango Chutney*.

I read the email over the noise of flesh-eating mutants attacking American soldiers:

Dear Alice,

I see that you must begin every email with a subject. This is rather difficult, as there is so much to tell you in this letter and there are so many subjects. Nevertheless, I have done my best.

Anthony Andrews is meant to be holidaying in Australia at the moment. Have you seen him? I saw a photograph of him this week in the Radio Times. *He has hardly changed since he was in* Brideshead Revisited.

There is a special offer on Pears Soap at the moment, so I bought twelve for the price of eight. Would you like me to post you some?

I tried to ride Dad's old bicycle the other day to the chemist to buy the Pears Soap. Unfortunately I fell off because I was wearing Dad's old Barbour and the cord caught in my spokes.

Nash rang to say you have left some overdue library books in the flat but he has been unable to reach you by telephone to discuss the fine. Would you mind calling him? (I am so sorry to have to pass this on, Alice, I do realise he is a complete wanker.)

My God. I had no idea that word was even in my mother's vocabulary, but there it is, in black and white.

My Nanny had a marvellous recipe for Mango Chutney which I will send you in my next email. Now that you are in Australia I am sure you can buy mangoes very cheaply.

All my love, Mummie xx

I move on to Nash's emails, even though I am thinking about Joel as I read them.

He is annoyed that he can't get me on the phone and wishes I would switch it on again. Is it because I've run out of calling credit, as usual?

Oh, shut up.

He is sorry about Sarah (again) and wants me to know that if it hadn't been for the breakdown in our relationship, he wouldn't have been tempted. It meant nothing to her, and it means nothing to him.

He says he will post me all the stuff I left behind if I send him the money to pay the shipping company.

Finally, he wants me to know how much he still cares about me, and that when things go wrong in Australia, I only have to call.

When things go wrong? He clearly wants me to be eaten alive by a shark feet first, just so when I call him he can be smug down the phone line from Romney College while my lower limbs are being severed from my torso to a der-der-der-der *Jaws* soundtrack.

There is nothing about the fact that Lisa is no longer in The Believers (the quiz team or the band) and nothing about Sarah replacing her. Well, quel bloody surprise, as Suzanne always says.

After that, it's time to sell Robyn's stuff on eBay. I feel guilty, I feel embarrassed, I feel ashamed – but I am also desperate. There's no point even pretending any more. I'm at my cousin's mercy. If I don't get some dollars on my credit card soon, I'm going to be in serious trouble, and this time there's no Nash to bail me out.

I am too scared to open an Australian bank account yet – just the thought of all the forms puts me off. Sydney isn't as cheap as I expected, either. I was completely mad getting a taxi from the airport. I didn't have much choice, because of my luggage, but it cost me half my weekly food budget.

I log on to eBay to register as a seller. It takes me four attempts, mainly because I can't understand the wavy words at the end.

Tharways?

Pernifor?

Weebur?

Isbun?

When I finally master the wavy word, the computer makes a sad little 'beee' sound, trailing off at the end, and crashes. I sit back in my seat and breathe out. There's another sad little 'beeee' sound and the screen goes black.

'Bloody computer.' I kick the grey plastic box under the desk.

'Speak nicely to it,' a cockney voice says behind me. 'Don't kick it like that.' The voice is definitely English. You can't hear the letter 'T' at all.

I turn around and see a tall, tanned man wearing a Ben Sherman shirt and cut-off denim shorts. He is ridiculously good-looking in a chav kind of way.

'Sorry. I've just had enough,' I tell him.

'They'll kick you out of here if you kick the computer,' the man says. 'What's the problem?'

'I can't do the eBay code thing.'

'I can sell stuff for you.'

'Can you?'

Oh no. A cockney cyber-spiv. I have come halfway around the world and run into someone from a Guy Ritchie film.

'I take 20 per cent and I sit here doing it all, so you don't have to.' The man holds out his hand for me to shake it and tells me his name is Matty.

'Alice,' I say, wishing it wasn't such a drivelly posh name.

'Are you interested then?' he asks.

I look at the wavy passwords. There's no contest really.

'It's just stuff from my cousin's flat,' I say. 'Before I move to Byron Bay.'

'Nice. I love it up in Byron. I live just round the corner. Drop in any time. It's a party house. Very friendly. What did you do in London then?'

'A bit of everything.'

I really shouldn't be talking like this to a complete stranger, but Matty is the first human being I have had a proper conversation with since I landed.

'There's nothing wrong with a bit of everything,' he says, putting his trainer on the side of my chair so I can admire the inside of his tanned, lightly fuzzed thigh. 'I do Bondi Markets as well.'

'Oh! I heard it's really good. My friend Suzanne told me about it. I used to look after her stall in Camden.'

'Ever meet a bloke looking after a second-hand book stall there? Alan? Down the back of the market?'

'Yes!'

'He used to live in my manor,' Matty says. 'Why don't you come round now for a cup of tea? You'll like Jade, my girlfriend.'

Oh. So I won't be having an ill-advised fling with an eBay trader then.

'We've got an open relationship,' Matty continues. 'Maybe you can take over the stall when she goes to Perth. We'll 'ave a talk about it.'

Aha, so Jade is going to Perth and Matty wants to let me know they have an open relationship. Very well. Matty has quite a kissable mouth actually, if you can possibly forget how many drugs have no doubt been crammed down his gullet. *Oh, stop it, Alice.* I just haven't had sex for a while. That's all.

I glance at Matty's business card. It's not been printed out on a machine at a supermarket, as I feared. It looks serious, glossy and expensive. Matthew Riddup – Web Commerce. I'm surprised he hasn't engraved 'Diamond Geezer' in copperplate below his name.

'Thanks,' I say, and follow him out. I will be really annoyed if I accompany Matty back to his flat and discover that he and Jade are the Bondi Beach equivalent of Fred and Rosemary West.

Matty recognises at least three people on the way.

''Allo, Charlotte, alright?' he says to a girl in a sarong.

'John! Wot you up to then?' He gives a bald man a thumbs-up.

'Phil! Over 'ere!' He waves across the street.

He reminds me of an old boyfriend of Suzanne's who was a roadie for some Britpop band who've since disappeared. She now refers to him as Ageing Lad. Matty's too young for that, but he is certainly keeping laddism alive, all by himself, in this distant corner of the world. I suppose, with Matty, there will always be some far corner of a foreign field that is forever *Loaded*.

We get into the lift in his building and I am overwhelmed by his aftershave. Or is it his aftershave, his cologne *and* his deodorant? I can just imagine what his bathroom looks like. He presses the button marked Penthouse and tries not to look smug. I don't think I've ever been in a penthouse before. I steel myself for potted palms, polar bear rugs and sofas shaped like lips.

Their flat is like Robyn's – another white, light-filled shell – although it's about five times the size. There are ashtrays everywhere, along with bits of clothing, odd trainers, empty CD cases and old pizza boxes. And hey, I was right! Copies of *Loaded*.

Matty tells me they're looking after the flat for a friend who's gone travelling. I suppose things like this happen to him all the time.

Jade appears, and offers to put the kettle on. She's a stunning six-foot black supermodel. If they are having an open relationship, I'm sure she's doing alright out of it.

'Alice's from Camden,' Matty says as he introduces me. I don't bother to correct him.

'I used to work on the market there,' I tell Jade. 'I looked after my friend's stall. Vintage clothing, that kind of stuff.'

'Up the back?' Jade enquires, crossing her legs.

'Yes. Her name's Suzanne. The stall has Union Jacks all over it.'

'I love that place!' Jade shrieks, and waggles her foot at me. It's encased in a giant platform sandal. 'These are Terry de Havilland,' she says proudly. 'I got them last trip.'

'They're amazing.'

'So what you up to in Bondi then?' Jade asks, switching the kettle on.

'I said she should help you out on the stall when you go away,' Matty cuts in.

'That would be nice,' Jade agrees. 'I want to go to Perth. Oh, baby, I am so dying to go to Perth! I want to see some dolphins.'

Matty brings out a bowl of jelly babies while we're waiting for the kettle to boil, and gives me an intense look. He appears to be waiting for some kind of reaction. Are they special jelly babies? Do they have Matty and

Jade's cocaine stash sprinkled on them? Suddenly I realise – they're proper Bassett's Jelly Babies. Rare exotica in Australia. A bit like the silly second-hand Union Jack tea towel I packed. I've already made it into a mini-skirt.

'Fantastic. It's so nice to see these again,' I tell him, and he passes the bowl to Jade, satisfied.

'You been down to Bronte yet?' Jade asks me, with a mouth full of jelly baby. I thought supermodels weren't supposed to eat that kind of thing.

'No. Should I go?'

'Get yourself down there,' Matty points through the window, 'and follow that path along the top of the cliff. There's signs everywhere. See that swimming pool underneath Icebergs?'

'Icebergs has the most fantastic bar,' Jade interrupts him.

'Yeah, well, just get yourself as far as the baths underneath it, and go from there.'

Oh no. More incomprehensible Australian directions. I have been following this kind of well-meant navigational advice for a week. You have to pretend you understand when people are trying to help you, though, or they get offended.

'Thanks, Matty. I might try Bronte this afternoon –'

'Watch out for the yucky lizard sculptures though,' Jade interrupts me.

'Yeah,' Matty adds. 'Jade thought they were real. Nearly fell off the cliff. Keep walking and you'll get to a beach called Tamarama. Don't go swimming there though, 'cos you'll drown. Keep going and you'll end up at Bronte.'

'Tell her about the blue jellyfish though, Matty.'

'Yeah. If you see people running about and screaming, and they've got red marks on their legs and there's these little blue tentacle things on the sand, get straight outta the water.'

'Okay,' I promise. I decide I am never, ever going to walk to Bronte.

I finish my tea and Matty and Jade invite me to watch *Eastenders* with them. Jade's sister sends them the DVDs from London every week.

'I'd absolutely love to, but I think I should go back and sort out this stuff for eBay.'

'Oh, yeah.' Matty remembers. 'Well, when you've got it sorted, give us a call and I'll come and get it. We take the photos, do the auction, post it out – the lot.'

'Wow. Thanks.' I wonder which English backpacker minion he employs to do all that for him.

They walk me to the lift and I am asphyxiated by Matty's aftershave again. I wonder if Jade dresses like this every day – tiny denim shorts, platform shoes, transparent pink shirt – and what the locals think of her. They probably love her. Maybe they think she's Naomi Campbell, especially when she puts on her enormous sunglasses.

Once I'm outside again, I decide the time has come to draw my own map of my new home town. I can't understand Robyn's tiny drawings, and her Sydney street directory is mental torture. I have already worked out the things I need to find in Bondi: the bank, the supermarket, the phone box, the internet café, the sea, the funny little street with all the great shops I can't afford, and the bus stop. The map takes me all afternoon, but finally I manage it.

You've just got to stop mixing it all up with Brighton or Blackpool – that's all.

Will there ever come a day when I just know where everything is? Australia is so vast, it seems impossible. Bondi is sprawling. *Sydney* is vast. No wonder my taxi driver had to look up Robyn's street in his directory. In London, the cabbies just know where everything is.

I go back to the flat and sort through the pile of rubbish bags again. I have already taken a discreet glance at the clothes my cousin actually possesses, so I'm not surprised that she can afford to throw out so much stuff. Robyn has a wardrobe like a boutique. You walk in one door and out of another. She has an entire cupboard just for *shoes*.

Her bathroom is like a small section of the cosmetics department at Selfridges. Her bookcase would make the librarian at Swiss Cottage weep. I have no doubt at all that my cousin is well off. It's quite different from English well off though. Everything about this flat is new. Everything about rich English homes is very, very old.

I need a swim. It's hot enough now, and anyway . . . I'm Australian these days. It's what they do.

The Bondi Baths are built on a cliff jutting out over the sea. It's not like any public pool I have seen in my life. There is no smell of chlorine. There are no posters about disgusting verrucae. There are no cackling fat boys with tight nylon trunks and bottom cleavage belly flopping into the shallow end. Best of all, there's barely anybody in the pool at all – just one man with the body of a Greek god slogging up and down the far lane. I am so used to having to jostle for space in London that it's hard to believe I can have a lane all to myself – or even make a leisurely decision to swim under the ropes and choose another one.

I get changed, try to ignore how white my body is, and get in the water. It's clean and cool and within minutes it starts to feel warm. The sky is blue, and the sea is too. I have space above me and space all around me. Lovely, lovely *space*, a million miles from my horrible relationship with Nash. I have absolutely no idea what I am doing here yet, or even who I am any more, but why would I want to be anywhere else?

With every lap, the fines on my overdue library books (oh, you wicked woman, Miss A. Templeton) seem further and further away. When I'm doing backstroke, I look up and see glamorous people in sunglasses standing above me at the bar having cocktails. This never happens at the Tooting Bec Lido.

I suppose Matty and Jade come down here all the time and do laps. Or maybe just Matty by himself. I allow myself a small, forbidden fantasy that he might come along for a swim one day (when I have developed a suntan and bought a stunning pink bikini) and invite me upstairs for a pina colada.

Then I get real, get changed, and go to the Bondi Beach post office to send my mother a cheque.

thirteen

A few weeks later, when my tiny savings have almost gone, I'm cleaning Robyn's flat, ready for her arrival, when I hear the key turn in the door.

'Alice!' she squeals. As she rushes towards me, I realise she's not wearing a bra. She's like a poster for an Australian gym come to life – all muscles, bounce, white teeth and perfect skin.

Robyn has short, jet-black spiky hair, enormous diamond studs in her ears, and is wearing a pristine white tank top (what my mother would call 'your father's vest') and black tracksuit pants. Her socks are white, her trainers are white, her watch is white. She makes me feel so . . . Swiss Cottage International Travellers Hostel.

I am trying not to think about the lesbian thing, but it's not working – mainly because the first thing she does is unpack her suitcase in front of me and throw out a thing that looks like an egg with a long cord and a battery charger. God, is that a vibrator or a piece of kitchen equipment?

'I've got a present for you here somewhere,' she says, squatting on the floor like a frog. 'Where the blardy hell is it?'

Eventually she pulls a small box out of the front zipper compartment. Please let it not be an egg with a battery.

'Balinese pearls,' she explains, before I can open the box.

'Robyn, thank you. You really shouldn't have.'

I put them on immediately, to please her. I suppose she thinks because I'm English I like my jewellery to be the same as Princess Anne's.

Once Robyn has finished unpacking, we sit down and open her duty-free vodka and drink it with the mint and fresh limes she picked up at the supermarket on the way home. My cousin is impressively well-organised. I would never have thought of doing that in a million years. I suppose that's what happens when you manage a hotel. You organise everything so it comes with ice-cubes and a swizzle stick.

'Welcome home,' I say. 'How was your holiday?'

'Oh, man,' she pushes her hair behind her ears, 'it was fantastic. I just chilled. I did yoga on the beach every day, then I just hung out. You have to go to Bali, Alice.'

'Well, places like that are so close now that I'm living in Sydney, aren't they?' I say, sounding like my mother.

'So what's the story with Nash?' She assumes a cross-legged yoga position on the sofa.

Aha. The story with Nash. I suppose it *is* something best explained methodically. Instead, it all comes out in a mad rush.

'The thing is, he always thought he was better than me. Anyway, he basically had sex in a jacuzzi with his ex-wife, Sarah. And this other woman, Lisa, who was on our quiz team, covered for them. Then Nash went behind her back and took her job, so she rang me up and told me about him and Sarah. I really did love him at the beginning, but that was before I realised how awful he was. I got this book out from the library called *Should I Stay Or Should I Go?*, and in the end I just thought, Go . . . The only trouble is, when I found out about Nash and his ex-wife, it felt like he'd left *me* first.'

'Wow,' Robyn sympathises. 'What a total prick.'

It is intensely gratifying to hear someone insult Nash like this and I savour the moment. Until my cousin comes over and starts massaging my shoulders. I try not to leap away, because that would be hurtful and insulting, but it's a relief when she has to go to the door to let in a delivery man.

'Looky, looky here!' she says, accepting a huge bouquet. Then she checks the note and pulls a face. 'Huh. Just corporate wank as usual. *From all at Phaeton Financial Management Solutions, in appreciation of your efforts at our annual Christmas party*.'

She goes off to find some old family photos – more Polaroids. There are three of Joel as a teenager, and I have to stop myself from lunging at them.

'That's a nice photo of your dad there,' Robyn says. 'He didn't really get on with Roland, did he? My dad was such a hippy back then. Yours was pretty straight, I reckon.'

'I suppose so. My dad was all about Derek Rose pyjamas. I expect your dad didn't even *wear* pyjamas.'

'So how was Joel when you saw him?'

I go pink. She notices and I go even pinker and can't stop. She pours us both another vodka.

'You saw him then?' She tries again, watching for more blushing.

'Yes.' I fight the urge to talk and talk about him. 'He came and stayed with Mum for a while.'

'He really likes you,' she says.

'Oh.'

'Rilly, he's got a crush on you. I can tell. But I don't think he wants to make a move on you because he's worried you'll think it's weird.'

'Well, it is a bit weird.'

'Not rilly. Put some more vodka in that. It's hot today, isn't it? Yeah, I think Joel's holding back because he thinks that *you* think it's all wrong. Even though you're not related and that.'

I hug the knowledge that Joel likes me to myself, while Robyn sloshes more vodka into my glass. She's just like her brother. Strangely honest and straight to the point – as if all communication has to take place as simply and quickly as possible, because life is far too short. Maybe it's an Australian thing. In this climate, you don't want to faff around, the way everyone seems to in England. Australian television, I have already noticed, is wonderfully unsubtle. There was an ad late last night for some kind of herbal pessary for men that consisted of a woman shouting 'CAN'T GET IT UP? GET THIS UP YER!'

Just look at the way Joel told me about Helena and his faintly embarrassing status as a bastard in the Templeton family. With anyone else – Nash, for example – the whole paternity thing would have taken days, even weeks, to uncover. It would have involved complicated tactical manoeuvres, awkward silences, changes of subject and all the other things that usually happen in England when anything personal is up for discussion. It took Nash five months to manage to tell his parents about me.

'Oh, look, Alice. There's a party on,' Robyn says, checking the text messages on her phone. 'There'll be lots of Pommies there. It's their Australian citizenship celebration. Do you want to go?'

'I'd love to.'

'Hey, how about that chick from the Department of Immigration? She was keen! I had to beat her off with a stick!'

'You mean the woman you had to talk to to sort out my application?'

Robyn smirks. 'I had to do more than talk to her. But it's cool. She's fallen in love with someone else anyway. Do you know about Dykes on Bikes?'

'No. Sorry.'

'Well, anyway, she's in love with one of the dykes. Hey, what are you doing tomorrow morning?'

Robyn's energy is relentless. She's sitting still but it's pouring out of her, like sweat. I feel tired just looking at her.

'I've got to work at Bondi Markets tomorrow morning,' I explain. 'I said I'd help someone out with her stall. She's trying me out, really.'

'Who is she?'

'Her name's Jade.'

'Really gorgeous? English? Black?'

'Yes.'

'Everyone knows everyone around here.' Robyn jerks a thumb towards the window. 'It's the Bondi Mafia. Or if you're a lesbian, the Bondi Muffia.' She laughs at her own joke.

Wow. So Matty and Jade are having an open relationship, and Jade is possibly a lesbian. Or bisexual. I have a sudden mad thought that Jade may actually have once been a man – she has enormous feet. I am about to dismiss it when Robyn puts me straight.

'Jade used to be John in London,' she explains. 'She's a trannie. She came out here to have the operation because it's cheaper. Everyone in my spin class is in love with her. She's got a boyfriend but they're pretty free.'

'Matty.'

'Oh, you met him, did you? Did he try to sell you anything?'

I suddenly remember the eBay sale and go pink again. I have sworn Matty to secrecy, but if Robyn ever finds out what I've done, I'll never be able to look her in the eye again.

I try to change the subject but she's having none of it.

'Matty's the sheikh of eBay,' she laughs. 'That's what they call him at the gym. I should have got him to sell all my stuff.' She winks at me.

'Well, actually –'

'I saw you beat me to it though.' She elbows me in the ribs. 'Someone emailed me and said "How come your tennis racquet's on auction?" Good call to ask Matty though. He rakes it in.'

'Sorry, Robyn.'

'Don't be sorry!' she shrieks, looking genuinely shocked. 'I don't care! Hey. You should join our gym. It's called Bondi Hot Bods. Jade and Matty *live* there. It's rilly social.

By the way, do you want another voddie? Shall we go out tonight? Do you want to come salsa dancing?'

Robyn and I are about the same age but she makes me feel very, very old. When I decline, she salsas around the sitting room anyway, clicking her fingers and throwing her head back as if she's in a video.

Right now, I just want to lie on my bed and take in what she said about Joel.

I want to gaze out of the window, at the stars above Bondi Beach, and daydream. It's a very, very long time since I felt like this. I think I'm in love. In lust. In-fatuation. Insane, because I have only recently become single and, besides, he's my cousin. Maybe I'm just inebriated.

'I'll leave you to it then,' Robyn says, once she's changed into the tightest no-bra black dress she can find and a sparkling pair of gold flip-flops. 'If you want me, I'm on my mobile. Hey!'

I look up.

'It's so great to see you again.' She blows me a kiss from the door. 'I'm *so* glad you've come to live here.'

The next morning, I am at Jade's stall at Bondi Markets at 7 am, as instructed. Jade, however, is nowhere to be seen. Maybe she went to the same nightclub as Robyn. I sit on the wall near the table bearing her name and a reserved label, and wonder how long I'm going to have to wait.

A man selling goldfish in empty fruit-juice bottles sets up on my left side, and I watch the fish swimming around for a while. I have a terrible headache from Robyn's vodka. Slugging water from the kettle throughout the night had no effect. If I don't find something to drink soon, I may become so desperate that I have to decant a live fish.

There was no sign of Robyn in the flat this morning, so I expect she got lucky. I imagine she probably has dozens of admirers, quite apart from the woman from the Department of Immigration who is now with a dyke on a bike. Apparently, Robyn is on the Sydney Gay and Lesbian Mardi Gras committee, so I'm sure she has plenty of takers.

While I'm enjoying the sun, a psychic sets up on my right, with a garden table and umbrella and a fold-up chair. She doesn't shave under her arms but she clearly uses a lot of aromatherapy oil – the smell of peppermint and eucalyptus wafting my way is amazing. She's wearing a leotard under her skirt, and boots that lace up at the front. A fringed shawl goes over the garden table and a hand-painted sign goes up: *Blossom Promise's Psychic Readings*.

I have never had a psychic reading in my life, but I really want one.

Blossom Promise looks my way and smiles. 'You're better off without him,' she says.

'Sorry?'

'Your man. Better off without him.'

Well, that was a lucky guess. It could have been any man, from any point in my history.

'The new one's better,' she continues.

'Really?' I leap on this information.

'Kissing cousins.' She smirks.

Oh. My. God.

'You've got two saints looking after you,' she goes on.

'Which ones?'

Blossom Promise shakes out her fringed shawl and settles herself in the chair. 'You got Saint Vincent and Saint Martin, sweetie.'

I check to see if the goldfish man is listening to this impromptu psychic reading, but he's too busy on his mobile phone. What does she mean, I have two saints looking after me? I don't even go to church.

'Saint Vincent de Paul and Saint-Martin-in-the-Fields,' she says. Then she closes her eyes and sinks into meditation. I watch her, hoping for another prediction – preferably about Joel – but nothing happens.

'Mim, mim, mim,' Blossom chants to herself. 'Mim, mim, mim.'

An official in a bright green vest comes over and moves her on. 'You're in the wrong possie,' he says. 'You're supposed to be at the car park end.'

'No, I'm not,' she says, rather unspiritually.

'This is goods. You're services.'

He shoos her along, and I catch a flash of hairy armpit as she scoops up her things.

'You need that book!' she shouts at me as he helps her with the chair, the umbrella and the fold-up garden table. 'Buy that book!'

Goldfish man smiles at me and twirls his finger at the side of his head. I expect he thinks Blossom is – what was Heidi's memorable phrase at the café that day? – one thermos short of a picnic.

I make up my mind to find her later. I want to know more about Joel. Why does Robyn think he has a crush on me? Was it something he said? Something he wrote in an email? I have to know.

And perhaps I *was* being looked after by someone up there in heaven the night I went to St-Martin-in-the-Fields and Heidi found my purse. Without Robyn's rubbish bags for the St Vincent de Paul shop, what on earth would I have done?

I think about the possibility that my father might be my guardian angel, then dismiss it. He played snooker, drank whisky and voted Conservative. If there was one thing he couldn't stand, it was people talking about ghosts. He's the last person I'd expect to actually become one.

For some reason, Blossom Promise's verdict on Nash makes me feel comforted. It's the same feeling I had when I was reading *Should I Stay Or Should I Go?*, when Dr Stein asked if I'd feel relieved if my family and friends staged an intervention and told me it was alright to leave. I suppose Blossom Promise is a kind of intervention in a way.

''Allo Alice!'

Jade appears, talking through a cigarette as she hauls a suitcase and two fold-up chairs past the goldfish stall. I try not to look at her breasts. Or her man-hands. The fingernails may be long and pink, but the fingers are still like sausages.

Jade is half an hour late but doesn't mention it. Instead, she's fizzing with good news about her Australian citizenship test. She and Matty passed with flying colours and will soon be lining up to receive their certificates before what she promises will be the biggest party in Sydney.

'My cousin Robyn told me there was a party on,' I say. 'She goes to your gym. Robyn Templeton.'

'Yeah, we know her. Everyone knows everyone, darling. I'm just gonna get the rest of the stuff from the taxi, alright?'

Jade teeters off in her platform sandals, her shorts and – new addition – an ancient oversized Madonna T-shirt. I recognise it immediately from Robyn's garbage bags and make a mental note to tell Jade not to wear it in her presence. Matty was supposed to have sold that.

She comes back with two more enormous suitcases on wheels. 'I got more stuff at home if we run out,' she says. 'And Matty's on the way.'

While we wait for the market to warm up, she explains the Matty/Jade business model to me. It seems to consist of selling the possessions of every departing English person in Sydney at a 20 per cent commission on eBay, and flogging the rest at a slightly lower commission at the market. The rest of their stock they find at auction. Australians are frightened of auctions, according to Jade. They're too laidback to bid.

Jade specialises in old swimming costumes from the '50s and '60s. She also snaps up Hawaiian shirts when she finds them, and natty little beach accessories – striped duffel bags, ancient towels with fringing on the ends, enormous Mexican sunhats, and beach wraps with boomerangs all over them. It's a fantastic stall, but she hasn't got enough stock. I could use Aunt Helena's fabric and make all kinds of things to sell here. Wrap skirts and sundresses, maybe, with headscarves and bags. The skirts and dresses would be easy enough to run up using my in-between sizes idea. I could do them for pregnant women as well. Maybe I could photocopy the photo shoot in Twad and pin it up at the front of the stall.

My dad was so right about me. He used to say I was a born capitalist without capital. Still, a woman can dream. Even in the middle of a credit crunch.

Jade suddenly clicks her sausage fingers at me. 'By the way, Matty did well with all your gear. He's gonna come over later and give you the dosh. That was lucky for you, your cousin having a throw-out, wasn't it?'

She's embarrassing me now and making me feel poor. I change the subject. 'Do you know that psychic, Blossom Promise?'

'Never heard of her. Here – tell me if you could get these questions right, alright?' She crosses her long, long legs and reads from her Australian citizenship test. 'What's Australia's floral emblem?'

'I don't know. Gladioli. Something to do with Dame Edna Everage.'

'Wattle. What's mateship?'

'No idea.'

'What percentage of all Australian migrants are born in the UK?'

'I know that one. About 20 per cent.'

'Yeah, too bloody many,' she laughs. 'Which creature can be found on West Australia's flag?'

'Kangaroo. Koala. Platypus. Dame Edna Everage. Pass.'

'The black swan,' Jade says, tutting at me. 'Can you sing the Australian national anthem?'

'No. Something about girt. Our home is girt by sea.'

'What role did Private John Simpson Kirkpatrick play in Australian affairs?'

'No idea. Actually – hang on. I do know.'

'Come on, time's ticking away.' Jade taps her wrist.

'It was in the First World War. Simpson was a medical officer. He used to put the wounded men on the back of his donkey and take them back to camp. Simpson and the donkey were both killed. They were at Gallipoli. It was so sad.'

'Ah, bless.' Jade pulls a face. 'You're absolutely right. I'm impressed. 'Ow did you know that one?'

'I used to go to this donkey charity shop in Finsbury Park. There was a poster on the wall of the change room. I must have read it a hundred times.'

Matty turns up, wearing a baseball cap with a lightning bolt on the front and pulling more wheelie suitcases.

'Gewd morning,' he greets us, as if this is the first time he's seen Jade in twenty-four hours. Maybe it is.

'I've just been telling Alice about the citizenship test,' Jade says.

'Piece of piss,' is Matty's verdict. 'You going to do it, Alice?'

'I might,' I say. 'Actually, maybe I should.'

'Ooh, you've made her go all serious.' Jade nudges him. 'Hey, did you bring Alice's money, darlin'?'

'All good, all green, all tax-free,' Matty says, and I try not to look too desperate as he counts $100 bills carefully into my hand.

'Well, I probably will declare the tax,' I tell him, but Matty and Jade are already off in a world of their own, rolling cigarettes and reading this morning's screed of text messages from London.

'I think I'll go and get a coffee,' I say. 'Anyone want one?'

'Yeah, ta,' they say in unison.

The coffee's hard to find. What did the man in the green vest say about services? Were they near the car park or away from the car park? And where is the bloody car park anyway?

I check the money Matty's given me and put it straight back in my purse. Then I stuff my purse down the front of my bra, just to be certain. I can't expect St-Martin-in-the-Fields to look after me all the time.

As for St Vincent de Paul, I'm determined to give him his cut from Matty's pile of cash. It's one thing to be skint. It's quite another to be cheap, and I want to be able to look Robyn in the eye when I see her next.

She explained the rubbish bags to me last night. She said she space-cleared her apartment in preparation for her detox in Bali, so she could bring in good chi for the New Year, realign her meridians and get the energy pumping in her love corner. Sometimes I have absolutely no idea what my cousin is talking about.

I see a second-hand book stall and go over, remembering Blossom Promise's parting comment: 'You need that book'. What in the name of merry jingo, as my dad used to say, was she blithering about? I see the book she means immediately. My old friend, *Should I Stay Or Should I Go?*. I suppose Nash will give my copy back to the library eventually, if he doesn't burn it first.

I flick through the book, remembering every word. I don't need it any more though. I shouldn't have stayed, Dr Stein – and I didn't.

There's a cheap batch of books underneath it marked 'AUSTRALIANA – HALF PRICE'. I pick it up and untie the string. One of the books is about the First World

War. I look in the index and find Simpson's donkey. There is a photograph of them both in the centre pages and I immediately want to buy it. Maybe Blossom was talking about this book instead. It could be good for the citizenship test.

I will take the citizenship test eventually, for exactly the same reasons that Matty and Jade took theirs – I want an Australian passport. I want to make it easier to get a proper job here. Maybe, one day, if a miracle occurs, I'd even like my future son or daughter to have an Australian passport too. I can't think of a better country I'd like my descendants to belong to; if I ever find a man to have descendants with, of course. I want to belong to this country too. I don't want to feel like an interloper. I already feel I owe Australia that much, even though I've only been here a short while.

I look at the other books. *The Story of Phar Lap, The Greatest Racehorse Australia Has Ever Seen* (so great, it seems, that they stuffed him) and a very smelly book called *Selected Poems of Henry Lawson*. I'm not surprised it's whiffy; it was published in 1918. Someone has also scribbled all over the first page.

A nosey woman in big sunglasses is looking over my shoulder.

'Do you want that lot, love?' the stallholder asks me.

'Yes, please.'

I hand the money over, and get a filthy look from Big Sunglasses as the stallholder puts the books into an old plastic bag.

I collect three cups of coffee in a cardboard tray and go back to the stall. Jade and Matty are snogging, ignoring their customers while they investigate each other's recently whitened teeth. I suppose if I didn't know that Jade used to be John, Matty's insatiable lust would be quite understandable. Then again, maybe her man-hands turn him on.

'Been shopping?' Jade enquires, when Matty finally gets up and lets me sit down.

'Just some Aussie books. I thought if I had to do the citizenship thing, they'd come in useful.'

'Yes, dear,' Jade says, as she spots a customer hovering. 'Can I help you?'

It's Big Sunglasses, but she's not interested in Jade's old clothes, she's interested in my books.

'My husband would love those for his birthday,' she tells me. 'In fact, he had his eye on them earlier. I was about to pick them up. Would you take $100 for them?'

I'm just about to be all middle-class English about it and say, 'Oh God, sorry, of course. I do apologise,' when Matty cuts in.

'Come on, love, if it's his birthday you can afford to be generous, can't you,' he says, watching her like a hawk.

'I spent loads and *loads* on Matty's birthday,' Jade says sweetly, backing him up.

Big Sunglasses waits for my reaction, then storms off – as much as any woman can storm in a pair of Birkenstocks.

'Give us a look at the books then.' Matty inspects each page with his fingertips.

'You wait,' Jade promises me. 'He'll sort it for you.'

'It's the Henry Lawson,' Matty says. 'Not that I know anything about Henry Lawson – although I prolly should, having just sat the bloody Australia exam – but that's his signature there in the front.'

Jade and I look carefully at the name, written in spidery copperplate in ink that dried a long time ago.

'Signed first edition,' Matty says. 'And that woman knew it.'

'If she was offering you $100, girlfriend, it's probably worth ten times that,' Jade says, fanning herself.

'Guard it with your bloody life, Alice.' Matty waggles his finger at me. 'I'll put it in the safe at home, orright?'

And then, just as St Vincent de Paul and St-Martin-in-the-Fields join hands and set off joyful fireworks in the shape of exploding dollar signs above my head, my world comes to a kind of mini-end. Coming towards us is Joel. And he's holding hands with a pretty, dark-skinned, dark-haired woman in a sarong who can't stop gazing up at him.

I duck my head, but it's too late – and anyway, Robyn probably sent him to look for me.

'Hey, Alice!' He kisses me on the cheek.

'You're back,' I say stupidly, before introducing him to Matty and Jade.

'Came back a bit early,' he says. 'This is Rebecca.'

Well, thanks very much, Blossom bloody Promise.

fourteen

The Henry Lawson poetry book is worth one hundred times what I paid for it. So Blossom Promise was right about that bit anyway. Matty photographs, prices and then auctions it for me on eBay and we watch the bids increase by the hour, until time runs out. Jade punches the air with her man-hands and yells 'Yessss!'

I do sums on the back of an envelope, converting dollars into pounds, and realise I can afford to send Mum another cheque, pay off my overdraft at last, and pay for Nash to send my things from London. Even more importantly, I can also afford to have Aunt Helena's trunk sent over. I am desperate for my things now – even Ducky the rubber duck. I feel as if half of me is still stuck in London.

Once Matty has paid the money into my account, the first thing I do is write to Nash. *Shipment to Australia* is my very businesslike subject header. All our emails are like this at the moment – keeping it sensible, keeping it civilised. It's still a competition though, to see who can be more grown-up about breaking up.

An email comes straight back – Nash has bought himself a laptop now, and seems to be on it first thing in the morning and last thing at night. He's typed a list of everything I left behind the day I stormed out of the flat. It's not exactly an auction catalogue at Sotheby's. *Bangles, dental floss, face-flannel, loofah, packet of felt-tip pens, melted pink candle, petition against scrapping of Routemaster London bus* (damn, I forgot to give that back to Suzanne)*, Swiss Cottage library card, rubber duck, four pairs of black knickers . . .*

I am surprised at how much I left behind. The Duran Duran keyring I was given for my sixth birthday, for a start. Oh, and the inflatable dolphin lilo Nash and I took to Cornwall on our first summer holiday. Maybe I could float around Bondi on it. I appear to own a lot of relationship self-help books too, all from charity shops. Funny about that. I tell Nash to chuck those. Apart from that, I want everything – mainly because I have only four suitcases to my name and feel as if I have nothing.

I notice that anything Nash and I bought together is not on the list. Mysteriously, he seems to have interpreted these shared purchases as his property. If I argue about that though, I'll never see my packing crates. *Thanks for making the list, and offering to pack everything up*, I write, gritting my teeth. *Hopefully you'll have more room in your new flat once my stuff is out of the way*.

The last time I was this polite with Nash was the first time we met. Because I wanted him so much, my restraint was incredible. He was polite too. When the relationship really took off though, he used to take my bra off at the front door.

The memory of it now makes me feel surprisingly wobbly. Why is it that your brain knows when a relationship is over, but your heart always lags behind?

I try to persuade myself that Nash was just a habit, like smoking. That was hard to kick as well; even when I was long past the cravings, I still used to walk into a room and look for an ashtray.

I read Nash's email again. He is quite happy to organise the packing and delivery of my stuff, as he thinks it's only practical that I have my things around me in Australia for the time that I'm there. *For the time that I'm there*. So, he still thinks I'm coming back. Does that also mean he hopes I might be coming back to him at some point?

Well, he can stuff that. I might be marshmallow on the inside but I'm hard on the outside. I'm a human Wagon Wheel now, baby. There's no going back.

I like my new country. I like the way everyone sounds the same. Nobody is posh, nobody has a *background* clunking along behind them. There's no class system for stamps. You can make your dream come true here. Everything I thought was impossible in London suddenly seems possible. Everybody says 'yes' here, almost all the time. Even if they think you're bonkers, they still say 'yes'.

I saw a kookaburra the other day and it cackled with laughter, just as the guidebooks said it would. It had a punk mohawk and a big beak – and it seemed properly Australian.

I have braved the walk from Bondi Beach to Bronte and I loved it. The lizard sculptures didn't scare me at all. I didn't see a single blue jellyfish. Instead, I dived into the water at Bronte like a madwoman, and stayed in the sea for an hour. Australia has see-through water. You can see sand and shells at the bottom, instead of murk and crisp packets. I want to stay here forever.

Matty and Jade have been teaching me about Sydney property. You save up for a deposit on a cheap unit (not a flat, a unit) in an up-and-coming area, then you rent it out and use the money to rent somewhere even cheaper for yourself – usually miles out of town, because nobody wants to live there.

'Distance don't matter though,' Matty advised me a few nights ago, when we were looking at a map on the internet. 'They've got the cheapest trains in the world here. The Aussies don't like them – they live in their cars. We're Brits so we're used to the pain. Use it to your advantage, Alice. Save up and get yerself a deposit then move to Woop Woop.'

Woop Woop, Matty explained, is local parlance for the middle of nowhere. But Woop Woop is also the only place to live, if you are broke like me and want to buy your own home. It is a shock to realise that I might own a flat one day – or even a house. It's always seemed like some mad dream, but Matty and Jade are talking about it as if it's a perfectly normal thing for me to consider.

I discover that Matty is right about trains – Australians don't like them, or at least Danielle Coles doesn't like them. When I ring to tell her I will be arriving at Byron Bay station tomorrow evening, she sounds deeply shocked.

'You're not bringing your car up?'

'I don't drive actually.'

'You're not flying to Ballina?'

'I thought I'd take the scenic route on the train. See a bit of the country.'

'But it's nine hours, Alice!'

'Oh well. Hang on, I need to put some more money in the slot.'

More shock. 'Are you in a *phone box*'?

I am fairly certain Danielle Coles is a rich woman. I have googled her to the very limits of Google and found her in the happy possession of not one but three dog-related businesses in New South Wales. Along with Bark's of Byron Bay, she also owns Pampered Pooches of Parramatta and Diva Doggie Day Care in Double Bay. I've asked Nash to send my packing crates to Robyn's address, because I don't want them to arrive at Bark's of Byron Bay. Danielle will suffer even more shock if she sees me unpacking tatty old underwear and a face-flannel.

In the meantime, I need to go shopping for some dog-friendly work clothes. Perhaps it's time I paid a visit to my good friend St Vincent de Paul in Paddington.

The real reason I'm going is because I want an outfit that will impress Joel. We're having dinner tonight. I know he has a lovely new girlfriend with long, dark plaits, and I also know she's a much better human being than me because she works for Joel's charity and helps Tibetan refugees. (Robyn, as always, has been a goldmine of information.) Nevertheless, I live in hope. I *have* to hope. As Joel himself said on the hill above the English Channel that day, it's the only proper response to life. Even if it's hope of the pointless and deranged variety.

I get the bus to St Vincent de Paul's and try not to look in the other shops, which are not second-hand and have eye-watering prices. Instead, I buy two chicken satay sticks and revel in the luxury of eating takeaway food for a change. Along with my pedicure budget (yes!) I am letting myself keep a small amount of spending money from my amazing Henry Lawson book miracle.

When I go into St Vincent de Paul's life begins to feel even more luxurious. The first rack I look at has nearly new English labels, recently shed by well-dressed expats on their way back home. I try everything on and realise I have more than enough in my spending fund to buy two pairs of jeans, three skirts, a bundle of tops and even a coat for next winter. Australia's like a fruit machine. Every time I do another pound-to-dollar conversion in my head, I find more gold coins in the tray.

I realise I have also lost weight. Result! All that swimming, and tramping around Bondi Beach and Bronte, has given me back the shape I had when I was a silver-painted key woman. Now all I need to do is stop looking so English and white.

Joel would really like one of the tops. It's white cheesecloth with drawstrings and looks a bit Indian. If I bleach the red wine stain out of the sleeve, it could even pass as new. I try not to obsess too much about Joel as I pay for the clothes, but dinner with him is just a few hours away now and I can't wait.

Suddenly, he walks past the window. What?

I rush out in time to see him disappearing into a jewellery shop. It is definitely Joel. Scruffy dark hair, tennis shoes, beaten-up old shoulder bag . . . Maybe I should just sneak off. I have no foundation on, and I'm carrying three big plastic bags full of clothes, exactly like the kind of hopelessly superficial capitalist shopaholic he'd cross the road to avoid.

I edge towards the window of the jewellery shop so that he can't see me but I can still see him. God, he's gorgeous.

Then he looks up, sees me, smiles and waves. Shit.

'Hey Alice!' He emerges and beckons me into the shop. 'Come and tell me what you think of this.'

I go in, trying to breathe normally. The woman behind the counter looks me up and down then looks away, as if she wishes she hadn't bothered.

'I really like this bracelet.' Joel shows me a bangle decorated with unmatched stones. 'On the other hand, I also like this necklace.' He shows me a huge piece of amber on a long silver chain. 'What do you think?'

'Nice,' I say mechanically.

'It's for Rebecca,' he explains. 'It's her birthday on Saturday. She's back in Sydney for a while.'

'The necklace,' I say, at the same moment the shop assistant says, 'The bracelet.'

'Both then,' Joel jokes.

I try to keep the smile on my face, but I can't maintain it forever or I'll develop paralysis of the jaw. I go and look at the rings in the front window instead. Why buy Rebecca a necklace *and* a bracelet together? Oh God. Joel must be really in love with her.

'Thanks for that.' Joel squeezes my arm once he's made his purchase and we're outside again. 'What are you doing over this way?'

'Just getting some work clothes for the new job at Bark's. I'm off tomorrow so you and Rebecca can have my room,' I say, testing him.

'Alice. Are you okay?'

'Fine. Just a bit tired.'

'That makes two of us. Do you want a cup of tea? Maybe we could do that instead of the dinner thing – if you're really tired.'

'Sure.'

We walk, in silence, to the café in the park at the end of the road. Suddenly he stops, and makes me look at him properly.

'What's wrong?'

'Dunno.'

He links his arm through mine and we walk into the park through vast stone gates and past two strange sphinx statues. It's like Victorian England transplanted halfway across the world.

'This is a good place to sit,' Joel suggests, showing me a bench overlooking a pretty nineteenth-century bridge.

'I suppose the English were so homesick once they got here, they tried to recreate London in Sydney,' I say.

'Is that the problem?' he asks. 'Are you feeling homesick?'

'Dunno.'

He laughs. 'Could the problem possibly be that I bought a bracelet and necklace in there for Rebecca?'

I give in. 'Maybe.'

'She's in Sydney till her birthday, then she's going back to New York,' Joel tells me. 'She runs the marketing department for us, in Manhattan. Anyway, I was her holiday fling. That's what she said on the weekend. And that's perfectly fine by me.'

I note the tense and try not to feel too excited. *Was* her holiday fling.

'Alice,' Joel squeezes my hand, 'you're going to Byron Bay tomorrow and I'm probably not going to see you for a while. We're also cousins – not genetically linked, but still part of the same family. You just broke up with someone. I've been by myself for a long time. My last relationship went nowhere because she said I couldn't commit. I'm not . . . *good* at this stuff. There's something there between us, but I don't know what it is yet and I'm not even sure we should act on it. Does that make sense?'

'Yes. Alright.' I look at his steady, serious eyes and feel his hand in mine and fight the urge to kiss him.

Then he sees the chicken satay sticks poking out of the paper bag in my pocket and gives me a lecture about battery hen farming.

'Sorry,' I say. 'I was absolutely starving.'

He nudges me. 'Come and stay with me in Bellingen. Once you've seen real chickens, laying real eggs, you won't want to eat the ones stuck in cages.'

'Can I really come and stay? I'm dying to see your place.'

Joel smiles. 'Any time. Just leave your plastic bag collection at home, okay?'

'Oh God, Joel. I'm such a sinner, aren't I. Any more lectures?'

'Not right now. And I've booked a vegetarian place for dinner – if you're still up for it?'

The next day, I catch the train to Byron Bay. After a farewell breakfast with Robyn, I go to the station with Joel, who takes one photo of me after another on his ancient 1970s Polaroid.

Central Station is like a grand old London station, complete with old-fashioned clocks and marble walls. There is something incredibly romantic about trains – I can't believe Australians are so reluctant to use them. Or maybe it's just Matty talking rubbish. My train is heaving with passengers, all equipped with pillows, chocolate, magazines and bottles of water. I look at the timetables and realise that the trains to Queensland will take all day and all night to get there – and that's only one state away. Imagine going to Perth. The train must be full of skeletons holding coffee cups when it finally arrives at the other end.

Joel kisses my cheek on the platform, and shakes my hand for good luck through the window. Once the train sets off and I'm by myself, I know I will hug that perfunctory kiss to myself for hours. Soon Joel will be back on his block of land at Bellingen, and then I can go and stay. He's going to buy two second-hand caravans and use them as a temporary home until he's ready to build his mud-brick house.

I wave goodbye through the window, until I finally lose sight of him. Then I worry that all the other single women on the platform will leap on him as soon as I've disappeared. Or that the beautiful and good Rebecca will change her mind about New York and stay in Australia after all.

The train finally leaves Sydney and its houses far behind, then crawls on between roads cut out of mountains and past tiny islands I didn't even know existed. I fall asleep somewhere between Woy Woy (the legendary Woy Woy!)

and a place name that sounds like a man falling down a fight of stairs. Tumble-along? Thud Wallop?

The woman in socks who has been doing sudoku next to me since we left Central Station disappears halfway through the journey, leaving me with a spare seat to lie sideways on. I am so tired – I was up all night talking with Joel for hours after we left the restaurant. I eventually wake up to an announcement about our imminent arrival at Byron Bay. I have seat-creases on my arms and sleep in my eyes, and all the make-up in the world isn't going to make me look presentable, even though I am wearing a new work outfit from St Vincent de Paul's. There's an old fashion rule about double denim (and Suzanne would kill me if she could see me now) but the faded jacket and skirt I found somehow look right together, with the addition of a stripy T-shirt from Jade's stall. Right now I feel ready for anything – even Bark's of Byron Bay.

fifteen

I stagger off the train and realise the sun is setting. Bondi Beach must be hundreds of miles behind me now. Then I see a tanned forty-fifty-something woman (a new breed I have noticed in Australia) with flaming red hair and three dogs on a lead. One of them is a worried-looking Pekinese wearing gingham rompers. The other two are excitable Labradors.

'Hello, Alice!' Danielle Coles pumps my hand. 'Let me take this luggage! I can't believe you wanted to take the train, you crazy girl!'

In common with many forty-fifty-something Aussie women I have seen, Danielle is wearing her gym gear at eight o'clock in the evening, although her hair is beautifully blow-dried. She has a bottom like two boiled eggs in a handkerchief. It is a Pilates bottom – a phenomenon I recently discovered in Bondi. You roll around on a plastic ball for an hour and develop a kind of rubber bum.

'These are some of the little fellows you'll be looking after.' Danielle introduces the dogs as we wheel my mother's old suitcases to her car.

Dad would have been impressed. It's an enormous silver BMW with BARK'S OF BYRON BAY painted on each side and the company logo, featuring dogs in crowns waving sceptred orbs around. It has a lot of stickers on the back window. Magic Happens. I Heart My Dalmation. I Heart My Corgi. No McDonald's for Byron Bay.

'Now, Alice. A bit of info for you. Mr Chang we've spoken about – he gets carsick, so we'll have him in the front by himself in case he does a little chuck on the way. And these two gorgeous boys are called Zoltan and Tikyo.'

Zoltan and what? It hadn't occurred to me that I will have to memorise the names of all the dogs at Bark's of Byron Bay. These two sound as if they've been named after alien fighter missiles.

'What I'm going to do with you, Alice, is drop your bags with the dogs back at the kennel, then take you straight out to dinner. I thought you might like to meet up with some friends of mine.'

'Lovely.'

We bundle into the big silver BMW and Danielle insists I call her Dani. 'Put the iPod on shuffle, darl,' she instructs me, and I try my best. Soon we are listening to random Sting, followed by random Enya and then more random Sting. By now, Nash would be sticking his fingers down his throat and pulling faces.

When we finally arrive at Bark's, I take in as much as I can, even though it's dark. The place is vast, like a health farm, and appears to be bordered by live electric fences and monitored by a Colditz-style CCTV system.

Dani takes the two Labradors in first, while I'm left to talk to Mr Chang, who has indeed been carsick down the front of his gingham rompers. I suppose the rompers have a nappy built into them. I wonder where his famous incontinence cushion is. Poor thing. I pat him on the head and he tries to lick my hand off. I'm sure nobody ever shows him any affection. Should I be doing something? I'm not sure. Perhaps I still have guest status at the moment so I'm not obliged to carry out any dog-wrangling duties. Then again, Mr Chang looks desperate for a wee.

Before I can make a move, Dani is back, wearing a pair of rubber gloves with frills on the cuffs.

'He can pee like a brewer's horse,' she advises me, before lifting Mr Chang out of the front seat and taking off his rompers. I wonder if he has a selection of pants to choose from. I certainly hope so. Otherwise I will probably be handwashing the gingham rompers once we return from dinner.

'There are about fifty dogs here on the weekend,' Dani explains, once she's lugged my cases into the house and we're driving again, towards the centre of Byron Bay. 'We have our regulars too. I call it my little dog therapy clinic. Mr Chang is a permanent resident from Friday to Sunday – his parents have a weekender up here. They'll be at dinner, by the way. Robert and Georgie. Robert's got a few vineyards along the north coast.'

Poor Mr Chang. He must be like one of those forgotten children of Hollywood celebrities, left with the nanny while their parents jetset around the world. No wonder he pees everywhere. So would I.

Dani's a terrible driver, mainly because she talks into what she calls her Blueteeth while she's supposed to be keeping her eyes on the road. Blueteeth appears to be some kind of invisible telephone. She can hear the person who's rung her up but I can't. I can hear her replies though, which, along with the sound of her GPS tracking device's robotic monotone, makes for a very odd atmosphere in the car.

'Yiss, he's been having a bad trot lately,' Dani says, as we narrowly avoid crashing into a lamppost. 'So I basically said, "Up your nose with a rubber hose darling, I couldn't care less". If his brains were dynamite, they wouldn't blow his hat off,' she goes on, and I realise she must be talking about my predecessor at Bark's. I find myself wondering how many kennel assistants Dani has actually employed – and what happens to them. Maybe she rolls over them with her Pilates ball.

We go into the restaurant after an amazingly bad piece of parking by Dani and there is suddenly a copious amount of what Nash would call mwah-mwah kissing among her friends.

The group of smiling, kissing people around the table is a silver blur of platinum rings, metal chairs, gleaming candlesticks, shiny hoop earrings and metallic handbags. All the silver contrasts with the tans, which are deep and golden, and the whole thing is reflected in an enormous mirror on the back wall. I am introduced to everyone and instantly forget their names – except for Georgie, wife of Robert, because she's sitting next to me.

The restaurant is BYO so everyone is drinking wine from Robert's vineyard. Because he's slightly drunk and not listening to me properly – and because the music is so loud you can't hear anyway – he makes the mistake of thinking I'm a businessperson too. We order our first course and Robert starts talking. And talking. He talks across Georgie and Dani and then across me, occasionally sending tiny bits of spit flying across the table.

'See the way Danielle parked her truck out there?' he asks me, without waiting for an answer. 'She's a shocking driver. Women shouldn't drive at night. Man's got the right-brain spatial ability. He's got the hunting vision.'

I try to think of a reply. 'But a woman can see better in the dark than a man,' I tell him at last. 'That's been proved.'

Now Robert doesn't know what to say either.

'Do you hunt?' he asks.

'No. It's been banned in England actually.' (Much to my mother's disappointment, but I'm not about to tell Robert that.)

He immediately loses interest and moves on to the man sitting on the other side of Georgie, who is the first straight man I've ever seen with cosmetic surgery. He looks most peculiar, like a fifty-year-old fifteen-year-old.

'So you're working for Dani,' Georgie says, leaving her wine untouched.

'I think I'm looking after Mr Chang. He's yours, isn't he?'

'He's Robert's dog,' she says. 'Actually, he belongs to Robert's son, Ryan – but then he got his tennis scholarship.' Georgie sounds as if she doesn't know whether to be smug or annoyed about this. 'Dani said you were over from London,' she continues. 'That's exciting. Byron Bay's so bewdyful. I'm doing a big detox spa next week. You must try it.'

'Sounds great.'

'Are you here in Byron on your own?'

'Yes.'

Georgie has nothing left to say to me, and I have nothing to say to her. She is the detoxed wife of a successful vineyard owner with a son on a tennis scholarship, and I am a sad, single, toxed-up Pommie dog-minder in second-hand clothes – a distinctly unbewdyful creature wearing double denim in the middle of bewdyful Byron Bay.

Robyn told me that Byron Bay is where the sea-changers go – people who sell their homes in the city and move to the coast so they can live the Australian dream, in enormous houses with all the swimming pools, yoga classes, ocean views, silver handbags, four-wheel-drives, flat-screen televisions, expensive restaurants and designer dogs this entails.

Poor incontinent Mr Chang. He must be the only part of Georgie and Robert's dream that didn't go according to plan. I suppose that ultimately they'll have to have him killed.

The following day I discover that Georgie and Robert do, in fact, want to have Mr Chang put down. 'If you could just run him to the vet later on for his . . .' Dani pulls a face because she is too delicate to say the words 'lethal injection'. I don't know what to say. This is the first task I've been asked to perform in my first Australian job and I'm not sure I can do it.

As I listen to Dani making calls in her office, I realise that although, according to her car sticker, she hearts Dalmatians and hearts corgis, she doesn't actually seem to have a heart at all. Nor does she actually own any dogs. Danielle and Heidi Coles share a surname and an Australian vocabulary (little black ducks, mad cut snakes, various rooted situations) but that's the only thing they have in common. Heidi is nice and Dani is clearly not.

I am in the Bark's kitchen – vast, stainless-steel, indisputably doggy – when it occurs to me that I may not stay here beyond the trial month. The list of instructions is overwhelming and the smell of canine crap is overpowering. And I'm not taking poor Chang to the vet to be put down. I have decided that already. Georgie, Robert and Dani can give that task to someone else.

Dani has lists everywhere, laminated and decorated with dog stickers. Under the heading *Kleptomaniacs* are the names of lawless animals who must be watched night and day in case they make off with anything on the premises. Dani is particularly concerned about a spaniel called Johnny who's been known to take other dogs' squeaky toys, and a mixed-breed named Whispering who digs up other animals' bones.

It doesn't stop there. When I add up the items on Dani's computer printout, I come up with forty-seven things I must – or must not – do as part of my duties at Bark's.

- Stereo tuned to bass notes only, no high-pitched music, and especially not violin. Dogs howl at Nigel Kennedy, Dexy's Midnight Runners, 'The Devil Went Down To Georgia' etc, etc.
- The following dogs will break into delivery vans if doors are left open: Hickory, Sophocles, Meatball, Twinkle, Zack, Punkboy, Rabbit and Travis.
- Bruce (Boston Terrier) pulls down washing.

- The following dogs jump up: Kisser, Cisco, Otis, Mr Whippy, Winchester, Teddy, Mooch, Nike, Psycho, Woody, Hollyoaks, Zed, Tubs and Mr Chang. (Aha. The unfortunate Mr Chang.)
- Buddy, a Maltese Terrier, attacks any human seen watching television – particularly if they're watching *Oprah* – and must be squirted with water.
- The following dogs are whiners: Lady, Calvin, Monsieur Henri, Robertson, Scoop, Tricky and Leroy.
- The following dogs attack lawnmowers, motorbikes, skateboards and cars: Cinnamon, Frosty, Monty, Mavis, Mr O, Rambo, Jet Boy, Bunny, Cooper and Farfalle.
- Nipper regularly goes into a trance. (Oh, please let Nipper not fall over dead like Goggles, so I have to carry him home in a plastic shopping bag.)
- The following dogs have criminal records: Pegasus, Willow and Jock.
- The following dogs are leg-riders: Outrageous, Lily, Chunky, Jelly and Whistler.
- Ollie (Kelpie-Staffie cross) is a licker and must not be allowed near anyone with bare arms.

It goes on for several pages. No wonder Dani Coles has been through so many staff.

I find out exactly how many when I do a full inspection of my carer's quarters. Everyone who's ever stayed here has written their name on a piece of concrete underneath a loose tile in the fireplace. It's an unofficial visitors book with a variety of one-star reviews.

Will I end up hating Bark's as much as all the other staff who have lived and worked here? I'm not sure. But

I now understand why Dani was so quick to take me on as a full-time employee, sight unseen, from the other side of the world. She's also quick to remind me of how much trouble it took to get me here.

'I've taken some admin costs out of your first week's pay,' she tells me as I'm trying to sort out the many sacks of dog biscuits in the kitchen. 'All that business with Immigration cost us a bit, Alice. Just so you know.'

She is looking at me as if she wants me to be grateful. I take my cue.

'Thanks so much for that, Dani. I really appreciate it.'

'It was a pleasure to be able to help yew.' She turns her back and her Pilates-perfect bottom on me and strides out.

At the end of the day, the subject of Mr Chang comes up again.

'Sometimes yew just have to be cruel to be kind,' Dani says.

'But he's not in pain. He's just incontinent, isn't he? Lots of dogs are like that. And he gets a bit carsick.'

'I think his owners are the best judge of that.'

'I thought this was a boarding kennel. I thought I'd be walking the dogs, feeding them, playing with them, bathing them. I didn't expect to be doing this.'

'There's a little saying we have in Australia: Love it or shove it.'

'It's exactly the same in England,' I tell her.

In the end, I obey orders and take Mr Chang to the vet, Phil Hodain, but only because I want to hear what he has to say about his health. But the vet turns out to be a she, not a he, and she's on my side. She says she can't possibly proceed with the lethal injection.

'This is a Bark's dog, I suppose. Apart from anything else, you're not authorised to do this. There's no signed letter here from the owner.'

'Dani said Phil would look after it,' I tell her apologetically.

'Phil's on leave. I'm the relieving vet – I usually work at Ballina. I don't know what kind of arrangement Phil has with Dani, but I'm sure he wouldn't proceed on this basis. Was this an impulsive decision by the owners, do you know?'

'Sorry. I haven't been told anything.'

'Well, you'll have to take Mr Chang back. But I'd advise against this procedure altogether – he's not in any pain or extreme discomfort. And the incontinence can be controlled with medication. It's no big deal.'

Poor Mr Chang. He looks terrified, shivering in the corner of the surgery in his ridiculous rompers (tartan today) and his matching collar.

When I take him back to Bark's, Dani is furious. She says she has better things to do, because she's training for a triathlon, and she'll have to sack me if I don't clean up my act.

'Alice, I don't have toim for this.'

'Can I take him then?'

'Take who? The *dog*?' She looks at Chang and then at me as if we are both completely mad.

'I'm happy to take him. Georgie and Robert won't care, will they?'

'Do what you like with him but you're not keeping him here.'

'I might have to leave then. Sorry.'

'You're quitting?'

'Well, you were about to sack me anyway, weren't you? It'll save us both a lot of time and trouble in the long run.'

'It's been a frigging *nightmare* to get you over here, Alice. Are you crazy?'

'I'm sorry.'

Before Dani can shout at me any more, I jog-walk back to my poky little carer's flat with Mr Chang and pack up my suitcases on wheels at record speed. I know there's no point in talking to Dani about money. Instead, I stand on the side of the highway and hail a taxi. Once I'm in Byron itself, I head for the nearest phone box. Oh, please let Joel be at Robyn's still.

It's wonderful to hear his voice when he finally answers.

'It's Alice. I'm having a problem,' I try to sound businesslike and fail.

'Where are you?' he says.

'In Byron Bay with this Pekinese dog, Mr Chang. I've run away from Bark's – *we've* run away. They were going to put him down. I don't know what to do. I've got a dog, all my suitcases, my sewing machine and I'm in a phone box.'

Joel doesn't miss a beat. 'Come to Bellingen and stay with me. I've organised the caravans – they're already there. There are no locks – just go in. There should be cooking stuff there too. I bought the vans with the contents.'

'Joel, I can't walk down two consecutive streets in Australia without getting lost. How am I going to get to Bellingen?'

'Get a taxi to the station and jump on the train to Urunga. But you'll have to hide the dog.'

'Aaargh!'

'Alice! Don't sound so worried. People do it all the time. I'll call Wiz, my neighbour, and ask him to pick you up at the other end. Have you still got that map of my property that I drew for you?'

'Yes. Oh, Joel, it was so awful at that place. It was like Colditz for dogs.'

'It's over now. I'll be there as soon as I can. Okay?'

'I don't want to drag you away from Sydney.'

'And I don't want you to be by yourself at the moment. How's Mr Chang feeling?'

'We can't call him that any more. It's just Chang. He already seems a bit happier.'

'He'll love Bello. It's dog heaven.'

Bello. Anything with three or more syllables in Australia is automatically shortened. Even two syllables is too long sometimes. I suppose at some point I will be magically turned into Al.

I flag down a taxi. My ticket to Urunga uses up a precious $50 note, but at this stage I'd give anything to put some space between me and Bark's of Byron Bay. Not to mention Dani's boiled-eggs bottom.

Because I board the train with so much junk – old suitcases, a sewing machine and various plastic bags – Chang, hidden in a cardboard box, goes undetected. I traipse through carriage after carriage, dragging my stuff behind me, until I find two unoccupied seats in the full blast of the loo doorway. Every time I open the flaps of Chang's cardboard box to give him some air, he wisely declines. I wish I could. Instead, I try to fall asleep.

After a long journey during which I veer between dreaming and waking, the driver finally announces that we are approaching Urunga. I turn to the window and see two pelicans flying overhead.

Please let that be a good omen.

sixteen

'G'day.' A bearded man walks up to me in the car park and offers his hand. He says his name is The Wizard Formerly Known As Wayne, and he's Joel's neighbour. Joel has told him all about me and the situation, he adds 'whatever that is', and if there's anything he can do, I only have to ask.

I look at him properly to see if I've heard the wizard thing right. He doesn't look particularly magical. His beard is short and clipped. He has no pointy hat. No purple cape with stars. No shoes that curl up at the end – although he does have tanned, bare feet and a toe ring.

'I'm Alice,' I say.

'Call me Wiz,' The Wizard Formerly Known As Wayne offers.

Then he takes my bags while I let poor Chang out of his box, and we make our way to his VW campervan. I see that Wiz drives with a can of beer on the dashboard. He also walks like John Wayne after a week in the saddle, and when he sits in the front seat, his legs are so far apart that his knee keeps bumping into mine. What the hell has he got in his underpants? A jar of pickled onions?

'Got the dog on the train alright, did ya?' He nods at little Chang who is cowering at my feet.

'They didn't seem to want to check. Maybe they were just being nice. Chang's been very good though. He didn't pee anywhere and he wasn't sick. That's a bit of an achievement for him.'

That is the extent of my conversation with The Wizard Formerly Known As Wayne as we begin the journey. I try, but give up. He'd clearly rather keep his eyes on the road and concentrate on the art of truck-dodging.

As trucks scream past us, I check my phone. There's no reception.

'Depends where you are,' Wiz informs me. 'Stand outside the back of the pub and see what happens.'

Instead I take in the countryside. I am slowly getting used to the Australian landscape. So far, I have only seen it framed by car and train windows, but there are some things that are becoming familiar – the enormously fat, healthy cows, for a start, and the brilliant green grass. In this part of the country, at least, there is no drought. It looks positively lush.

I see a river through the trees and assume it must be the Bellinger that Joel loves so much – where you can famously drink the same water that you swim in. Suddenly, I long for a swim – and a drink, come to that. I wanted to explore the beach at Byron Bay too, but I suppose I'll have to do that another time. Another year. Another decade.

We pass a swimming pool and a golf club, and then we are in Bellingen itself. It's just as Joel described it: one street, one pub, one supermarket, one chemist, one newsagency, one garage, one library, one war memorial.

There are Christmas lights up everywhere, even though Christmas is long gone, giving the impression that the whole street is celebrating something.

'Well, it's not London,' says The Wizard Formerly Known As Wayne, offering me a bag of nuts.

We drive for miles, leaving the war memorial far behind. I am too afraid to ask Wiz how far away Joel's property is, in case he loses concentration and runs into a truck. Trucks in Australia don't carry orange juice or chocolate, as they do in England. They invariably have huge logs on board, or herds of cattle.

'You're probably wondering about me,' Wiz says, although I'm not. 'I used to be known as Wayne O'Halloran. Then I got in with some bad mojo people and they took away my power. I had to change my name for business reasons.'

'Did you get the idea from Prince?' I ask him.

'Yeah.'

He gives me a sly look and turns on his cassette-player – whereupon I am blasted by 'Little Red Corvette' ('Whoo! Whoo!' hoots Wiz) accompanied by much finger-clicking and foot-stamping.

Eventually we turn from the sealed road onto a bumpy dirt lane, then rattle our way down a winding track at the bottom of a long mountain range. I recognise the hand-painted, numbered sign at the entrance to Joel's property from his hand-drawn map and try not to get too excited.

'You're Joel's cousin,' Wiz announces rather than asks.

'Yes, but we're not related.'

'Yeah. You'll like it here,' Wiz says. 'Do you do much astral travelling?'

'Not really.'

'That's a shame. You can go a bloody long way from here,' and he points upwards.

Wiz parks the van, hands me Chang in his box, and drags my cases and sewing machine over to the two caravans parked side by side in a clearing beneath a canopy of trees.

'Thanks so much, Wiz. You must come round for dinner.'

My new neighbour looks at the caravans, looks at me, and smiles – at last. I suppose it's the most ridiculous thing he's heard all week.

'Tell Joel some goat's runnin' around,' he grunts before he drives off.

I take off Chang's dreaded rompers and let him loose – which is when I spot the goat. It's white, like a goat from a children's fairy story. He eats the grass sideways, his jaw shunting backwards and forwards, while the rest of his furry face remains immobile. Chang is thrilled and gives little barks of excitement; it may be the first goat he's ever seen. Or maybe he thinks it's some kind of gigantic poodle.

I go inside the larger caravan first. It's lit by fluorescent strips, and when I look in the mirror it's like seeing some kind of vampire woman. I find a packet of tealight candles in a drawer and light them instead, turning the caravan into a shadowy cave.

I open and shut every drawer in turn. All I find are ancient saucepans, bits of old picnic-set cutlery, smelly newspapers and the occasional mouse trap. Then I check my phone reception – nothing.

I sit down on the mattress and read one of the newspapers dating from last year. I discovered that the Bellingen Potato Festival featured an Iron Man competition in which each contestant had to spring 40 metres carrying a 20-kilo bag of potatoes, drink a raw egg, eat a cold meat pie, and blow up a balloon until it popped. Prize: a 20-kilo bag of potatoes.

The annual Bellingen Chainsaw Races were replaced by Bovine Bingo, due to lack of interest. There was also some news about the Urunga Swingers – but it turned out to be a ladies golf club.

I give up on the newspaper and look in the second caravan. It's even emptier, but the sheets and pillowcases seem cleaner – and there's even a proper bath-sized towel. I decide to settle in there, and put a blanket under the van for Chang.

As I sit on the caravan's step that night, London has never seemed further away. I can't wait for the stars to come out. Joel said you can see everything from his property, including the Southern Cross.

I wonder what Wiz's house is like, and imagine a purple-painted shed with silver-foil wallpaper and a lot of incense. My God. I hope Wiz doesn't astral travel into my caravan tonight. The way he was grinding his thighs together while singing along to Prince was just awful.

I go to bed and try to think of something else – preferably Joel. When I wake up again, it's almost seven o'clock in the morning and there's a goat trying to get into the caravan and what sounds like a rooster coaching him.

Suddenly, I realise that Chang is on the end of the bed. Oh no. I lift him off and look for the wet patch. The blanket and sheets are dry.

'Chang, did you sleep on my bed and not pee? Did you? Did you manage to stay here all night and behave yourself?'

He snorts as if I am a complete tosser, and skips out of the van and immediately chases the rooster away.

I step outside into the sunlight, still wearing my clothes from the night before. I'm already dreaming of a new look for Australia, of course. A straw hat with an old 1950s gingham belt . . . and as much denim as I can bleach, stretch and fade in the sun. It is already warm, and looks as if it will be boiling hot by lunchtime. Joel said there was a creek on the property that I could use as a temporary water supply until he buys a rainwater tank. I try not to think about the king brown or red-bellied black snakes on my wall chart from Australia House as I go looking for the creek. Instead, I concentrate on the nice-cup-of-tea aspect of finding water. I have left a lot of my old life in England behind, but one thing I can't get rid of is my addiction to builder's-strength tea.

I find the creek at the bottom of a steep slope then realise I haven't brought anything to carry the water in. I go back to the caravans and eventually find four tin buckets in the storage cavity underneath the beds. I return to the creek to fill them up. The water is incredible. Clear, cool and up to my knees. No pollution. No murk. No old crisp packets or tyres.

I make a cup of tea.

I take Chang down to the creek, where I strip down to my bra and pants and sit in the water as if it's a bath, hoping that Wiz's bearded face won't suddenly appear around a tree trunk. I am quite alone, though – and after my bath, I spend the whole morning exploring the deeper parts of the creek while punk-rock kookaburras cackle at me through the trees.

By now, I'm starving, but there's no food in either caravan. I suppose I could do a hippy fasting thing until Joel gets here, but I'm beginning to feel faint.

Chang seems to read my mind. He leads me to a grapefruit tree, like Lassie.

'Good boy!' I tell him.

He loves the attention and jumps up at me – the forbidden jumping-up that Danielle Coles so loathed – then lifts his leg on a gum tree to celebrate his own cleverness.

The grapefruit are sweet and juicy; not like London supermarket grapefruit at all. There is also a patch of spinach nearby, just as Joel promised. Then I discover rhubarb, tomatoes, potatoes, cabbage, pumpkin and even, once I taste-test it, coriander. Although Joel's been away, the vegetables are flourishing all by themselves.

Chang keeps exploring, so I let him lead the way and eventually we find a henhouse. There are a few chickens inside, asleep, but I can't see any eggs and I don't want to disturb them. I imagine them as feeling like me at Huddersfield University, riddled with performance anxiety and desperate to stay in bed all day. If there was a television inside, they'd be watching quiz shows and eating pot noodles.

I try not to feel anxious about when Joel's going to get here, but it's like every other time I have waited for anything nice to happen. The more I count the hours, the less time seems to move on.

I fall asleep, with Chang lying on my stomach, and am woken by Joel whispering my name.

'Hey, Alice,' he says, standing in the doorway.

'It's you!' I say stupidly.

We drink a vat of tea and I tell him all about the horrors of Bark's, and then about not wanting to disturb the chickens.

He laughs at me. 'Just lift them up. The eggs'll be right under there.'

'Oh, Joel, you know I think that all eggs come from Tesco's.'

Joel shows me a deep waterhole further down the hill that we can use for our water supply. I never thought about water in London, but I am beginning to see how much it matters here.

We have good intentions of christening the caravans with the bottle of wine Joel has brought up from Sydney, but we're so busy talking that we forget to open it.

He tells me that my preferred caravan can be my home here for as long as I like. So that's it then. We'll be caravan neighbours. Non-kissing cousins. Any silly daydreams I've been having about an instant relationship vanish in a second. I should have known that Joel is far too sensible for that.

'So you met The Wizard Formerly Known As Wayne?' he asks.

'God, yes. How could you do it to me?'

'Wayne's alright. He's just done too many mushies.'

'Magic mushrooms?' I ask, and am pleased when Joel nods. I am learning to translate the Australian language, slowly but surely. You just stretch out every compressed word and phrase until you've added back all the letters or syllables the locals take away.

The next day, Joel suggests we buy bicycles. We can't rely on lifts forever. He was lucky to hitch a ride yesterday, he says, but he can't count on it happening again.

'I should hope not,' I say. 'You could have ended up in pieces in someone's car boot.'

We still have to hitchhike today, but the Wizard Formerly Known As Wayne kindly picks us up on his way into town, and drops us at the second-hand shop. Unbelievably, they have a few bikes to choose from. Mine is a girl's bike from the 1970s – pink, decorated with daisy stickers, and equipped with a funny straw basket at the front and a big vinyl carry-case on the back. I ride around Bellingen with Joel, pinging the bell for the hell of it, then go to an internet café to pick up my email.

There's nothing from either Danielle or Heidi Coles. I feel bad about Heidi, so I write her a short email about Bark's using the magical phrase 'it just didn't work out'. Suzanne taught it to me years ago, and although Nash used to curl his lip in utter contempt any time he heard me saying it, it's the emergency life raft of the English language. At one point in my career, though, I would really like *something* to work out. Is that too much to ask? All my good intentions about Vintage Alice seem to have been defeated by Bark's, money, time, life, the universe and everything else.

Danielle Coles's silence is deafening. I suppose she will never contact me again. She and her horrible friends should be grateful for one thing though – I saved them a vet's bill by kidnapping Chang.

My mother's sent three messages with the same information reworded each time, because my silence over the last few days has convinced her that her googles to me aren't getting through. She's excited about an online dating site she's discovered called Greydates UK, for widows and widowers of a certain age, and wonders if I agree with her that it's time to make new friends again. Oh my God. Greydates UK? And what does she mean, *friends*?

I can't think about it properly now, but I tell her she's free to Greydate as much as she likes, if she feels ready. It's been three years since Dad died.

She also tells me she's sent Aunt Helena's trunk to Bark's of Byron Bay. I can only hope Dani sends it on. Oh God. What if she chucks the lot in a fit of revenge? Or, worse, makes natty little dog coats out of the Mary Quant dress?

While Joel picks up provisions at the supermarket, I trawl through the rest of the latest from London. My friends want to tell me about everything I'm missing on the television, and all I want to do is tell them all about Joel. Instead, I sit on my hands. How can I possibly explain any of it to anyone? I don't understand it myself. Underneath everything lurks the thought that although it feels right, right, right, it's wrong, wrong, wrong. Even if I did go to a phone box now, ring Suzanne and get her out of bed to talk about it, I still couldn't find the right words.

Nash has sent me two emails. One is headed *Communication to Australia* and insists that I make more of an effort to stay in touch. We may have broken up, he says, but that is no reason why we can't remain friends.

Yeah, right.

I write back and tell him I'm staying in a caravan on a country property with no water, a generator, no phone line and no proper loo, thus *Communication to Australia* is a bit limited. That should shut him up. I don't tell him about the Bark's disaster. Just the thought of entering into a discussion with Nash about that makes me feel overwhelmed.

All I really want to do is get back to the grapefruit tree. And the chickens. And the creek. What did Joel say last night? 'Welcome to the real world.' I think I'm beginning to understand what he means.

Nash's second impossibly polite email is about the packing crate he's just dispatched – and, like Mum, he's sent it to Bark's of Byron Bay. My God. I hope Danielle Coles doesn't open that either – once she sees my donkey charity shop tights collection she may never recover.

I don't think the internet is a very good idea at the moment. Every time I read messages from England my head feels like it's going to explode. Even Suzanne's emails are too much – full of Camden Market news and local celebrity gossip. It all seems too far away.

While I wait for Joel to finish at the supermarket, I wonder how long I should wait before ringing Dani about my shipments from England.

Maybe I should tell her I know Sting or something. That might help.

We cycle home, unsteadily, in the heat – it is the kind of day when the roads seem to shimmer and wobble. That afternoon, I help Joel clear the weeds from a patch of land south of the caravans, which he thinks would make a good home for a worm farm. We wear thick rubber gloves as we pull out the weeds and I try not to sneeze as pollen flies everywhere.

The previous owners poured a concrete slab in this spot, and left behind a rusty car trailer without tyres. There's also a black, leathery corpse lying on the ground.

'Poor old flying fox,' Joel says. 'Must have hit something on the way home.'

Chang inspects the corpse and makes little whining noises. I think it may be the first bat that either of us have seen. Australia is continually presenting me with real versions of things I have only experienced on television, even if sometimes they're dead versions.

'So tell me how the worm farm works?' I ask.

'Everything organic goes into the tank,' Joel explains, as we sit down on the concrete slab for a rest. 'Paper, cardboard, sewage, the lot. The worms process it, to put it nicely. Then it all goes back to feed the fruit trees and vegies, as a kind of super juice.' He looks at me. 'Are you okay with that?'

'Oh yes,' I swallow hard. 'You make it sound so lovely. I can be an Australian worm farmer.'

He picks up an old stone tool lying on top of an old car battery near the slab. 'Someone else found this before me,' he says. 'I'd forgotten I left it here. It's Aboriginal.'

'Wow.'

'The other Australia,' he says, as he helps me up.

'So they were here, on this land?'

'Yeah. Before they were driven out. Who knows when that got left here. It might have been hundreds of years ago.'

We go back to work, and don't stop again until the sun's heading towards the mountains. Joel tells me he'd like to build a house here using solar power.

'I'm so hopeless,' I say, feeling very Swiss Cottage all of a sudden. 'I don't know anything.'

'Neither do I!' he says. 'I'm going to teach myself while I'm living here. But imagine this place in a couple of years' time. Everything on your plate could be grown here. You could cook using the sun for your electricity. Drink rainwater from the tank. Gather honey from your own beehive . . .'

'Get milk from your own goat,' I add, as the goat stumbles towards us, bleating.

'You can give him a name if you like,' Joel says. 'He's not mine. He probably belonged to the squatters.'

'What squatters?'

'I've been hearing about them in town. Apparently a bus just rolled up one day, when I was in India, with half a commune, kids, goats, chooks – the lot.'

Joel looks completely untroubled by the idea. I think of Nash, who hates the squatters in London so much that he's been known to pelt gravel at their boarded-up windows.

'They probably left the chooks and goat behind as payment,' Joel goes on. 'That's often the way it works around here. Anyway, the animals seem to have found a way to get by.'

Later, when Joel thinks I am not looking, I sneak a glance at him, swimming in his boxer shorts. The fact that he is so untroubled by my presence bothers me. At the beginning with Nash, when I was falling in love with him, and he was falling in love with me, we were so twitchy and self-conscious around each other that we could barely get through a night out without jumping every time our legs touched under the table. Joel just doesn't seem to care. Does he really think we can stay like this for months, living side by side in a couple of caravans and just being neighbourly cousins, or cousinly neighbours?

He's seen me in my bra and pants in the middle of the night, wandering off into the bush for a pee. No response. Meanwhile, I care more about his close proximity to me every day. Maybe his lack of interest is because of Rebecca with the plaits. Maybe he likes her a lot more than he's letting on. In any case, I'm beginning to feel as if nothing will ever happen between us.

seventeen

Now that I have a new life in Australia, with a new dog and a new home, I make a new financial start. I decide I am going to pay Joel back for everything, even if it kills me.

We are having a beer at the pub in Bellingen one evening when I push two $100 notes across the table.

'What's this?' he asks.

'The bicycle you bought me. Our food, loo rolls, this beer. Everything you've spent on me so far.'

'I'm not keeping a tally. Are you?'

I feel embarrassed. 'Sorry.'

'Don't be sorry – I get it. But if I was broke and you had some cash lying around, wouldn't you want to send it my way?'

'Yes.'

'Well, then, no tally. You'll be helping me out soon enough when you get going with your clothes, the Vintage Alice thing.'

Joel gives me one of his funny, friendly, crinkly smiles, and I try to smile back, although I feel like a complete fraud. There are dozens of pregnant women in England just waiting for me to make them frocks – but at this rate, they'll have given birth by the time I've managed to organise myself.

The next day – the hottest morning yet – I cycle all the way to the Bellingen library and borrow a book about goats. I also give ours a name – Henry, after Henry Lawson. He is not the donkey I want – who will be named Simpson – but he's a start.

There's a lot to learn. Henry has lice, which is why he's scratching all the time, and unless I'm careful it appears the lice may hop onto Chang and then, presumably, onto me. The solution is a large teaspoon of sulphur every day, for as long as Henry can stand it.

He also needs a doe if I am ever going to make goat's milk yoghurt, but I have to make sure she doesn't have big knees. Big knees, apparently, are a huge problem in the goat world. I must tell Suzanne that in my next email. It's exactly the same in the world of fashion: one big knee and you're out of the collection; two big knees and you'll never work again.

I talk to Joel about Henry the goat and his lice. 'Maybe we should try sheep instead,' I suggest.

'Except they get blowfly strike and pulpy kidneys,' he tells me.

Bugger; or, as they say in Bellingen, buggery. If I have to deal with a sheep's disgusting pulpy kidney after a hard morning's work throwing buckets of sewage at worms, I think I may have to throw in the towel – or, as they also say around here, chark it all in.

Joel cheers me up by bringing home some mint, parsley and basil plants from Wiz, which he has exchanged for a box of fresh eggs. He is dripping with sweat in the heat.

'Wiz says he can help us with a beehive,' he tells me, 'but we'll have to change our clothes.'

'Why?'

'Bees hate black.'

'You're joking. That's almost everything I own.'

'They don't like beards either. Wiz had big problems with his bees attacking his chin.'

We have peanut and spinach loaf for dinner, made with Joel's spinach, and something he calls apple ambrosia, which I have never heard of but think I may become addicted to. I suppose I am becoming an accidental vegetarian. I used to eat vegetarian food sometimes in London, when Nash and I were particularly broke, but now it feels like something I could live with consciously, for the rest of my life. I don't even mind Joel's lectures any more. In fact, I'm beginning to understand the point of them. All those farting cows and global warming – how could it possibly hurt to eat asparagus instead?

Oh my God. Suzanne was absolutely right in her last email. Thanks to Joel, I am turning into a fully fledged, card-carrying Aussie hippie chick.

The days roll by and the heat builds – abnormally so for late summer, according to the locals – and we make plans for the autumn, to make ourselves feel cooler.

Joel and I continue to say a polite goodnight to each other from our caravan doorways, then wake each other the next morning with billy tea, boiled in a tin billy on a campfire and served with unpasteurised cow's milk, with blobs of yellow cream on top. We could just plug in a kettle, of course, but Joel prefers his tea this way. He's a romantic. And yet, for all our late-night stargazing and convivial beer-drinking at the Federal Hotel, we seldom seem to get any closer.

I long to talk to Suzanne about it, but she's so busy that even when I manage to get through on the phone, all I get is her voicemail. She seems very, very far away. Sometimes, when I'm particularly missing her, I look at an issue of Twad in the Bellingen newsagency. It comes on a ship, the newsagent tells me, which is why it's always three months out of date.

I am dutifully pulling out more weeds near the concrete slab on another intensely hot morning when the postman delivers a kind of instant Christmas – Aunt Helena's trunk and all the boxes from Nash, both sent on from Bark's of Byron Bay. I kiss the trunk, which has been squashed inside a wooden crate. Thank God for Nice Heidi. She must have talked Nasty Dani into sending everything on, because her aunt still refuses to reply to my emails.

I notice something stuck on the side of the trunk – a polite note from Dani on Bark's of Byron Bay writing paper, decorated with the usual dogs wearing crowns and carrying orbed sceptres. Perhaps she's forgiven me after all and I won't wake up one day to find myself issued with a deportation notice from the Department of Immigration.

Joel helps me carry the crates into my caravan and I rip off the tape with the bread knife. Suddenly, all that remains of my old life in England is decanted onto my bed.

'You look like you're going to enjoy this,' Joel says, smiling. 'I'll leave you to it.'

I prop myself up with pillows against the caravan wall and sort through the bits and pieces of my recent past. Nash hasn't included a note. It's still strange to see his handwriting on the boxes though.

I pick my way through my grandmother's button collection, which he's wrapped up in one of my old pink towels. I wonder if I could make jewellery from them and sell them at the Bellingen Market? The market is my discovery of the week, along with a chicken-food recipe that's supposed to prevent fowl pox.

I find a black beret that saw me through several hard winters in London. If I wore it here, our new black-hating bees may attack me. I try out a half-full tube of concealer that I made Nash send, and a lipstick I used to love. I squint at myself in the sunlight in a tiny hand-mirror also from the box, now cracked on one side. Not only is my face divided into two halves, I look like a Goth panda. The red lipstick is too hard in the bright sunshine, and the concealer is far too white. Without even trying, I have picked up a tan in Bellingen.

My A-Z of London is in the second box, scribbled with arrows pointing to long-forgotten locations of job interviews, all the way from Kentish Town to Putney. There are other scribbles on the dog-eared pages, reminding me of parties I went to in the days when it was still possible to have a good time with Nash.

Oh, look. He's sent me *The Best of Motown* – now there's something I never thought he'd let me keep. He's such a dictator about music. I can't believe he's passed up the opportunity to edit my collection at last – but no, he's carefully packed it into the box with everything else. My

God, all those petty annoyances seem so far away and so long ago. I wonder how The Believers are faring with Sarah on board? The news must be either very good, or very bad, because in either case Nash is saying nothing about anything.

I unpack old soap-making equipment, four fat, dusty paintbrushes left over from my pottery days, a stripy scarf hand-knitted with glittery wool. These were all ideas I had before Vintage Alice. Suddenly I'm not sure if I should feel comforted by my old possessions or depressed by them.

I find a family tree I half-started and gave up on. How funny. There's Joel's name next to Robyn's, growing out of the left-hand fork in one of the trees. And now here I am, living on the same branch.

eighteen

Suddenly, he bounds into the caravan.

'Hey, guess what I've just found?' I wave the family tree at him.

'Get up on the bed.'

'What?'

'Just hop up on the bed, Alice, quickly, and look at the wall. Don't look down.'

I step up onto the caravan bed and, despite his instructions, immediately look at the ground, following his eyeline. And then I see it. A long, skinny black snake slithering from the doorway towards the kitchen cupboards.

'Aaargh!'

'Shhh. It's fine, Alice. The snake won't hurt you. I just need you to stay up there on the bed, that's all. And *don't look*.'

I turn my head to face the wall. Please, please, Saint-Martin-in-the-Fields and Saint Vincent de Paul, make the black snake go away. I'm not sure how long I can remain standing on this wobbly mattress.

Joel pounds the floor in his boots, and I try not to whimper. Has he just stamped on the snake's head? What happens if you do that? Does the head explode?

'There you go. I've got him. No worries,' Joel mutters, reassuring himself as much as me.

I finally feel brave enough to turn my head, and see him holding a hessian sack at arm's length from his body.

'Take it away!' I yelp.

'One red-bellied black snake to go,' Joel jokes, and takes a huge jump off the caravan step, swinging the sack as he goes. 'Stay here, Alice. I'll be back.'

My legs feel as if something is crawling all over them – probably of a reptilian nature – and I am momentarily paralysed. Should I run out of the van or stay where I am? What if the snake has a wife? What if there's another one in here, right now? Or a whole family of them, slithering around under this bed looking for my legs?

Joel wouldn't have left me if it wasn't safe. I have to trust him. But maybe I should close the caravan door to be extra safe. Cringing, I step down from the bed, trying to avoid the few feet of lino where the snake was only a few minutes ago. I slam the door, whimper, and get back on the bed. I try not to worry about the fact that Joel seems to have disappeared. What if he's been bitten? Where's my G'day Australia handbook? I've already forgotten what you're meant to do about a snake bite. Do you pee on it, or not pee on it?

Suddenly, the handle of the caravan door turns and Joel bolts in, panting.

'Smoke!' he yells. 'That's why the snakes are all out. We have to get out of here.'

'What?'

'There's a fire coming.' He takes my hand and pulls me out of the van. 'I can see smoke down near Wiz's place.

On the other side too, which means the fire's already jumped the road.'

A fire *coming*? I am about to correct him when I remember where I am living now. It must be a bushfire.

'See that cloud?' Joel squeezes my hand and makes me look east. 'It's bushfire smoke. It's a long way off, but I'm worried about the wind changing.'

I suddenly remember the snake and ask him about it.

'I let him go. He's a long way off. Don't worry. But we need to get out of here.'

'Will all the snakes be trying to escape now?' I suddenly feel terrified.

'They won't hurt you if you don't hurt them,' Joel tries to reassure me, but I've heard that one before, and all I can think about is a whole army of them slinking down the hill.

Joel says Chang has detected the bushfire too, because he's shivering and won't leave my side.

Then I blink – there's something in my eye.

'Ash.' Joel looks worried as he holds out a finger to catch more of it – tiny black specks blowing around in the air. 'It's coming from everywhere. Alice – pack a case. We're going to have to bike it, so don't overload yourself. I'll take Chang if you can get him in a rucksack. We'll have to leave Henry and the chickens. I think they'll be okay – but we have to get out.'

'What about all my stuff from England?'

'Leave it.'

'Oh God, Joel. Helena's trunk. My sewing machine. It's everything I have!' I feel like crying.

'We have to go, Alice. Leave the sewing machine – I'll get you another one. Bring your passport, papers, photos, some clothes. I'm giving you three minutes.'

'What?' Suddenly I feel like killing him.

'Two minutes, now,' he says.

We run to the vans, puffing in the heat, with Chang following us. For the second time in a few months I find myself grabbing as much as I can of everything that is precious to me. I cram my passport into a plastic bag and stuff in everything else I can see – all the while conscious of Joel yelling at me from his caravan.

There. One minute left – and I've done everything I can. Maybe the bushfire won't get us. Maybe the Mary Quant dress will be okay. Maybe Joel's over-reacting.

'Come on.' He pulls me out of my van and bundles Chang into the rucksack. He swings him on his back, squashing his head down, but Chang's head pops straight up again.

'There's even more smoke now,' I tell Joel. A dirty grey cloud plumes high over the tops of the trees. We're panting now, breathing in the thick dust and ash.

Suddenly we hear a honking sound and see Wiz in his campervan at the top of the road, waving frantically. 'Got another five minutes,' he shouts through the window.

'You sure?' Joel shouts back. I am already tearing off down the hill again. All I can think about is the extra room in the back of Wiz's van. I can put Helena's trunk in there after all. I have to. If all those clothes and fabric burn, I'll never forgive myself.

Joel catches me up. 'Get all the blankets from your van and soak them,' he pants. 'Fill everything you can with water and bring it. We might be able to get some of the chooks and Henry in too – not sure.'

I try to shoo the goat away from the caravan door and in the direction of the van, but he won't go. Instead, he stumbles towards the creek. There is no sign of our hens.

'He'll be fine. It's okay.' Joel gasps for air.

It feels as if all the oxygen is being sucked away from the land; at the same time, some enormous fan heater is blowing dust the other way. I try not to think about the little bits of black, flaky ash that must be going into my lungs. My eyes are already starting to water.

'Now!' Wiz yells, leaning out of the van window and beckoning us over.

We stumble towards him juggling bottles of water and sopping wet blankets, Chang swinging in the rucksack on Joel's back.

'Helena's trunk . . .' I hear myself saying.

Joel cuts me off. 'Can't go back. Water's more important.'

I start to thank The Wizard Formerly Known As Wayne as he helps us into his van. 'Wiz, we're so glad to see you –'

'Git in there,' he says, before I can force any more of my time-wasting English politeness upon him.

The smoke cloud is enormous now, hanging high above our heads.

'Nothing tethered?' Wiz asks. I suppose he means the animals.

'No,' Joel reassures him.

Then I realise we are sharing the back seat with a large dog and an ancient cat. No wonder Chang is now trembling like a jelly under my arm. It takes me a few seconds to realise what's in the front seat. A large goanna, flicking its tongue and waving its tail from side to side. It looks like a junior extra from *Jurassic Park*.

'Kiss me,' Joel whispers.

'Shit!' I can't stop staring at the awful goanna, which stares back at me with its cold reptilian eyes.

'Kiss me, Alice.' Joel pulls me towards him and I breathe in mint, lemon and patchouli and all the other wonderful hippyish things he always smells of.

'You just want to take my mind off that . . . thing,' I whisper, once we have come up for air.

'But was it good?' He nudges me.

'God, *yes*!' I blurt out, like some deranged, sex-starved idiot. I give myself the giggles, and they go on and on – until Wiz gives me a fierce look in the rear-view mirror and I realise I may be having some kind of hysterical fit. But . . . he kissed me. Joel kissed me. Goanna or no goanna, it's happened.

The van lurches forward over the unsealed road and suddenly the fire has raced ahead of Wiz's van so that it's now either side of us. My heart starts banging and won't stop, and suddenly I want to go to the loo more than anything else in the world. My brain wants to be brave but my body wants to be a coward. Wiz looks straight ahead, hunched over the wheel as if his hands are glued to it. The beautiful, sunny day has turned dark. Where did all the light go?

'Wet your face,' Joel tells me, and passes me a water bottle, and one to Wiz.

'My eyes are stinging,' I croak. 'My throat's burning.'

'Keep blinking hard and try not to rub your eyes.' Joel squeezes my hand. 'Breathe normally, as much as you can. Take little sips of water. Don't talk.'

I realise the roaring sound that I thought might be wind is actually the fire. It has now raced across the road in front of us, making it impossible to pass.

'Can't go back,' Wiz says, looking in his rear-view mirror. 'She's all gone back there. I'm gonna put the headlights on and drive straight through.'

'Shit,' Joel says. 'Are you sure?'

'Sure as I'll ever be,' Wiz says, and punches the cassette player. Prince bursts into life.

I suddenly realise what we are about to do. Our lives are completely in Wiz's hands. We are driving through a fire listening to 'Purple Rain'. I bury my head in Joel's T-shirt and breathe in the smell of his minty, lemony chest. The shirt stinks of smoke but his skin is still the same, thank God.

Whatever happens now, I think, it has to be right. Everything about the last few months has been right, so this must be too. And . . . it feels like we're together now. We've jumped the fence, just like one of the chickens, and now we're on the other side.

I stroke Wiz's cat and dog, who are wide-eyed, panting and terrified, while Joel holds Chang. The dreadful goanna huddles low on the passenger seat.

'Good on ya,' Wiz says, and pats the goanna absent-mindedly.

The water bottle goes around the car again, and this time we sluice it over our skin. Wiz pours a handful over the top of his head, and licks his lips as it runs down his face.

Flames go over the bonnet of the car and I try not to look. Joel pushes the animals down on the floor so they can't see either.

A horse runs past us, away from a burning property, and I find myself praying that he won't race into the fire. Perhaps he's on fire already, but we can't stop to save him. We have to keep driving through.

Then, without any warning, the engine stalls.

'Shit,' Joel says.

'Shit,' Wiz echoes him. He tries the engine. Nothing.

'We'll get through,' Joel reassures me. 'We're nearly there now, Alice. Town's not that far away. There'll be a firebreak soon. Just hang on.'

Wiz tries a second time, and a third. The car springs into life and we drive forward again – just as a burning tree crashes to the ground behind us.

'Prince is a real master of his game, isn't he,' Wiz says to nobody in particular. The goanna sticks out its tongue.

'So tell me again why you're known as The Wizard Formerly Known As Wayne,' I ask, trying desperately to take our minds off the flames outside.

'My ex-wife got nasty,' Wiz explains croakily. 'She made a voodoo doll out of scone dough and wrote Wayne on its back – and this happened . . .' He keeps one hand on the steering wheel while he lifts up his T-shirt with the other.

Joel whistles. 'Those are some spots.'

We drive on through the smoke and I rub my eyes over and over, trying not to think about Wiz's horrible spotty back. I bury my face in Joel's shoulder, wishing it could all be over. It feels like some kind of mad dream.

'Look!' Joel yells and points out the window. 'Blue sky, Alice. Just a patch. But you can see it now.'

'Yeehar!' Wayne whoops, and honks his horn.

I think about the poor horse running along the road and realise I've been crying steadily for the last five minutes without knowing it. My eyes are so sore from the smoke I barely registered the tears.

We keep driving. Two policemen appear in the middle of the road. They shake their heads at us, grin and wave us on. In reply, Wiz's thumb appears over the steering wheel and he waggles it backwards and forwards.

'You're a miracle man,' Joel says, and slaps him on the back, but Wiz still only has eyes for the road.

'There!' I yell, spotting a large State Emergency Service sign propped up outside what is normally a row of cafés and a car park, but has become a makeshift rescue centre lined with trestle tables, bottles of water and fold-up chairs.

Wiz stops at last, and we fall out – hot, dazed, and shocked at the way the fire has turned his van from pale blue to dirty black.

Wiz carries his goanna in his arms to the nearest bowl of water. Chang follows Wiz's cat and dog straight past the line of fold-up chairs, the rows of parked vans and cars – all charred black like ours – and into the nearest stretch of grass. In just a few weeks, the lush green fields I saw on the way in from Byron Bay have turned straw-yellow. Still, there is water over there somewhere, and the animals seem to know it.

'Let him go.' Joel puts his arm around me as I watch Chang run off. 'He knows what he's doing.'

Wiz has been recognised by locals, despite his dirty face and singed beard, and is being given bottle after bottle of cold water, which he doesn't know whether to drink or pour over himself. I realise we are both shaking – Wiz quietly and me uncontrollably. Joel, by contrast, is perfectly still.

Fire trucks are pulling in everywhere. People seem to be reacting in two ways – smiling and laughing far too much, from relief and nerves; or staring into space like stunned mullets.

'Do you want to sit down or lie down?' a woman wearing a bright orange SES waistcoat asks me. I see there are dozens of blow-up air mattresses lining the street.

'I don't know. I saw a horse trying to get out,' I tell her. 'We had to leave our goat. We had to leave our chickens.'

'I know, love.' She has kind eyes, like Heidi Coles.

Wiz collapses into a fold-up chair, still shaking.

'They need to treat him for shock,' Joel says.

The SES woman puts her hand on his shoulder. 'We're treating you *all* for shock.'

The rest of the day is a blur. I panic about Chang and Wiz's animals – but they are eventually found and then kept inside an air-conditioned rescue truck. There are radios everywhere, blaring news bulletins. There seems to be a fire update every ten minutes, and I hear a rollcall of unfamiliar place names that were also caught up in the blaze. Suddenly, I feel unbelievably tired.

Wiz's relatives arrive from Taree to rescue him, his animals and his few possessions.

'He saved our life,' I tell his nephew, a man with red hair. 'Wiz saved our life. I'm never going to forget it.'

'We still call him Wayne in the family,' the red-haired man replies.

Bits and pieces of conversation drift past my ears. It's the worst fire Bellingen has had for ten years. Half the houses on Darkwood Road are expected to be gone by tomorrow. The fire was deliberately lit; or, in another version, it was an accident, started by tourists who left a barbecue burning.

'Hey, Joel.' A dark-haired man approaches us. It's John, a friend of Joel's who has come to volunteer.

Joel gives him a huge hug. 'John, we're homeless, mate. This is Alice. And the dog's called Chang.'

'No worries,' John says. 'Come to my place.'

'Is it safe?' I ask stupidly. Everything feels unsafe at the moment.

'I live on the beach,' he explains with a small smile.

We pile into John's huge truck. There's room for all three of us on the wide front seat, and I put Chang on my lap. Our sad collection of bags, blankets and water bottles are bundled in the back.

'Chang was incontinent,' I tell John, trying to make conversation as we drive. 'But now he's not. Obviously.'

A pause, then Joel and John both howl with laughter, and I find myself joining in, until I can't stop. I remember my grandmother telling me about the mad giggling that went on during the worst days of the war. If you've been badly scared, you'll take the chance to laugh at anything.

* * *

John's house by the beach turns out to be wonderful – an old-fashioned wooden bungalow with a separate studio in the garden. We sleep there, with Chang at our feet, and throw all the blankets off because it's so hot, until we are covered only by a sheet. A fan chops away on the ceiling, and tiny frogs stick to the window, the suckers on their feet fixing them to the glass.

'All this cousins thing is going to be weird, isn't it,' I say to Joel as I snuggle into him.

'Too much explaining.'

'It's going to be *very* hard work trying to make people understand.'

'Already is.' Joel pulls me towards him.

We both stink of smoke and have mild burns, like painful sunburn.

'I'm so tired. I've wanted this forever and ever,' I tell him, 'but now I'm just so tired.'

'Sleep.' He kisses me. As I fall asleep, I catch myself thinking that I will always associate the smell of singed hair with a strange kind of happiness.

We both have nightmares. Mine have nothing to do with the fire; instead they're about snakes in their hundreds all over the property. Joel's are all about the fire, and at one point he has a lucid dream that the horse we saw running along the road is trying to push us off the edge of a cliff.

I can't believe how angry I feel the next morning. It is a generalised anger – at the fire, at the person who started it, at Australia itself.

'The bush can be a bitch,' John agrees, as he pours us some orange juice.

Joel and I are both so dehydrated that we can't stop drinking. We gulp down anything from tap water to coffee, like people who have been walking through a desert. Then we have the longest, coldest showers in the world. I have never craved water so much.

We laugh at our bloodshot eyes in John's bathroom mirror. They look exactly like the eyeballs you see in silly fake glasses in fancy-dress shops. Even Chang's little round eyes are red.

We ring Wiz at his nephew's place, but he doesn't answer the phone.

'At the pub,' John jokes. 'Bet you. First place you're going to find Wiz after everything he's been through. I've got to take you back into town to fill in your rego forms,' he goes on. 'Otherwise you're going to be a missing person statistic.'

We listen to the news on the radio as we drive back to Bellingen. The fires have been widespread and two people are dead, with three missing. Joel and I look at each other, terrified. Then he starts blaming himself for not evacuating us earlier, for not having a plan, for not reading the weather more carefully.

'Stop it,' I say, and put my hand over his mouth.

The makeshift emergency centre, so crowded yesterday, is now reduced to a neat little camp of buses, trucks and ambulances. Joel and I register our names and address, and supply Wiz's as well, in case the police haven't heard from him.

'Alice Templeton,' I say.

'Joel Templeton,' Joel says.

We are unable to let go of each other, or of Chang, who's on the other end of my long stripy scarf from London, a makeshift lead. Joel and I wear each other like security belts.

'You two are married?' John asks, overhearing. 'You kept that one quiet, mate. Congratulations.'

'Not married.' Joel looks embarrassed. 'Cousins.'

Now it's John's turn to look embarrassed.

'Not actually related by blood,' I try to explain. 'Don't worry.'

'It's a long story, mate.' Joel puts a hand on John's back. 'I'll tell you another time.'

'You goin' back to your property?' a woman from the SES asks. 'They've given the all-clear now. You can get a lift if you want one.'

'We are going back,' Joel confirms. 'Who do we speak to about a ride?'

'Becky can drive you,' the SES woman tells us. We thank John and bid him farewell, then go to look for Becky – another volunteer in a bright orange vest with large bottles of water in both pockets.

'Get ready,' she warns us as we drive off in her van.

All we see for the first mile or so are dead or dying cows.

'I can't stand it!' I hide my face in Joel's shirt.

'What are they doing about the animals?' he asks Becky.

'They're onto it. We've got Wires, the RSPCA, the whole lot up here. Don't you worry about the animals. You're priority one. They're the *other* priority one.'

Trees are still on fire everywhere we look. Even worse, houses have been reduced to burning shells, only their frames still standing. The smell of smoke in Becky's van is inescapable, even with the windows up.

Finally, we reach Joel's property.

'I only had a couple of caravans here,' he tells Becky before she has to ask. 'There wasn't much to lose.'

He doesn't tell her it's everything that he and I own in the world.

The three of us get out of the van, leaving Chang in the back, and walk down the hill. There is nothing left of the postbox. Neither caravan has survived. Instead, there is a black mess covering around half an acre of Joel's land. It's hard to tell what used to be caravan and what used to be trees. Even our bicycles have burnt to nothing.

'You save much?' Becky asks.

'Just bits,' I reply, then I realise the enormity of what I've just said and start feeling shaky. I want to cry but I can't. I'm too tired.

We find Henry the goat; his feet, nose and ears are red with blood. Joel's eyes fill with tears as we lead him to the van for the long drive back to the Bellingen football oval, which has been set up as an emergency animal shelter.

'We should have put him in the back of Wiz's van,' I say.

'No time,' Joel says sadly.

The chickens are dead. We find other animals too that couldn't get out in time – possums, wombats, kookaburras and even a poor little wallaby. It is so unfair, I can't stand it.

'How did the fire start?' I ask Becky, whose eyes are as red as mine.

'Vandals,' she says, looking grim. She tells me she's been back and forth to six properties in two days, all destroyed, with dead and dying native animals everywhere she looks.

'Your friend's house is alright,' she says, and I realise she means Wiz. 'He left his hoses running over the roof, and he'd been soaking the grass since the sun came up. He's lost about half of it, but there's enough there to build on. Not insured, though.'

'Not insured?' I echo, looking at Joel.

'Crazy.' Becky shakes her head. 'You wouldn't believe how many people weren't. But he's The Wizard Formerly Known As Wayne, yeah? So he's obviously got,' she makes quotation marks, 'supernatural powers.'

We get back in the van and Henry lies across our knees. He puts his head in Joel's lap like a human, as if he's asking for help.

And then I see it – a lone brown hen with wet tail feathers running towards us, clucking in panic, from the direction of the creek.

'Hey ho,' Becky says. 'Some old girl had the brains to sit it out in the water.'

Joel and I cackle at each other like idiots.

'She's alive!' I say, pointing at the hen, which is excitedly making bock-bock-bock noises.

Joel laughs at me, then we start cackling again. The van is almost shaking now. I suppose Becky's used to it – probably everyone she's driven around lately has ended up in hysterics.

'You're staying up at Urunga, is that right?' she asks us, once we've calmed down and we're on the way back to town.

'For the moment. Then we'll probably go and stay with my sister in Sydney,' Joel tells her.

'My cousin,' I say at the same time, and get a strange look from Becky.

'Then make a fresh start, eh?' she suggests, catching my eye in the rear-view mirror.

'I'm sort of getting used to it,' I tell her as I put my hand in Joel's.

When we get out of the car, Joel, Henry and I are immediately snapped by a newspaper photographer. It's only when he stops to reload his camera that I realise I am still holding Joel's hand.

'It's just for the appeal,' the photographer explains.

It seems a fund has already been started for all those who lost their homes.

'People round here aren't rich but they'll give everything they can,' Joel explains.

'We can't take money from them,' I protest.

Joel shrugs. 'It's just neighbours being neighbours. We'd do the same if we'd escaped and other people had got stuck. It's like that round here. People look after each other.'

Then he kisses me and this time I don't care who sees. I only wish I was wearing my ultimate media opportunity outfit for the photographer – my white Marilyn Monroe frock, and one of Helena's old paste brooches, turned into a necklace. 'Hey,' Joel notices my attention wandering and pulls me back. 'Come here.'

nineteen

Joel rings Robyn to let her know we are okay, then he rings his parents. Robyn tells him we can stay as long as we like. She's been desperate to get hold of us, she says. 'She called us crazy hippies,' Joel says, 'but she's glad we're okay.'

I go into Bellingen on the bus so I can pick up my post from the post office, which is holding mail for all the people who lost their homes in the fire. I also want to call my mother before she has a chance to find out about the north coast bushfires on the internet. I needn't have worried. She is more concerned about a forthcoming bicycle ride with Greydate UK. They're cycling to a village where Princess Alexandra is rumoured to have friends, and because the Greydaters are having lunch at a restaurant afterwards, Mum's worried that Princess A will swan past their table and see her tatty old shoes.

'Just wear your wellies, Mum. They're very fashionable at the moment.'

'Oh, I don't think I can do that!'

'Look, I've been staying in Bellingen with Joel. We had a bushfire, but we're okay. We might go and stay with Robyn at Bondi Beach for a while though.'

'Oh dear. What sort of bushfire?'

'Joel had a couple of old caravans, and we had two bicycles. Everything melted. Our chickens died. Well, all except one.'

'The chickens are *dead*?'

'Our goat is at an RSPCA shelter. They've set up a special centre for all the livestock. He couldn't get away. It was awful – he's covered in burns.'

I then stand in the phone box for half an hour while my mother forces me to work backwards through the story – *all* of the story.

'Cousins can marry cousins,' she says thoughtfully, after I've confessed about Joel. 'It's perfectly normal in the Middle East. Though I believe it's illegal in America. What about Australia?'

'Mum! I'm not even considering marrying Joel.'

She asks me about my job at Bark's.

'This woman Danielle was going to do *what*?' she interrupts as I'm telling her about the day I was supposed to have Mr Chang put down.

'She's a bit of a fitness freak,' I explain. 'I think that comes first.'

She sighs. 'I really don't like those giddy gym bunnies.'

'She did Pilates as well.'

'Oh, how ghastly. It sounds like a disease.'

My mother asks me what I have left after the fire. Three black skirts. Five T-shirts and shirts. Three pairs of knickers. One pair of flip-flops – which Joel insists I should call thongs because I'm Australian now. One book on Yves St Laurent. My passport, immigration papers and address book. My photographs.

'It's making me cry,' I tell her. 'Can we talk about something else?'

'Ooh, Alice, yes. Do you know, I have 250 friends in my Greydate UK local forum? I only found out this morning. I had no idea. I feel as if someone has filled up my dance card without me noticing.'

I think of Mum's spatial skills, which have never been particularly good, and imagine her with hundreds of other similarly confused Greydaters, cycling in a pack up the M23 while an out-of-control truck careers off the road somewhere near Princess Alexandra's friends' village.

'Anyway, darling,' she finishes, 'if you've been in a fire, that really is an emergency, isn't it. So I'm going to put some of Dad's money into your account this evening.'

'No. It's for you.'

'He meant it for both of us.'

'Mum! First Nash and now this? There'll be nothing left!'

'Don't argue, dear. There'll still be plenty left. You can't live in three pairs of knickers.'

I feel like two people. One of them is New Australian Alice, who can manage perfectly well on her own – no matter if the problem is a worm farm, a bushfire or a snake. The other one is Old Alice, who is so relieved and excited to hear about the sudden arrival of some money that she simply gives in.

In the end, I make peace with both of me. If Mum puts too much money in my account – more than I need to get by, anyway – I'll deposit it straight back.

* * *

On the way back to John's on the bus, I read the classified jobs section in an old newspaper someone's left behind. I am not a backhoe operator, boiler-maker, bus driver, butcher, cabinet-maker, concreter, driver, electrician, forklift driver, glazier or panel-beater though. Are all Australian jobs designed for hearty women?

I spot two jobs Joel and I could do, if we were desperate enough: selling advertising for volunteer magazines over the phone (call Jason now!) and selling boutique wine over the phone (call Trevor now!). We've already talked about asking Robyn for jobs at her hotel, but neither of us wants to do it. We feel we are imposing enough as it is. There is a small part of me that wishes she would just offer though – even if it means hurtling back to my days as a cleaner. I never thought I'd be grateful to have the chance to vacuum up other people's mess again, but now it seems like a lifeline.

Joel is convinced we will be better off going back to his property, pitching a tent and slowly building up the chickens, vegetable patch and fruit trees again. We could live on the very last of his savings, he tells me, while we try to live off the land once again.

The bus hurtles on towards Urunga while I worry about all this. The cool change the locals were talking about has now arrived, and the sky is pale grey through the windows.

Perhaps I think about money all the time because Dad did too. My father worked like a dog – or at least a Bark's dog-carer – for all of his life, but, like most of his friends, seemed to spend his time like a hamster going round and round on a gigantic wheel. The second-hand Jaguars and Mercedes he bought had to be repaired, cleaned, insured and maintained. Expensive security systems had to be installed to protect the cars from thieves and any drunk who felt like chucking a brick. After that, the tax usually finished him off. My memories of my father revolve around paperwork, late-night accounting, frantic sessions with calculators, and a constant supply of aspirin washed down with a glass of red wine after dinner.

I love the idea that Joel and I might be self-sufficient one day. I am longing for a time when I never have to think about money again. It seems impossible at the moment though, with only one chicken left and burnt-out trees all around us.

I remember my post, and open it. There's nothing remotely interesting – just bank statements that Nash has redirected from London. Amazingly, one of the letters actually manages to spell my name right. I am usually known as Miss A. Templeeton to the HSBC, but this is an envelope from a rival bank. It's a credit card offer. I can transfer my debt from my old card and pay no interest for six months. There's a toll-free number to ring, and a promise that a decision can be made over the phone. The card can be mine in fourteen working days.

I stare out the window at cows lying on their sides in the sun. I have only just managed to escape being a serial debtor, with any number of collection agencies threatening me, and already some finance company is trying to woo me all over again. It's hard not to be tempted. Then an enormous bull standing near a fence at the side of the road craps dramatically and at length on the grass.

'Thank you,' I mutter. The universe has spoken.

* * *

When I arrive at John's house, Joel is in the garden on the phone. After he's finished, he pours me a beer – John brews his own – and tells me that we've been offered a new caravan if we want it. And a tent. And a new generator.

'Wow. Where from?'

'People I don't even know,' Joel says. 'Someone's started a donation centre in Coffs Harbour. They've just had a whole container of new sheets offered by a department store in Sydney. Look – I've written it all down. All we have to do is turn up and put our names on the waiting list.'

'Mum's offered to put some money into my account,' I tell him. 'From Dad's emergency fund.'

'Did you say yes?'

'I don't want to. But part of me has to.'

'Okay.'

'Some bank's offering me a credit card as well. No interest for the first six months.'

'Do you want to take it?'

'No.'

'*Good.* Now come here.' Joel holds out his arms. 'Let's go for a walk on the beach and watch the storm coming in.'

We pick our way over a range of sand dunes, then crisscross through a jungle of trees and bushes to get to the beach. As we walk along the sand, Joel shows me the full list of things that people have sent to the donation centre in Coffs Harbour. Almost everything we lost is on there, from hairdryers to boxes of baked beans, pillows to pots of paint. The list reveals an incredible outpouring of generosity, and I know it's coming from areas outside Sydney where there is very little money. These are the places that Matty pointed out to me the day we were talking about buying a unit and getting onto the Australian property ladder. Nevertheless, everyone seems to be giving what they have.

In the days when I was still weighing up the wisdom of moving to Australia, several people told me I'd find the people impossible to deal with. They're too taciturn, they said. Too hard to get to know. Too rough. They might have been describing Wiz – or even John – but Wiz is also the man who came to find us in his van, checked that Henry wasn't tethered, waited for us to pack our belongings, then drove us through miles of flames. Meanwhile, John has opened his home to us – and everything in it – as if it were our own. Joel says he's always been like that, even though they don't know each other particularly well.

I think about Wiz's burnt-out house and promise myself I will do whatever it takes to help build another one. Even if I have to sew pyjamas out of charity shop sheets and sell them on Jade's stall, I'll try to repay him for saving us, Chang and Henry.

'Here comes the rain,' Joel says, and we run to shelter underneath a tree growing out of the marshy land that runs behind the sand dunes. In London, rain was always irritating, boring, and something to be avoided. Here, I don't mind if I get wet. Anything's better than fire.

I am still having nightmares about our escape. The snakes have gone, but now it's flames chasing me down the road. I haven't said anything to Joel yet, but when we finally go back to Bellingen, I'm not sure I can live indefinitely in a tent or a caravan – or, more importantly, without a water tank.

When I was a teenager, like everyone at my school, I went through a horse-mad stage. I used to ride across the South Downs with a friend called Lucy. One day my horse bolted and I came off and broke my arm. I was told to get straight back on again as soon as my arm healed. It didn't work though. I stopped riding, and don't want to get on another horse as long as I live.

I feel differently about the threat of another bushfire though. The other night John told me that if we'd had a proper house instead of the two caravans, we could have stayed on and saved what we had.

Even if we have to build everything ourselves, I need to live somewhere I can stay and defend. Time and again this week, I've heard about people who stayed on their land and fought back the fire. If I'm ever going to return to Joel's property, I have to know that next time we can beat nature before it beats us. I talk to Joel about it as the rain pours down across the beach and lightning flashes on the horizon.

'I don't know how we're going to do it, but I need to live in a house if we're going to stay there permanently,' I say.

Joel puts his arm around me. 'The fires won't come again for years. There's nothing left to burn. A house is going to take time, Alice. I've got some money left, but it's not enough.'

'That's it.' I make my mind up. 'I'm going to get the money.'

'How?'

'I don't know. I'm just going to make it. We've got to have a house, Joel.'

Meanwhile, I mourn the loss of my tartan wellies and umbrella. Perhaps some kind person will have donated something I can replace them with.

The rain pours down, but I look along the beach in both directions and count my blessings. Nobody in their right mind would be here on such a wet and windy day, but it is still incredible to see miles of white sand, all unoccupied.

'It's so beautiful here,' I say.

We agree that Australia really is an upside-down country. We have seen dolphins cresting the surf on this beach, in water so warm you can dive straight into it. Joel has also seen sharks though, swimming so close to the shore that he could see them snapping at anything that moved. He once saw a shark bite into driftwood here too, and was out of the water in ten seconds flat. Just when you think Australia is some kind of postcard paradise, it bites you in the bum – as The Wizard Formerly Known As Wayne would say. But still, I haven't changed my mind about it, even since the fire. I want to belong here. I want my name on a citizenship certificate, beneath the emu and the kangaroo, so I can frame it and hang it on the wall of the house we're going to build.

'Will you come with me to my citizenship ceremony?' I ask Joel.

'It would be an honour and a privilege,' he says, kissing me. Then: 'This rain's not going to stop.' He takes my hand. 'Do you want to make a run for it?'

We race back to John's house, ahead of the thunder, and find a message on his answering machine telling us he's gone fishing. We settle down on the sofa together and play an old Led Zeppelin album – John still believes in vinyl and record players. Led Zeppelin were banned from my life when I was with Nash. They were too low down in his musical class system. It feels good to have them back.

Joel produces a box from one of his bags. 'Tibetan incense. It's good for Lhoong. I think we should burn some.'

'I can't believe you saved that from the fire! What's Lhoong?'

'A disequilibrium of mental and emotional events,' Joel reads from the label. 'It's also said to be good for tinnitus, swelling in the abdominal region and a dry tongue.'

'John's beer is pretty good for that too.'

We sit and stare at the incense for a while, without talking. The music makes me think of Nash again. 'There was a moment in the caravan when I looked at some photos of Nash and really had to think about whether I should save them,' I tell Joel.

'Hmmm. You know you'll have to tell him about us some time.'

'Joel, do you mind me mentioning Nash?'

'Not at all.'

'Damn.' I pout, pretending to be annoyed.

He squeezes my hand and smiles. 'You know, I wasn't going to tell you this, but when we were driving through the fire, I realised I was happy to die with you.'

'Me too.'

'John won't be back for hours,' Joel says. He leads me to the studio, and throws his clothes on the chair.

'Your skin.' I touch his shoulders. 'It's still so red.'

'Not all of it.' He smiles, and pulls my shirt off.

I have fantasised about sex with Joel so often, it's a shock to realise how completely unlike my daydreams it actually is. In my imagination, it's always urgent and intense. Now it's finally happening, everything seems to go in slow motion.

It's hard not to compare him to Nash. But I am already amazed at how brown he is, how warm he feels, how different he smells. There are no chemicals on Joel Templeton.

My bra comes off, little by little, and finally my pants.

'So wet down there.' Joel touches me softly with the tip of his finger. Then he finds a condom, and unwraps it for me as if it's a chocolate.

Nash was a woman whisperer but he always made me feel as if he'd done it all a million times before. Joel makes me feel as if everything is being made up on the spot, just for me. He strokes my hair as he guides himself inside me, then meets me halfway as I find myself bucking against him. I want him so much I don't think I can wait.

We hear John's truck in the driveway. He's home early.

'Later?' Joel says, and stops and kisses me. But I have no desire to wait. I've already waited too long.

'Shhh!' I hold my hand over his mouth.

But it's no good – once I've switched places and got on top, I come before he does, and I can't stop my own moaning, let alone control his.

'God,' Joel says at last as I roll off him. 'Oh my *God*.'

We lie together side by side, and I realise the sheet is soaked with sweat. It is, in every sense of the word, the hottest sex I have ever had in my life.

We fall asleep, and when I wake up Joel has gone. I get dressed and wander into the sitting room to find him chatting to John and drinking his homemade beer. I suppose it's the Australian way.

I go back to the beach for a moonlit walk and try to work out what I am going to say to Nash. I don't owe him anything really, but I'd like to be more honest with him than he ever was with me. Besides, there's a small, smug part of me that just wants to boast about my new boyfriend. Even if he is my cousin.

In true Alice Templeton fashion, I spend the rest of the night dithering, and then all of the following morning in Bellingen trying to do everything I can except go into an internet café.

I go to the post office as a distraction. There's a postcard of Bondi Beach for me, from Matty and Jade. Their stall will be available from – oh my God – next weekend for three months. The postcard has been sitting there for days. The address is simply: *Alice Templeton, Bellingen*.

I ring Matty immediately, and try to deflect all his questions about the bushfire – and Joel – and make him tell me about the stall instead.

'It's paid in advance,' he says. 'Just take that out of whatever you make on the gear. You going to put your own stuff on there too?'

'I want to. Once I get another sewing machine.'

'Sweet,' he says. 'I'll tell Jade.'

'I'll be on the next plane to Sydney,' I promise, then I call Robyn, who says I can have her spare room.

Next I call Joel, who's helping John in the garden and takes a long time to answer. As always, the more I flap, the more unflappable Joel becomes.

'It's alright,' he reassures me. 'You go now. I'll come down later, when everything's settled with the property. John says he can give you a lift to the airport, so ring up now and book a flight. He reckons you should be able to get a seat, no worries.'

The rest of the morning disappears in a frantic rush as I book a flight, rush back to John's place, pack up everything I'll need, blow-dry my hair on John's old travel hairdryer, and find at least one clean pair of pants – all in the space of three hours.

John drives Joel and me to the airport, with Chang on our laps in the front seat.

'Good luck,' Joel says, and kisses me at the airport door. John hovers behind us, looking embarrassed. 'Say hi to Robyn for me.'

The flight to Sydney is just under an hour, and I have only just finished my plastic tub of water, my suspiciously mouldy-tasting sultana cake and my free magazine when our tray-tables have to be folded up again as we prepare for landing.

I can still taste Joel's kiss despite the sultana cake. I wonder who his father really was. Maybe Helena did shag some famous actor at a '70s party, as Robyn once joked. Someone has to take responsibility for those long, long legs.

twenty

I am beginning to understand Joel's love of roughing it, but there is no substitute for a bath that doesn't have insects landing in it. Robyn's bath has bubbles instead, which I decant from her Doctor Who Dalek bubble-bath container. It's bliss on a stick, as Robyn says – although I have to point the Dalek's exterminator stick at the wall.

'You and Joel are insaaane,' Robyn drawls, when I have finished my bath and she's made me one of her wonderful vodka and lime drinks. 'The eco-hippie thing is great, but you've got to be contactable. When the bushfire was happening, I didn't know if you were dead or alive. You've got to stay in touch with the real world.'

After that, she goes off to Hot Bods for her spin class and tells me I can check my email on her computer.

My first message is from Heidi Coles. It seems that Dani is selling Bark's of Byron Bay and her other branches, and that I am (apparently) the last farking straw that broke the farking camel's back. Heidi is writing to let me know that nobody blames me, least of all her. I suppose I have been forgiven then.

I move on to my mother's email. She is marrying a man from Greydates. *What?*

I read the long paragraph again, to make sure I've got it right. But all the details seem to be there. The Greydates man is called William Bastable, and my mother met him playing conkers at a Greydates UK Back-to-School dress-up party. William worked in the music business for years, and before he retired he invested in *Saturday Night Fever*. Consequently he is now a multimillionaire with homes in France and Rye, East Sussex.

Mum says he is in his late seventies and 'rather attractive'. She has enclosed a photo, or, as she insists on calling it, a J-Peg, as if it's a clothes peg. It looks like a 1980s corporate ID shot, taken for the purposes of an annual report or possibly a name-tag at a seminar. William Bastable has a stunned look, like a fish that's just had its head banged on a rock. Still, he had a nice tan back then, and most of his own hair. It's obviously the photograph that lured my mother to his Greydates UK profile.

I read on. For no apparent reason, she has enclosed a recipe for homemade lemonade, along with the news that she is sending me all her old fur coats by sea mail, because winter is coming in Australia and we can wrap Henry the goat in them, as she is worried that his coat won't grow back, after the fire.

As always, she leaves a chain of PS's at the end of her email.

PS: I hope Dad's money is now safely in your account.

PPS: William wants to buy this house, so he can sell his home in Rye and move in with me. We plan to live between Hove and Provence. Hope this is OK with you.

PPPS: I have decided to give you half the proceeds from the sale of the house. Please don't try to argue.

PPPPS: William and I thought we might hire the Bee Gees for our wedding. Could I have your candid opinion on the wisdom of this?

I sit back in my chair. I can just imagine what William Bastable will be like when we finally meet – a giant overgrown schoolboy in baggy shorts, with some horrible disco past. What would my poor father say? I should never have let Mum loose on the internet in the first place. I am sure her relationship with William Bastable has been aided and abetted by constant emailing, and at her age she may be about to make a terrible mistake.

She's only known William Bastable for a few weeks. I know almost nothing about him, apart from the fact that he looks good on paper. She's about to make a life-changing decision based on nothing more than a night of passion (probably blotto on cheap Greydate UK punch) and a misguided sense of what love is. In other words, my mother is reminding me of myself when I raced into living with Nash. I would be a total hypocrite if I tried to stop her. No wonder it's making me feel wobbly.

I contemplate the idea of having some old conkers-playing reprobate in shorts as a close relative. And what does she mean, can she have my opinion on the wisdom of hiring the Bee Gees for their wedding? I can't even begin to think about the old fur coats for Henry or the recipe for homemade lemonade. I wish she wouldn't try to cram everything she would have discussed with me over the course of a fortnight into the same paragraph.

And she's selling the house and giving me half. Already, it sounds like the kind of good news that's too impossibly good to be real. It will never happen. I wonder how much a house in Hove is worth these days. I hope Mum's going to do it all through a property agent. In which case . . .

I let myself have the forbidden fantasy. In which case, I need never worry about money again. Joel and I can build our own house. On his land. With a new henhouse and new hens. And I can get a baby donkey!

If my father were here now, he'd have his head in his hands and be asking my mother for three aspirin along with his red wine. It is utterly typical of me that my greatest concern at this crucial crossroads in my financial destiny is the purchase of a baby donkey.

I mentally move my mother's offer into the 'Too mad to be real' category, which has taken up a lot of my brain space over the years, and move on to the other emails. They're all from friends – mystified at the rumours they are hearing about me and my cousin; worried that I have gone completely broke; deeply miffed that I have apparently been involved in a bushfire without bothering to let them know.

I knew it. You can try to keep your secrets, but even in a small town like Bellingen, sooner or later the smoke signals will cross the world and that's the end of you.

Finally, I move onto Nash's email. It seems that a photograph of Joel and me kissing after the fire appeared in *The Guardian* in some worldwide weekly round-up. *What?* I thought those photographs were for the local paper. I didn't realise that Joel and I would end up as *The Guardian*'s whacky Australian photo of the week.

Snide remarks about keeping things in the family follow. It's a horrible email and I wish I hadn't opened it. I can hear him laughing at me, even though he's thousands of miles away.

I decide I've had quite enough of the computer for one day. There is something about very emotional matters being transmitted by very unemotional electronic messages that is not good for the soul. Especially when Nash is at the other end of them.

I walk from Bondi to Bronte along the cliffs, and think about the importance of tea in my life. All the things I've just faced in my email inbox would normally have resulted from fairly measured developments in my life in London accompanied by long conversations and many cups of tea. They don't tell you this when you go to your interviews at Australia House, but once you live upside down on the other side of the world, ten hours in front and two seasons out of sync, everything goes pear-shaped. Cups of tea and long conversations become things of the past. The normal unfolding of everyday events stops. Suddenly, you just get *news* all the time.

Other Brits in Australia – like Matty and Jade – have told me that the price of emigrating is learning to let go. Joel said it best: you have to accept that life is going to concertina around you from the other side of the world, and you won't be there to stop it from happening.

I was worried that my mother would come down with a stroke while I was at the other end of the planet, and instead she's come down with a bad case of love. I was worried about how I was going to tell Nash about Joel, and he found out for himself, in a newspaper. These are things that should happen over cups of tea – or possibly not happen at all over cups of tea. They should certainly take place with my active participation.

If I'm to remain in Australia, I need to get used to the not-invited feeling about life in England. And my friends over there will have to learn to let me live my life apart from them as well. I suppose, in time, everything will sort itself out. Once I've rung Nash and talked to him properly, maybe we can move on – until one day I'll look at his name in my address book and realise I haven't heard from him for years.

My mother's situation will eventually take care of itself too. There'll come a time when I no longer feel miffed if she makes a decision without me, and she will no longer feel moved to let me know everything that is on her mind every single day, no matter if it's William Bastable, Anthony Andrews, mango chutney or Princess Alexandra. When that day comes, that will be the real break-up with England. It doesn't happen when you're waving goodbye at Heathrow Airport, or even when you're standing in Trafalgar Square trying not to cry. It's only real when the emails slow down and the phone calls stop.

I don't regret leaving London for a minute. If I was given the choice between the Swiss Cottage laundrette and Joel's creek, I would take the creek any day. Even if insects do land on you. I used to live in a place where people wouldn't give up their seat for anyone on the train. Now I'm living in a place where a neighbour is prepared to give up his life for you in a bushfire. It's not what I expected to happen, but I am beginning to realise that Heidi Coles was right: nothing about this country is predictable.

I can't believe I seriously entertained the idea of moving to Wales, or Canada. Now that I'm here, with Joel, I feel as if I could never be anywhere else (despite everything, even the red-bellied black snakes). The homesickness is there alright, but it's like any other addiction. I may think I miss sundials, people dressed up as hedgehogs and Tunnock's tea cakes, but it won't last long.

I decide to sit at Bronte with a glass of wine and wait until the sun has well and truly set before I call Nash. As soon as the clock hits 6 pm Sydney time, I'm going over to the phone box. I'm sure he won't mind talking to me over his breakfast cornflakes. We have to talk. Properly. And I have to let him know my future lies with Joel.

I watch the locals walking down to the beach, and admire the mothers who disappear into the change rooms in their work suits and come out like Superwoman, in dazzling bikinis and with children hanging onto both hands. If Joel and I ever have children, I would love them to be water babies. More than anything else though, I would love them to have two passports, so they can have the best of both our countries.

I hug this thought to myself, finish my wine and gaze at the funny dark-blue line where the edge of the sea meets the sky. Maybe one day I can tempt Mum out here too – if it all works out with William the Conker Conqueror.

I order more wine and watch the day slip away. It's seven o'clock now. I can't put Nash off any longer. I drain the glass, hoping it will make me feel braver, and walk to the phone box armed with a purse full of gold coins.

'Would you mind telling me exactly what is going on with your Australian cousin?' is the first thing Nash says.

It is early in the morning so I suppose he's allowed to be bad-tempered, but his anger is frightening even at this distance.

'His name's Joel. And he's not really my cousin. You know that.'

'I rang Robyn as soon as I saw that photograph of you and him in the paper. All I got from her was "Yiss, yew'll have to talk to Alice".'

'Don't be like that. Robyn just did what she thought was best. We were in a *bushfire*, Nash.'

'What the hell are you doing in the outback with your bloody cousin, anyway?'

'Nash, I'm standing in a phone box on Bronte Beach looking at the most beautiful sunset. I do not need you shouting in my ear. Can you just calm down for a minute? Can you just *listen* to me?'

Listening is not Nash's way though. It never has been. The whole point is, you listen to him. The memory of his awful self-absorption comes flooding back to me as I listen to him barking in my ear. It's the same old thing. He knows what's going on and I don't have a clue; he's right and I'm wrong. I feel as if I have time-travelled back to my old life in London in a nanosecond, even though I'm staring at a beautiful red Sydney sunset over a dark blue sea.

'Nice one, Alice. There was a solid chance there for a while that we might get back together.'

'Not with me there wasn't. You screwed your ex-wife behind my back.'

'Whatever.'

'Whatever. You must be screwing now. How *is* the quiz team going?'

I slam the phone down, feeling shaky and slightly drunk from the wine. I wonder what the photograph of Joel and me is like. I'll have to get a copy, even though it's caused all this trouble. I decide I'm not going to tell Nash about my mother's impending marriage to William Bastable, or the fact that she wants to sell the house and give me half the money. I refuse to discuss anything about my life with Nash ever again – unless I absolutely have to.

I walk back to the café and consider ordering another wine with my remaining coins, then see Jade and Matty toasting each other with champagne in a corner. I hope they haven't seen me. I'm in no mood to talk. I slink away and sit on a bench near the phone box, fantasising about what I would say if I could call Nash again. It is so absolutely typical of him to refuse to apologise about either Sarah or Lisa, but to seize upon the fact that I've begun a relationship with Joel. Nash must be single – Sarah must have given him the flick – otherwise he wouldn't be this pissed off. I don't believe for a minute that he's genuinely jealous of Joel. He lost that particular nerve function about a year ago.

Nash and I were addicted to the most hormonally charged kind of love once, and now we're addicted to a kind of loathing. Of course, I don't hate him – not really – but the idea of bickering with him is so seductive it's hard to keep away. How can you resist an argument you know you're going to win? I thought Joel might have got me over that kind of thing, but the phone box is calling me. I must have the last word with Nash. I *absolutely* must have the last word. That's it. I'm going back.

Then . . .

'Over here, Alice!'

Matty beckons me over, while Jade waggles her fingers in a cool, supermodelly hello. They are celebrating Jade's new job in London, Matty tells me. There's a new soapie starting on ITV called *Australia Street* and she's been offered a one-year contract.

'It's a bloody load of rubbish,' Matty says. 'Poor woman's *Neighbours*, really. But the girl's done good.'

'It's like *Home and Away*,' Jade explains, 'except there's a lot of gay characters. So people are already calling it *Homo and Away*. They're really nice people actually,' she goes on. 'They said they were going to build the part around me. Apparently they saw loads of people but nothing really clicked for them. So they decided to rewrite the character. She's an Olympian gymnast. Or she was, before she became a nun.'

'It's a big co-production with English telly,' Matty explains, looking smug. 'It's gonna be huge. Loads of money. They're going to make her a *star*.'

'Congratulations!' I say.

'So, alright about the stall then?' Jade asks.

'Fine. Fantastic.'

Matty suddenly remembers what's been happening in my life. 'You okay after the fire and all that?'

'We survived.'

'I never really thought about acting before,' Jade goes on, slurring her r's, 'but my friend said they were looking for English ladies, so I thought I'd give it a try. It was so easy. I could quite get into the acting thing, I think.'

'Just learn your lines and try not to bump into the furniture.' Matty winks at me. 'Anyway, you was in the paper in London, Alice. Did you know?'

'Yes. My ex saw it. That's how he found out about me and Joel. We're sort of together now.'

'Oh my *God*!' Jade shrieks, pouring me another glass of champagne.

'Robyn said the house burned down or something,' Matty says.

'When Robyn told us, we was quite surprised. It's funny about him being your cousin, isn't it?' Jade twirls her champagne glass around in the candlelight.

'Yes, but we're not related. His mother only married my uncle after she'd become pregnant by somebody else.'

'Naughty, naughty,' says Matty.

The waitress brings over the pudding menu and they pore over it. I decide that from this moment forward I won't tell anyone that Joel is my cousin. It's all too hard. I'm going to change my second name to something else. My mother's maiden name was Tonks. I try it out in my head, while Matty and Jade choose between pavlova and banoffee pie. Alice Tonks. No, it's rubbish. It rhymes with honks and bonks for a start. Oh, why couldn't my mother have a normal name?

A few days later, Matty and Jade send me a farewell text message from the airport. The following Saturday, I go down to Bondi Markets and set up the trestle table with Jade's name on it.

I size up the stall from the front, as if I'm a buyer not a seller. It's an old trick that Suzanne taught me at Camden. Always get in front of the table before you sit down in your chair. Make sure you're seeing the stock the way the punters do. This is increasingly the way I'm beginning to see Vintage Alice too. I'm reading it from a customer's point of view. And not just any customer. I want to sell beautiful, affordable clothes to women who feel un-beautiful – and for women who don't think they can afford anything. I've just bought a whole box of discount denim from a website in Melbourne so I can do just that.

Selling Suzanne's vintage clothing at Camden was deeply satisfying. She has such an amazing eye for detail that I ended up selling exactly the kinds of things I wanted to buy. Her handbags are the kind you drool over, and she has the most extraordinary tulle party frocks and staggering pre-war velvet jackets. Vintage clothing is different in Australia. There's less of it, for a start. Jade has tried her best, but most of her stall is padded out with nylon flares that don't date past 1980 and retro-look sunhats bought cheaply in Chinatown then marked up for the tourists.

The only thing I think she's got right is the old swimwear and beach accessories. The sunglasses are priceless – like an entire wardrobe of Elvis Presley eyewear, boxed up and never opened since. She also seems to have unearthed a treasure trove of Australian bikinis decorated with palm tree designs, frangipanis, wattles and tiny kangaroos.

Australian vintage beachwear isn't my area of expertise but maybe I can ask Suzanne for some advice. If this is going to be my career for the rest of this year, I need to learn fast.

A tutting woman in an enormous hat and dark glasses looks through the few dresses there are on the rack, and heaves an enormous sigh.

'Sorry, we'll have more stock later,' I promise, as I search for something – anything – that might fit her, in the pile of suitcases behind the stall. She has the classic kind of body that fashion designers think is too hard to cater for – although it's the body that every other woman is born with.

'Hang on,' the woman says, taking off her enormous, jet-black sunglasses. 'It's Vintage Alice. Right?'

'Hello Vera!' I say, recognising the tufty orange hair, sticking out from under the hat.

'Long time no see,' she raises her eyebrows. 'Suzanne said you were in Australia now but she had trouble getting hold of you. So did I. You still got my card?'

'Oh yes. I'm sorry. I've been in the country.'

'In the bush, dear. That's what they call it. Hey, when are you going to make me some *frocks*?'

Blossom Promise walks past the stall carrying her fringed shawl tablecloth, her garden table, a pack of tarot cards and an enormous lump of crystal.

'Hiya!' she says and waves.

I wave back. 'You were right about buying the book!'

'Destiny works in mysterious ways!' she yells. 'Would you like a girl or a boy?'

'What?'

But she's gone, leaving a cloud of peppermint essential oil behind her.

I plonk myself down on the fold-up chair in shock. It can't be. Joel and I have been so careful. He's the king of condoms. What on earth is she talking about?

twenty-one

Mum and William Bastable are thinking about a May wedding, so William decides to introduce himself to me via video conference call. He wants to know if I have a camera on my computer so we can set up the call. I am too embarrassed to confess I don't even own a computer.

'I'm like Mum,' I tell him, during the phone call he's had to settle for instead. 'I'm a bit of a Luddite.'

'No problem!' he booms.

William has one of those old smoothie voices that I associate with the men who used to sell Dad their old Jaguars. I tell myself I must try to like him. I must try to trust him. Just because my relationship with Nash was a financial and emotional disaster doesn't mean my mother is similarly doomed. Sometimes bonkers, fantastic things just happen – and they even work. Just look at people who circumnavigate the globe in rafts made of orange-juice bottles.

I listen to William ramble on about the house. The sale is already underway and he will be moving his things from Rye at the weekend. They have done everything through a property agent, he says, to keep it simple. I try not to become too excited about the fact that the house sale might become real after all. I already feel guilty about looking up a Hove property agency online and trying to price my own family home. William wants me to know that I am welcome to stay with them any time. My old bedroom will remain just as I left it. The only change he intends to make is the addition of a swimming pool and a gazebo.

The addition of *what*? What about Dad's old potting shed? I suppose he's going to throw ten sticks of dynamite under it.

'Isn't he lovely?' my mother asks when she takes over the phone. I suppose he must be lurking in the background, eavesdropping. 'We're so excited about the swimming pool. William's very fit. He has a pool at the house in Rye, so we thought we'd put one in here.'

My God. What does a fit seventy-something look like? And it's been a long time since I heard my mother use the 'we' word. It may take me some months to get used to it.

I know that William has been married before – Mum says he doesn't like talking about it. Perhaps because he kept his previous wife in the cellar and made her wear rubber scuba-diving gear. *No, Alice!* I must stop being such a suspicious cow. I'm sure William is among the nicest of the Greydaters – and my mother wouldn't be marrying a mad, bad old cad. Would she?

'It's the *Saturday Night Fever* thing,' I tell Joel later. 'I wish he hadn't invested in it. I know it's made him a fortune, but every time I try to picture him I see some dodgy old disco bunny doing business deals with the Bee Gees.'

Joel's trying not to laugh. 'William probably invested in a lot of things. He was in the music business for years, wasn't he?'

'He probably bankrolled half the albums Nash loves to hate. I must find out.'

I am back in Urunga, on a cheap midweek flight, when Joel and I have this discussion – a precious break with him before I have to return to Bondi for Saturday's market. John has been the perfect host throughout our time here – ever willing to look the other way when I come out of the bathroom, always ready with homemade beer, always ready to drive us to Bellingen if we need to go into town . . . Nevertheless, both Joel and I are looking forward to moving out and being together again.

John drops us off at the internet café the next morning so I can check my email. Joel leaves me to it, and wanders off for a walk along the Bellinger River.

My mother has written to say that the sale of the house is now complete and she's deposited the money into my account. It won't have cleared yet so I won't get my hopes up. But I can't resist looking at my bank website anyway, just to make sure that I'm absolutely right. The money has cleared in three days – William Bastable must know how to do those kinds of things. I am so used to seeing the letter 'D' next to anything in my account that it seems quite wrong to see the letter 'C' there instead.

I am rich. Rich, rich, rich!

I can go to England with Joel and watch my mother become Mrs Bastable II.

I can have a pedicure.

I can start Vintage Alice.

I can buy a baby donkey.

I can do *anything*.

I have to find Joel and tell him.

I leave a pile of coins on the counter of the café – the first tip I've left since arriving in Australia – and race down to the river. When I eventually find him, he is swimming in his boxer shorts in a deep waterhole two miles upstream. The rest of his clothes are on the bank.

'Are you coming in?' he yells.

'I'm rich!' I scream – then jump in fully clothed.

We wade towards each other until we're close enough to talk properly.

'William's paid Mum and Mum's paid me,' I tell him breathlessly. 'It's all in my bank account. Oh my God. Come and look!'

He grins at me. 'I don't need to look.'

'We can build a house! We can do everything.'

We hug each other in the water, dancing around on the muddy bottom like mad people.

Is this what it feels like to be rich? Is this how the Queen feels? Or Bill Gates? It's not so much what the money can bring, I think, as I dance around with Joel – it's what it takes away. No more shampoo with Arabic instructions. No more out-of-control politician's eyebrows because I lost my tweezers in the fire and can't afford to buy new ones. No more skipping lunch. No more panic in the pub when it's my turn to buy drinks. Most of all, though – no more guilt. I am never borrowing money from anyone, ever again. Even if our house has to be built from hay bales.

'We should go to England,' I tell Joel. 'We can go to my mother's wedding. I can make you a suit. I've already found the fabric on eBay.'

'You want to?'

'I feel so cut off from everything that's been going on. I want to meet William Bastable. I want to be part of her life again.'

Joel grins. 'We could get tickets today.'

'We can do anything today. It's the *day* of days.'

The first thing I do after we take a taxi – luxury! – back to John's is ring Suzanne. It's midnight in London but I know she'll be up.

'Hello?' she yells, over the sound of some noisy club.

'It's Alice. I'm ringing from Australia.'

'Alice – aaaa!'

'I want to buy that red Dior coat from you. Have you still got it?'

'Sure. Of course. Alice, my God, have you come into money or something?'

'Yes. Don't laugh. Mum's marrying this rich bloke who used to be in the music business. He's bought her house off her and she's given me half.'

'Ooh, I say.' Suzanne puts on her best *Carry On* films voice.

'We're coming to England for the wedding,' I go on.

'You and the cousin?' she shouts over the music.

'Me and Joel.'

'When? When?'

'Soon. When everything's sorted out here.'

'The sooner the better. You should hear the things I've heard about you lately. Romantically involved with a goat!' she shouts down the phone. 'Completely destitute and living like a hippy in the outback . . .'

'Don't tell me.'

'You should stay in touch a bit more, Alice. Save us having to look at pictures of you in the paper.'

'I know. I'm sorry. I'm useless.'

'You're in love, that's what you are. Don't worry. You're allowed to go off the air. And listen. If you're into Dior coats at the moment, you need to see the stuff I just got in Paris. I've been at the flea markets all week. I've got Dior, I've got Yves, I've got Chanel, I've even got someone's old Galliano.'

'Really?'

'I'm gonna take this phone outside for a minute,' she announces over the doof-doof bass and the sound of screeching, inebriated Londoners.

'So, anyway, now I've got some money,' I start.

'Darling,' she interrupts, 'we should go into business together and create a global market empire! I can export to you!'

'Actually, Suzanne . . .'

She's got it the wrong way round but the right way up. We *should* go into business together. Instead of me buying from her though, she should be buying from me. If Jade is prepared to hand over her stall and a few of her secret auction addresses, then I can send Suzanne the kind of exotic Australian swimwear that Londoners only dream about. Suzanne's always moaning about the lack of decent summer clothes on the stall. Jade's discovered a goldmine of exactly the kind of vintage sarongs, shorts, bikinis, sunhats and sunglasses that Suzanne's after. There may not be much of it, but what there is, Suzanne can sell – probably at a huge profit.

'Listen,' I ask her. 'Do you know a swimwear brand called Speedo?'

'Yup. Of course. Legendary Australian label. People love it – especially if it's '70s. As long as the gussets are alright, of course. My customers seem to prefer an intact gusset.'

'I thought I'd bring as much stuff as I can over to London.'

'Sure, darling. Straight through the green channel and over to me. Perfect.'

I'm sure Matty would help with the boring paperwork side of things – and Jade would help with the sourcing. She may be a soap star now, but that won't last forever. I don't remember much about fashion college, but I do remember the golden rule about cash flow: have your first business on the go, then start your next one.

Vintage Alice is my next plan. At long last, Vintage Alice.

I do a little dance on John's rug.

'I'm dancing, Suzanne,' I tell her once she's agreed to my idea – and she immediately says she's going to dance too. So there we are, like a couple of nongs – a fine Australian word I've learnt – hopping around thousands of miles apart.

Afterwards, I bombard Joel with my plans. There's no Nash here to pour cold water on my dreams or moan about how much it's going to cost him. There's only Joel, massaging my shoulders on the sofa as I throw all my ideas at him.

I suppose I am doing what he talked about all those months ago in England – taking the wrong way round and the long way round. He's right: it's a lot more interesting.

A few days later, we pack our cases ready for Bondi Beach and buy John the new canoe he's been lusting after. We want it to be a surprise, like Wiz's new campervan. It's the least we can do, since he's volunteered to look after the property and what remains of the animals in our absence. We pay for the canoe and the campervan to be delivered from Coffs Harbour.

'Trust me,' Joel says, 'these aren't the kind of guys you want to make any kind of big gesture with. I think it's better for everyone if we're away when it all arrives.'

As we say our goodbyes at Urunga train station, John holds Chang in his arms and makes him wave his paw up and down.

'Thanks, mate,' Joel says in a very Aussie-blokey way. 'Hopefully there won't be a next time.'

'Gotta get on and build that mud-brick house and get that tank up, mate,' John replies. 'Anyway, me and the dog'll still be here when it happens.'

When we finally get to Bondi, Robyn's finished work for the day and is waiting for us with pizza (vegetarian for Joel) and her vodka, lime and mint speciality drinks. She wants to know all about my mother's wedding – where they're getting married and where the reception's being held. I explain that Mum is voting for Chelsea Register Office, because that's where Judy Garland got married; but William likes the idea of doing the deed inside a capsule on the London Eye.

'Jeez, no, you don't want them getting married inside a vomit comet,' Robyn says.

She rings my mother immediately to offer her advice on the reception. When she finally hangs up, she mixes Joel and me two more vodka, lime and mint drinks, then adds an extra slug of vodka to her own glass at the last minute.

'What's that English word that means a bit vague?' she asks.

'Dotty,' I supply.

'And what's that other English word that means a bit mad?'

'Potty.'

'It's great to reconnect with Auntie Penny, but this wedding is sending her dotty and potty,' Robyn concludes. 'She's running around like a chook with its head cut off. She hasn't even rung round for quotes. There's some place in Kensington that wants to charge them a fortune just for the hire of their rooftop. And it's extra for the farking pink flamingos. She has *no farking idea*.'

My mother has gone totally Lady Penelope after all, and gathered quotes from Claridge's, the Ritz and the Dorchester. There will also be an announcement in *The Times* and the *Daily Telegraph* this weekend. Nash would love it – not that he'll ever be invited.

'William Bastable is a Sir,' Robyn tells us. 'Did you know he was a Sir?'

'Are you sure?' I ask.

'Your mum told me to slip it into conversation with you, because she didn't want to be indelicate. Indiscreet. Impolite. Inappropriate. Whatever. Of course, as soon as she drops his name when she's talking to the hotels, the price just goes up and up. Maybe I should just get over there and do the talking for her.'

Robyn says she is definitely coming to the wedding now – nothing will stop her – and she says there's even a chance that Roland or Helena might also make it.

'Instant family reunion.' Joel shakes his head. 'I think this may be my first experience of the nuclear family. It's –'

'A bit weird?' I interrupt.

'Really great,' he says.

'Your mother's banking on two hundred guests including the website people – what are they called again?' Robyn asks.

'Greydate UK.'

'Yeah, them. Anyway, she's allowing one bottle of Bollinger per head, plus she wants asparagus rolls, chicken vol-au-vents, smoked salmon, pink fairy cakes, a four-tier wedding cake and probably all the Bee Gees jumping out of it. I'm just warning you,' Robyn raises her eyebrows at us, 'in case you weren't *todally* prepared.'

We spend the rest of the week at Bondi swimming and enjoying the luxury of having Robyn's flat to ourselves while she's at work.

I'm not sure what to do about the market plan with Suzanne, Matty and Jade. Dad would have told me to get a lawyer and organise contracts. Instead, I write the whole thing out on some Snoopy writing paper I find at the markets, lick the envelopes and hope for the best. Sometimes you just have to trust people.

Then, in the middle of the night, I get a text message from my mother: WEDDING NIGHTMARE. URGENT. PLEASE CALL.

I ring her, terrified that William Bastable has disappeared and everything – her happiness and my happiness – has vanished with him.

'Mum? What is it?'

'Oh, Alice. I don't know what to do. It's all gone a bit belly-up.'

'What do you mean?'

'The wedding has to happen next week, darling, or it's not going to happen at all this year. Everybody's booked up for months. The good news is, we've got the Dorchester. Both wedding and reception. Such a relief! So William and I were wondering – could you possibly catch the next flight over, do you think?'

'Is that all? My God, I thought William had buggered off.'

'Oh, no. Why ever would you think that, Alice?'

twenty-two

I manage to find someone to take on the stall the following weekend, and Joel and I fly to London after a long night with Robyn and her vodka and lime. I enjoy three completely new experiences in my life. One is flying with a hangover. Another is the novelty of paying for somebody else's trip. The third is travelling on a plane where there's actually room for my knees. This time I complete the journey without my mother's knockout herbal tranquillisers. Joel and I spend most of the trip greedily watching films. In the few months that we've been together, we haven't been to the cinema once. Joel doesn't even own a television.

When we finally arrive at Heathrow at 6 am, my mother is there with William Bastable. He's wearing a navy-blue jacket with shiny buttons. I'm worried about calling him Sir, and so is Joel, so we've decided to pretend we don't know about his title, thus avoiding the problem.

'Should I curtsey or something?' Joel jokes as we stagger through the green channel at customs, pushing all my luggage. I have somehow managed to pack Jade's finest selection of 1950s sunglasses and 1970s Speedo swimming costumes into two suitcases and two squashy nylon bags, and still found room to wedge in our own clothes.

'Alice!' William steps forward in the arrivals lounge and shakes my hand. 'Joel!'

'Hello, darling.' My mother gives me a hug and I see that she's wearing an enormous sapphire ring on her finger.

Joel kisses her on the cheek and congratulates her, and she holds the ring out for him to see.

'Beautiful,' he says, and William looks quietly pleased.

We all notice a horrible smell at the same time. It must be time for Heathrow's morning rubbish collection – either that, or someone has dumped a lot of illegal French cheese.

'There's a bit of a pong in here,' William says, looking around suspiciously. 'I think we should get a move on, don't you?'

His car is something far too new and shiny for my father to have ever sold. When he switches on the radio, it's tuned to Radio Four.

'I was worried he was going to play us *The Best of the Bee Gees*,' Joel whispers in my ear.

'Saucy,' William says, when my mother leans forward to fiddle with the volume knob and reveals too much bra.

He turns to me and Joel in the back seat. 'I'm just going to zoom straight up the M23 and then kick on home. Is that alright with you?'

'Fine,' Joel says, trying not to yawn. He has a bad case of jetlag. Neither of us slept much on the flight from Sydney after the first ten hours. Instead, we did what we always do, which is talk for far too long when we should be going to sleep.

I decide that William is what my father would have called a good egg. There is something about the way he overtakes the other cars – and the way he pokes two fingers in the air and tells the drivers to 'eff orf' – that reminds me of Dad, and Roland too. He seems like *family* somehow. My mother has found her man at last. Despite me thinking her mad for believing in rich husbands and effortlessly happy endings, she seems to have conjured up both. I have to hand it to her. She may be dotty and potty, but she has also been proved right.

There is something incredibly comforting about all the ordinary, English things I see and hear as we zoom (William's favourite word) towards Sussex. The voices on the radio, the sunken green hedges that line the motorway, even the crisp packets stuck between the hedges' twigs are strangely endearing. Ah, English litter. So familiar.

'I hope you'll get to see a little of this country while you're here,' William says, handing Joel a guidebook from the glovebox. 'You should go off for a few jaunts. See what you're missing in Aussie land.'

'Thanks.' Joel takes the book. 'I only had a few days here last time.'

I look over Joel's shoulder at the map and see Cornwall marked with wavy red lines. The homesickness was supposed to hit me when I was in Australia, not now, but I find myself longing to see the Furry Dance at Helston. I am dying to wander down to Land's End and have a bright yellow ice-cream. I am also desperate to walk around Cambridge again and remind myself what a cobblestone looks like, and a barge.

As we make our way towards the coast, I am filled with regret for the way that I left England – worrying about Nash, and the future, and what would happen once I left everything behind. I should have left this country dancing with hedgehogs, and instead I left worrying about debt collectors. I left England the way I left Nash – angry, confused and barely capable of putting one tartan wellie in front of the other.

Joel was right. I did have a huge empty space in my heart when I left London – and Australia filled it perfectly. Perhaps I let go of England too prematurely. It's a different place when you can afford to be here, and now that I can, I want to take my time. I want to pay my last respects in the appropriate manner, I suppose.

'I love this.' Joel shows me a photograph in the guidebook of a stone circle. 'The Hurlers. Do you know about them? They're prehistoric stones on Bodmin Moor. They used to be men who were turned to stone as a punishment for throwing balls around on the Sabbath.'

'I'd love to see them.'

'And look at this – Dozmary Pool, the mysterious lake next to Bolventor that's the last resting place of the sword Excalibur.'

'Good for tourists anyway,' honks William from the front seat.

'I want to see everything there is to see,' Joel says, closing the book. 'And I want to play cricket at Cricket St Thomas as well.'

'Oh, that's where they filmed Penelope Keith in *To The Manor Born*!' My mother gets thoroughly over-excited in the front seat. The only woman finer than Judy Garland, as far as she is concerned, is Penelope Keith.

Once we're home, Joel and I are installed in my old bedroom and handed two hot water bottles and two large cups of tea.

'We're just off for a walk,' Mum tells us through the door. 'Make yourselves at home, both of you. Have a look at the garden, Alice – you can see where the new swimming pool and gazebo will be.'

Joel and I fall asleep in each other's arms on top of my old pink eiderdown. The last time we were this exhausted was after the bushfire in Bellingen.

'It's still one of the most incredible countries in the world,' Joel says.

'Incredible in what way? I left it, remember.'

Joel tries to explain. 'It's just so hard in England. Really tough and really cold. But everyone still daydreams. It's quite incredible. It's all Alice in Wonderland, and the Queen, and Vivienne Westwood –'

'I'm glad you remember everything I taught you about her,' I interrupt.

'Everything's like a fairy story. Or a pantomime. Goodies and baddies. Beautiful princesses and evil stepmothers.'

'But it has to be like that, because otherwise it would just be too . . .' I try to think of a word and fail.

'You tried really hard to make it work here, didn't you?' Joel says.

'Yeah, but your history follows you round. You can never get away from your mistakes, or even the mistakes that your parents – or their parents – made. You don't have any of that in Australia. It's all new. You can be what you like, do what you like.'

I think of Jade, who is about to become a TV star, and Matty, who is creating a business empire. I can't imagine either of them would have dared stretching their luck that far in Camden. Jade would have been a hairdresser and Matty would probably have been on the dole and selling cocaine in the pub. Jade was discovered in Sydney, not here.

'The Witch of Wookey Hole,' Joel says suddenly.

'What's that?'

'A place in Somerset called Wookey Hole. I want to go there too. It's all limestone, and there are waterfalls below the ground. A witch used to live there, according to the locals.'

'Hmm. I think Nash's parents went there once.'

I see Joel's face and suddenly wish I hadn't mentioned Nash. I've been able to forget about him lately, but sooner or later I'll have to see him and talk about . . . everything.

'Does being back here remind you of him?' Joel asks, staring out of the window at the sea.

'I suppose so. The bad bits and the good bits. Mostly the bad bits, though. I seemed to spend that entire relationship freezing to death. No heater and no warmth from him either.'

'But you're going to sort things out with him now, aren't you? Once and for all?'

'Oh yeah,' I agree. 'Closure is such a stupid word, but it's right in a way. It's like closing the curtains on a theatre stage. Finishing things. When I bolted to Sydney, I didn't have time to close *anything*. Now I can. I'm going to ring him tomorrow.'

A few days later I go to Romney College to see Nash. It takes half a day to get there, and by the time I have missed my train (because the computerised ticket machines aren't working) and failed to get a packet of crisps (because the girl behind the counter was ignoring me) and lost another hour (because the bus was late on account of a late driver), I am well and truly fed up with England again. So much for *The Wind in the Willows*. So much for prehistoric stones that used to be people. It's all business as usual – complete and utter chaos. Nothing's open. Everyone's got a cold or a hangover.

I ring the train company to see if I can get my money back and am put through to a call centre in Scotland. I suppose it's an improvement on Mumbai. Once again, I bless William Bastable's money. In the old days, any failure to get my money back on a train ticket would have forced me to live on apples for the rest of the week.

The people in the queue for the train are so patient – in Sydney they would have started a riot by now. But this is England. There's a system. Even when it's not working, people still try to pretend it's worth going along with.

When I finally arrive at Romney College, Nash has finished teaching for the day. He's wearing his old grey tracksuit, from the time when he used to coach school football. His hair is shorter, the curls have gone, and he looks harder and older, and sexier too. Shit. I hadn't counted on being attracted to him all over again. I'd forgotten about his noble Roman nose. And the way he looks at me, long and hard, until I have to look away first. It's partly because he needs glasses, of course, but he's too vain to wear them.

'Come in,' he says, and leads me into his flat. I remind myself that he's all wrong for me now. Quite wrong.

The flat is decorated with posters that I've never seen before. Two are reproductions of jazz album covers from the 1960s, and another two advertise art exhibitions I've never heard of, although I can see by the dates that they both occurred in London this spring.

Nash smells different. Spicier, somehow, and slightly sweet. When I go to the bathroom, I see why. He's using new matching shampoo and aftershave.

We sit down in immaculately upholstered armchairs, which I suppose must have come with the flat, and I try to fight the feeling that he's still mine. It's just an old, dumb instinct really. Like automatically feeling a sense of ownership about our shared CDs – I can see them there on the shelf.

'Great to see you,' Nash says in a twitchy, nervous way. 'You're looking well. Very suntanned. Very Aussie.'

'The winter's so sunny over there.' What a completely moronic thing to say.

Nash gets up to make us a cup of tea and says he's sorry about the phone call when I was in Bronte, that he wasn't thinking straight.

'It's alright,' I call through to the kitchen. 'Neither was I.'

While he's fiddling around with teabags and asking me stupid questions like if I take sugar – how could he have forgotten so quickly? – I get up and inspect his shelves. All his old Bob Dylan books from Swiss Cottage are there, along with . . . hang on, some books I thought were mine. He also appears to have been buying cookbooks. I suppose he had to learn how to cook some time. Useless twat. There. That's better. I almost feel back to normal with him.

'So what are you up to?' he asks.

'I'm working full-time in Australia now. Well, sort of – organising a business between London and Sydney. And I'm starting up Vintage Alice.'

'Not skint any more then?'

'Mum gave me half the money from the sale of her house. Her fiancé bought it from her.'

There. That's knocked him for six, as my mother would say.

'Very nice.' Nash puts on a posh voice and I can see that my sudden fiscal turnaround has made him nervous.

'Anyway,' I change the subject, 'how's the quiz team? How's the band? How's life?'

'I've got some news actually.'

'Really?'

'I'm leaving the college. I've sort of been asked to leave. I've been seeing a girl here. Not everyone thinks it's a good idea.'

'Do you mean a *schoolgirl*?'

'It's all perfectly okay. She's eighteen, an outstanding sixth-former, and she's getting ready for Oxbridge. I've been tutoring her. She's incredibly bright, extremely mature – and I'm not the first.'

'Not the first what? Teacher?'

'It doesn't matter. Anyway, someone told the head and I've been asked to go more or less immediately. I expect I'll move to Oxford. She's bound to get in, and there's at least one place for me at one of the schools there.'

'Bloody hell, Nash.'

'Don't make a big thing out of this, Alice. It's really pretty straightforward. Some schools dig it. Some schools don't. This one doesn't. She's happy and I'm happy. You're happy with your bloke, aren't you? Your cousin?'

'Will you stop calling him "my cousin" as if he's my next of kin and it's all terribly weird? His name's Joel. I'm not telling you again.'

'Fine.'

'Yes, it's all absolutely *fine*. So it didn't work out with Sarah then?'

'I'm not going to talk about her.'

'What about Lisa? Any contact with her?'

'You're being cruel,' he gives me a lopsided smile, 'and that's not like you. Has Australia made you cruel? Is it living in those harsh conditions?'

'Don't be silly.'

'So you're rich,' he says.

I laugh, embarrassed.

'Lend me some money then?' he asks, and I suddenly realise he's serious.

'About my finances,' he says, twisting his hands together. God, the number of times those hands have been all over me – but I can't think about that now. 'The girl I've been involved with,' he goes on, 'well, it's all totally cool, but it did get a bit legal for a minute – with the school and her parents. That costs. And I'm not entirely sure about my next job.'

'You really want me to lend you some money?'

A long silence.

Then he says, 'There's absolutely nobody else I can ask.'

I write a cheque for the amount he once lent me – £2000. Then I get up to leave.

'I can't believe you're seeing one of your students,' I tell him. 'She's practically half your age. It's pathetic.'

Nash shrugs. 'So are you going to marry Joel then, and stay in Australia for good?' he asks as I walk out of his flat.

I don't reply. But it's all I think about on the train back to London.

twenty-three

Joel often goes off by himself, but I seldom do. When he's around, I want to be with him. Today, though, I am craving solitude.

'Alright?' he asks me as he rubs my shoulders at breakfast. He is the emperor of impromptu massages.

'It's all the Nash stuff, I think. I just feel like hanging out by myself. Is that okay?' I told him about Nash last night – the schoolgirl and the £2000 cheque. He was good about it, but I need to be by myself, just to take it all in.

'It's fine,' he says, and decides to go with William to see the Bluebell Railway, which he'd hoped was a train made entirely from bluebells but is actually just Pommie trainspotter heaven in the middle of Sussex. It turns out that William Bastable's other passion, apart from catchy chart music of the 1970s, is old steam engines.

Once they've gone, and Mum's out shopping for fabric for her wedding suit, which I've offered to make for her, I leap onto William's computer and look for Nash's schoolgirl. He makes it easy for me by emailing me all about her, as if justifying himself. She has a Facebook page and her photo is stunning. She's half Italian, apparently, and the recipient of several music scholarships. She is a regular little culture-vulture – I suppose that's where Nash's new posters came from. Not to mention the cookbooks.

I don't think it will last between Nash and his Italian schoolgirl, not for a minute, but I suppose I wish him some kind of luck. When I tell my mother, I know she will fall sideways on the sofa and fan herself with a copy of the *Daily Telegraph*. I'm not going to tell her about the £2000 though. The only person I'll ever tell is Joel.

I drift from Facebook to a relationship self-help site. I'm not entirely sure why. Perhaps it's a knee-jerk response to being back in England and seeing Nash.

There is a quiz on the site for couples who are breaking up. *Why did you fall in love anyway?* it asks. *What went wrong? When did it go wrong? When did you give up? Why did you give up? Do you think you could still make it work? Do you hate him/her? Do you love him/her? If not, then why not?*

I feel a sudden rush of sympathy for Sir William Bastable, who must have been down this route himself – if not via an internet quiz, then in some discreet corner of Sussex with a marriage guidance counsellor. He still doesn't speak to his ex-wife. I am glad William and Mum found each other. I can even forgive them for dressing up in school uniforms and playing conkers.

I wonder about every other couple I know and how they will fare. Matty and Jade? Yes, they'll probably be okay. As long as she keeps earning and he keeps dreaming. I think about Suzanne, who I guess will ricochet between London and New York until the day Sam finally commits and moves to London. Then I think about Richard from our pub quiz team, who I hold no hope for, with anyone, ever; and Michael and his wife, who I think will be fine. I remember Danielle Coles in Byron Bay and her obvious leanings towards an affair with any one of her friends' husbands, not to mention the local vet; then I take comfort in the fact that John, good, kind John, will probably, at some point in the future, bump into the beer-guzzling, fish-crazy love of his life at the Bellingen pub.

Love is a scratch-card. But what kind of scratch-card was I gambling on when I fell in love with Nash?

I return to Facebook and stare at the photo of his schoolgirl again and remember the time Nash was at a party with me and refused to dance to a song because it was Motown and he said he was bored with Motown. He walked off the dance floor and left me standing there by myself. Nobody was watching, nobody cared, but Nash couldn't bear to lower his standards. Then I think about how he told my mother we were moving to Australia before I could. And how he apologised for it, with a bloody text message.

He'll never make it with his schoolgirl – she'll reject him as soon as she meets someone her own age in Oxford. What a waste of time. But it's so typical of Nash. It's just like Lisa and Sarah all over again. I suppose he thinks he's a romantic or something.

I have a nap to try to shake off the very last bits of jetlag. Maybe I can dream Nash out of my system, and all the sadness he brings with him.

When Joel wakes me up, I smell him before I see him. He's brought his funny lemon soap from Bellingen with him, along with his mint tea habit. His smell is easy to become addicted to.

'Hello,' he says.

'Hi.'

I tell him about the photo of Nash's schoolgirl on the internet, and we make bad jokes about it, and then we try to rationalise it, but nothing works. Some things are so awful you just have to sit and digest them, like putting up with bad food on Christmas Day.

'I like William Bastable,' Joel says, changing the subject. 'He's a great dancer.'

'Is he? How did you find that out?'

'He showed me a video of his wedding reception the first time round. That man knows how to shimmy.'

'How can you shimmy in Hush Puppies?'

'Exactly. But he can. You should have seen him. And here's another thing. He wants me to call him Bill.'

'Does that mean I'm allowed to call him Bill as well?'

'Not sure.'

Joel grins as I hit him with a cushion.

Suzanne rings the following morning and tells me she wants me at her stall tomorrow so I can check the prices she's putting on Jade's Australian bikinis.

'I think I'll go out walking tomorrow,' Joel says hastily, before William can take advantage of my absence to show him any more steam trains.

On the way to London the next day, I read the newspapers. Floods and David Beckham's feet, as usual. Suzanne greets me at her flat wearing what she calls her

Benny Hill couture look – long shorts, a Fair Isle V-neck sweater, long woollen socks and brown lace-up boots. As always, she looks fantastic. On anyone else it would just look silly.

She shows me the price tags she's putting on Jade's stock and asks me what I think.

'You can't charge that, Suzanne! Flipping heck, woman. It's as much as a microwave oven.'

'Oh yes, I can, baby. It's a two-piece with matching skirt.' She smiles, and glides around with a pair of gigantic, hand-embroidered bikini bottoms held up against her hips.

'You're under-charging for that Pucci dress though,' I tell her.

'Mmm. I was rather hoping you'd say that. You do know your Pucci.'

She loads her trunks onto the back seat of her ageing Volkswagen, and I carry the rest of the stuff on my lap in the front. Plastic rubbish bags fill every inch of available space, from the floor to the bottom of my chin.

I tell her about Nash's schoolgirl and try not to feel embarrassed. Talk about humiliation by association.

'So is that it with Nash forever then?' she asks, turning a sharp corner into the least-full street behind Camden Market. 'Not even friends?'

'I don't know. I don't think so. He's moving to Oxford. I'm going back to Australia. Wow. Maybe that is it. Is that what happens – it just sort of comes to a complete stop?'

We drive past a towering block of flats with 1980s lettering on the mailbox, still trying to find a parking space.

'London's just dire,' Suzanne says. 'Isn't it awful? It's so crowded. Nobody knows what's going on. Everyone's got bags under their eyes. Everyone's on bloody drugs all the time. All they do is watch telly. Don't you just want to leave this time and never come back?'

'Stop it. You know I want my kids to be half-English. I want them to go on the Bluebell Railway, and go to Soho at night and dance around like hedgehogs.'

'Don't they do that in Australia?' Suzanne yells over the roar of her ancient engine.

'Put it this way. They don't take silliness as seriously as people do here.'

'Aha!' Suzanne shouts back. 'That's it. The English seriously believe in everything silly because if they didn't, they'd just throw themselves onto the *road*.'

We finally find a parking spot and lug the trunks and plastic bags past all the waiting hordes. I can moan all I like to Joel about the crowds in London, but there's nothing like a heaving queue in the early hours of the morning to give a casual stallholder hope.

'Here we go,' Suzanne chants under her breath. 'Here we go, here we go, here we go . . .' The Union Jack bunting goes up along the top of her stall, and I plug the extension cord into the generator and watch the fairy lights come on all at once.

'Boom shanka, boom shanka,' Suzanne chants as she pins Jade's polka-dot bikinis from Bondi Beach up on the washing-line that flanks the back of the stall. She lays out Ray-Bans, and imitation Ray-Bans, and rows of real shark's-tooth necklaces. She pins up tiki necklaces from New Zealand, and strange brooches made from abalone shells. The colours in the Mother of Pearl pendants remind me of the petrol you see in London puddles. If I could find a fabric that shimmered like that I'd make ball gowns with it.

A man in a huge tweed jacket stops and picks through the bikinis. He is followed by a woman in a beautiful pair of pink pants – Escada, late 1980s, I tell Suzanne – who can't stop cooing over the Hawaiian shirts Suzanne has just hung up next to her usual selection of white dinner shirts and silk-fronted waistcoats.

People descend on us from all directions. We are like the victims of a Roman battalion in turtle formation. They are above us, to the left of us and to the right of us. They are behind us, and sometimes below us.

'I should have put more on those bloody Ray-Bans,' Suzanne reflects half an hour later.

We both know she is joking. She has doubled her usual take, and she has four business cards sitting in her cashbox, all from professional stylists who can't believe how she managed to find quite so many pristine 1960s swimming costumes – and all with clean gussets.

'We're on a roll,' Suzanne promises me. 'We're on an egg and bacon roll, Alice, and, quite frankly, it's going to gather no moss.'

'When do you think I should launch Vintage Alice?' I ask her.

'In Australia or here?'

'Maybe everywhere. I was thinking I could get a website.'

'Launch in the European spring,' she says. 'That's what Chanel did. Be lucky.'

'That's it then,' I promise myself. 'The European spring.'

* * *

When we take a tea break, I see I have a text message – from Nash. I call him back straightaway, but almost wish I hadn't, because the first thing he does is cry.

'Are you okay?' I ask.

'No. Yes. I just wanted to say –' He can't get the rest of the words out.

'Are you sure you're alright?'

'I just wanted to say I'm sorry,' he finally manages, and hangs up.

In all the time we were together, I never saw him cry.

twenty-four

Uncle Roland is coming to England for the wedding. Helena can't make it, but he'll be here with ding-dong bells on, he says.

'Does your dad talk like my dad used to?' I ask Joel. 'I thought he'd be a bit more San Franciscan.'

'It's in the DNA. All Templetons of a certain age talk like that,' Joel replies. 'You will too, one day.'

The excitement of the wedding is turning my mother into an insomniac. When she does manage to sleep, she holds strange conversations with the strange people populating her dreams. One night I'm walking past her room on the way to the loo and overhear her.

'No. It's my badger,' she says. Then: 'You have NO idea.' Then: 'Take the asparagus and be done with it.'

I'd forgotten that she talks in her sleep. It's one of the most endearing things about her.

When I go downstairs the next morning, I find her wedding notebook on the kitchen table. It's full of scrawled ideas about what to drink, and who to invite, and, interestingly, who *not* to invite. Some of the Greydaters William has pencilled in have been carefully crossed out by Mum. Anne Horton-Bills has gone, with this comment from my mother: *Annus Horribilis!* Someone called Nicholas Lowry has gone too, on the grounds of his greenhouse gas emissions. Other than that, it seems hundreds of G-Daters, as William calls them, will be coming to the Dorchester on Saturday.

There are catalogues from Asprey and Dunhill on the table too, along with their congratulations cards to the happy couple, and a pile of business cards from photographers. Then there is my mother's scribbled sketch of her wedding suit – nipped in at the waist, flared out at the hips (but not too much), and pulled in at the knee with a classic pencil-skirt tapered pleat.

I am quite proud of the suit, which I made for her on my new sewing machine, but I drew the line at the lime green linen she asked for. We compromised on a beautiful bolt of raw silk from Suzanne's stall, dating from the '50s, which time has faded to the creamiest shade of coffee. The hat I have no control over. I think it looks like a small UFO trying to return to its mother ship, but this is something I have only confided to Joel.

He is out this morning, on one of his long walks along the seafront. Later on, he texts me and I join him at The Mock Turtle, where he is having a cup of tea and sorting out his family.

'Is everything okay?' I ask.

'Bit of politics.'

'What?'

'Roland's not coming. He's had second thoughts.'

'But why?'

Joel rubs the sleep out of his eyes. 'Roland created some problems for the rest of the family when he left Mum,' he says at last. My heart instantly goes out to him.

'I'm sure he did.'

'That's why your parents left us alone in Australia for all those years. I think your dad was furious with Roland. It's possible they didn't speak, although I'm only guessing. Nobody talks about it.'

'Wow.'

'Roland came back from India one Christmas when we were kids, and planted his stash on Helena. He thoughtfully decided that if he was going to take some hash back to Sydney, he may as well be really clever about it and hide it in her stuff. He nailed it into this painting she had – of the Buddha, can you believe it? – and they found it. She protected him at the airport. Robyn and I saw her do it. She took the rap, and she got busted.'

'Oh my God.'

'End of marriage. Enough was enough. But Roland's been like that his whole life. Totally selfish. Completely irresponsible. And he was never a good dad to me because he knew I wasn't really his son.'

'Oh, Joel.'

'He rang me last night, when everyone was asleep. And I blew it.'

'What did you say?'

'Just something stupid about Mum not coming, and how great it would have been for you to meet her again. Anyway. That was all it took to set him off, and then we ended up arguing about all that – the dope, the end of everything.'

'Mum has no idea you feel like that about him or she wouldn't have invited him to the wedding.'

'Families keep secrets. Are you going to tell our kids about Nash and all the stuff that's happened there? Of course you're not.'

'I'm so, so sorry Joel.'

We finish our tea and go for a walk along the seafront. 'Ooh, I've just remembered something that's cheered me up,' I tell him. 'When we go back to Bellingen, it'll be snake-free, won't it? Because of the bushfire.'

He laughs at me. 'Sorry, Alice. You're never going to get round it that way.'

'Oh, well. I miss Bellingen anyway.'

'I *really* miss it.' He gives me his sexy, serious look. It is the expression that made me choose him as Number Nine all those months ago, not so far from here.

'When we went back to the property that day, when the chickens had gone, and the mailbox had disappeared, and our caravans had been burnt to the ground,' I tell him, 'I finally understood why you went to work with the Tibetans in India.'

'Because . . . ?'

'Because they don't just lose their homes, they lose their country and their family as well. In a few years' time they may even lose the memory of who they used to be.'

'It's the same for all refugees,' he says.

'Well, I want them to have half my money from Mum. I want you to give it to Tibetaid. Maybe we can go to India and give it to them together. Honestly, I mean it. We had a really good life on your land before the fire came, and we did it without stupid money. Why do I suddenly need so much of it? We can do everything we want to do in our lives without all that.'

Joel laughs at me. 'Yes. We could. Except, as usual, you've got no idea about money.'

I grin back at him. 'I really have absolutely no idea, do I?'

'Nope. For a currently homeless woman, half your money is *way* too much. But we should definitely go to India and give them something – money, time, energy, whatever we're in a position to give. Some of my best friends are still there. You'll love them.'

We walk past a large tourist coach parked outside the West Pier and hear some Australian accents. The two women talking are annoyed about something and are telling each other how rooted it is.

'Wow,' Joel steps back and looks at me, 'I suddenly feel homesick.'

'It's not like any other language, is it?' I say.

'As good as French, or Italian or Spanish.'

'Better.'

We decide to keep walking, to give my mother a chance to catch up on her sleep at home, and cross the road to the gardens behind the Pavilion.

'Can you help me with something?' I ask him.

'Sure.'

'I've decided I want to apply for citizenship when we go back. Or even before. I could go and see Heidi Coles in London and ask her about it.'

'Wow. Okay.'

'I need to do my Australia homework. The only thing I know about is Simpson's donkey and it's pathetic. I bet those women back there on the coach know *everything*. I don't even know what the national flower is. I told Jade I thought it was gladioli.'

'Golden wattle,' Joel tells me. 'We've got it growing on the property. Or we did.'

'Let's plant some more,' I say, squeezing his hand. 'I want to plant a whole new garden when we get back.'

Having survived the bushfire, Bellingen is now enduring the threat of flood. It's been raining for weeks, apparently, and the river is steadily rising. John thinks we should buy a water tank and take advantage of the rain – and Joel's taken him up on the offer.

Joel gives me a progress report on Henry the goat. John – who has been charged with the task of keeping us updated – says that Wiz thinks his fur is slowly growing back, although he has become unbelievably randy and must be kept away from the other recovering goats when he goes for his regular RSPCA check-ups. Chang is alive and well and has taken to digging enormous holes on the beach. John thinks he is trying to dig to England, so he can see us.

'What about our chicken?' I ask.

'She's still around somewhere. We'll have to get her some friends, though.'

'Do you think she could become friends with a sheep?'

'I suppose so. What have you got in mind?'

'The French make cheese out of sheep's milk. It's a delicacy. I'd love to do that. Am I mad?'

'Not mad at all. The sheep will keep the grass down as well. And fertilise it. I know a guy who'll do the shearing, and then you can wash the wool and spin it.'

'This is such a nutty conversation to be having in the middle of Brighton,' I say, looking up at the pickled-onion domes of the Pavilion. 'So could we do it? What about foot rot and fly strike and all of that?'

'If we trim their hooves they won't get rot. It can't be all that different from a pedicure.'

'Aaargh! A pedicure. Do you know, when I was in Swiss Cottage with Nash, I used to dream about having a pedicure. And a facial. And a massage. And now I can afford it and I haven't done the slightest thing about it.'

'That's what weddings are for, aren't they?' Joel asks. 'It's about all the fun stuff. I think you deserve some fun.'

He buys a disposable camera in a gift shop – he's left his clunky old Polaroid at home – and takes some photographs of me. Then it's my turn to take some photos of him. I wonder if Joel looks anything like his real father. Perhaps one day we'll both find out. It's one of the things about him that I leave alone. I don't mind him knowing all about me – from my awful days as a Woman With Key In Back to the time the bailiffs turned up at my door. Something tells me that he'll always need a small, private space for himself though.

I follow him around the park, snapping as I go. I have never known anyone so determined to go left when everyone else is going right, or vice versa. If there's a shortcut, Joel doesn't take it. Instead, he'll choose the least likely option and stop and smell the flowers on the way. Life with him is definitely the wrong way round and the long way round, but I can't imagine how I ever lived any other way.

'Actually,' Joel says, picking me a flower, 'will you marry me?'

'Yes,' I say instantly. Then I laugh at myself because I sound like such a hopeless Bridezilla.

'Is it too soon?' he asks.

'I said *yes.*'

This time Joel laughs.

'Quick, let's take a photo.'

I grab the camera with one hand, and him with the other, and lean my head in towards his. I am sure it will be hopelessly out of focus, but I want a record of this moment.

When we return to the house, William is on the phone to a friend, giving motorway advice. 'Penny's gone into Hove to see about that Mendelssohn CD she wanted,' he tells us. 'I'd like something a bit more modern, but it's better than having her trotting down the aisle to "Here Comes the Bride, Short, Fat and Wide".'

We go upstairs to my old bedroom and I take Joel's jeans off on the bed. 'I love you,' I say. I've never actually said it, although it's always in the back of my mind.

'I love you too,' Joel says, then as he starts looking in his wallet he exclaims, 'Bugger, we've run out of condoms.'

'Later, then?'

'Bill'll have some.' He zips up his jeans and swings his legs off the bed.

Before I can protest – I do not want William, sorry, *Bill,* to know that we're doing it right now, in this room, above his head – Joel has disappeared. He returns with his prize – not one, but two condoms, which he says Bill keeps in an empty Maltesers packet in his briefcase.

'I told him we were engaged and he said "Congratulations, have two",' Joel tell me, and laughs.

'Oh, for God's sake,' I say.

Then we sit and stare at each other as we realise two things. Firstly, we have managed to terrify yet excite each other at the same time by agreeing to marriage. And secondly, there is no way we can embark upon a celebratory shag now that Sir William Bastable has provided the contraception.

In the end, though, I just want Joel too much. Oh please, let that never change . . .

The wedding is an absolute hoot, as my mother would say, from start to finish. It begins with her lying on the sofa at sunrise with a full face of Nivea cream, and ends with a drunken tour of their bridal suite at the Dorchester, where everyone agrees the bed is big enough to accommodate all of the Bee Gees at once. Of course the Gibb brothers do not leap out of a giant cake with their guitars strapped to their chests. Instead, we have my mother's Mendelssohn, and later on William is allowed to play what sounds like The Wombles.

I can't stop adding up the cost of the reception in my head. It's like the bad old days in Swiss Cottage when I used to stand in the aisles of ASDA with a pencil and paper and add up everything until it came to £4. Even though those days are long gone, I can still remember everything. Own-brand cola was 20p and own-brand orange juice was 16p. Own-brand crisps were 51p, and I can even remember the price of the loo roll – 38p for four. The lavatory paper at the Dorchester is so thick and soft you could make a blouse out of it. It's probably 38p a sheet.

'What are you doing?' Joel asks, when he finds me sitting on the stairs. He is covered in synthetic day-glo spaghetti, because Sir William went mad and seized all the cans that were intended for the bridal car and sprayed the lot on Joel's head instead.

'It was just his way of congratulating me on becoming engaged to you,' he says, when I complain. 'Everyone knows now. After you disappeared, your mother seized the microphone and broke the news. Then Robyn got hold of the mic and made everyone give three cheers.'

'Oh no,' I say. So much for our vague idea about keeping it low-key. I really wanted Mum's wedding to be out of the way before anyone began thinking about ours.

'Here.' Joel hands me a fistful of scribbled-on napkins, bits of paper and business cards. 'All these women want you to make them a suit.'

'Really?'

'They loved the silk most of all. I didn't tell them it was second-hand.'

'Vintage,' I correct him.

twenty-five

Joel and I go to London for a few days to escape the post-wedding madness that has taken over my mother's life. She and Sir William are going to Paxos for their honeymoon but it seems to be taking an awfully long time to get there.

We stay in Suzanne's spare room, which has become a vintage clothing emporium since her trip to Paris. There are so many Chinese silk dressing-gowns hanging up that the light is struggling to come through the window. I recognise my swimming costumes and sarongs from Sydney lying in dry-cleaning bags.

'Our new stock,' Suzanne says proudly. 'Isn't it great?'

'Fantastic.'

'Where are you off to today then?' she asks, as she and I sit in her kitchen drinking tea before she heads off to Twad.

'Joel's gone back to Mum's place to catch up on some Tibetaid work. And I'm going to Australia House to find out how I can become an Australian.'

Suzanne starts singing 'Jake the Peg' pretending to be Rolf Harris. 'While you're there, see if you can find out about a working visa for me.'

'Really?' I try not to sound too excited.

'If I'm going to go all the way to blimmin' Australia for your wedding, I want to hang around afterwards,' she says.

When I arrive at Australia House, Heidi Coles gives me a Euro-kiss – once on each cheek. Her accent seems to have changed as well. The twanginess has gone, replaced by strangely rounded vowels. She says she might be marrying her new English boyfriend, next year, if they can book the church in his village for summer.

'There's no point doing it any other time,' she says. 'We'll just get drenched. I attract rain, you know.'

I have to admit she's right. Every single time I've seen Heidi it's been pouring down – or threatening to – and today is no exception. We are standing in the foyer at Australia House when it suddenly buckets down without warning.

'You know, I can just give you all the right answers from the files,' she whispers as she takes me up to the library. 'You don't have to do the research thing. Hey, if you still want a job in the public service, I can give you all their old exam papers as well.'

'Thanks. Actually, I'm running a stall at Bondi Markets. And doing my fashion label thing.'

'You're joking!'

'I took over the stall at Bondi from these friends of mine.'

'Fantastic. Hey, sorry about Danielle.'

'I'm sorry too. Thanks for all that – it seems like such a long time ago now. But you got me to Australia. Really, you did.'

Heidi photocopies a book about Simpson and his donkey for me. 'Are you sure you're not going overboard with this?' she asks.

'It's just for me really,' I tell her. 'I've always liked donkeys. Joel says we can have one, once we sort out the cows, and the sheep, and everything else.'

'You were living in a hostel in Swiss Cottage and now you're running a farm – you're one of our success stories,' Heidi says.

'It won't be a farm. We just want to be self-sufficient, that's all. As much as we can be. You know how much organic tomatoes cost in London? We grow them just by accidentally dropping a few seeds on the way to the compost heap. Bellingen's incredible. Everything grows as you're watching it.'

'It's supposed to be bewdyful up there,' Heidi says wistfully.

I buy her lunch at the nearest pub, because we've both decided the café near the Strand is jinxed.

'How's your ex?' she asks, as I put our drinks on the table.

'Having it off with a schoolgirl.'

'You're kidding!'

'They've thrown him out of school.'

'Remember that day when you dropped your little purse? I was listening to everything you two said. I thought, "they're never going to make it".'

'You were right.'

I tell her that Joel and I are engaged, and she squeaks at me, then shakes my hand.

'You look scared,' she says. 'Don't look so blardy scared.'

'Maybe I've had too many Girl's Own Adventures lately.'

'Can't be any more frightening than moving to some place you've never even seen before.'

'I suppose not.'

'We get so many people wanting to move to Australia,' she says. 'The good, the bad and the ugly. Some people want to go because they're desperate. They don't give a stuff about the place itself but someone's told them their pounds will turn into thousands of dollars and the weather's really good.'

'That's Nash. That was why he wanted to go.'

'Yeah, and look what happened. Even if you had got on the plane together, Alice, I guarantee he'd have turned tail and come back to England. A lot of people do.'

'It hasn't been easy,' I tell her, 'but I never, ever thought I'd do that. I liked it too much the moment I got there.'

'That's because you're one of us,' she says, and I feel ridiculously pleased – until she adds that I am mad by nature and therefore ideally suited to life in a country which is upside down, back to front and impossible for most normal people to deal with.

'You know you'll get a question on mateship in the test, don't you?' she warns me. 'They ask everyone.'

'I was talking to Joel about that. We decided the definition of mateship is people we know in Bellingen. One of them, Wiz, drove us through a bushfire and probably saved our lives. The other one took us in after we'd lost everything.'

Heidi winces. 'Those fires were *bad*.'

'Australians just seem to keep on rescuing me for some reason,' I tell her. 'A bit like you and Robyn that day in the café, when I was worried Immigration weren't going to let me in.'

Heidi beams at me, and shows me a photograph of her boyfriend who is dying to go to Australia with her once they're married.

'Come and stay with us,' I offer.

'I'd rather stay with you than Auntie Danielle. Do you want to know what she's doing since she sold Bark's?'

'Another dog thing?'

'No, she's started a colonic irrigation centre. For humans. It's the scariest thing I've ever heard of.'

I laugh. 'Please don't tell me what it's called.'

Heidi clinks glasses with me and congratulates me on my forthcoming Australian citizenship. She won't be there, but she knows they'll take me.

'Are you going to have kids, do you think?' she asks.

'Not sure. I hope so. But not yet.'

'Have them in Oz, then they can have two passports. Best of both worlds.'

After I've farewelled Heidi at Australia House, I walk down to Trafalgar Square, where I tried to say farewell to England the last time – and failed.

I've been dying all day to use the pregnancy-testing kit I bought at the chemist this morning, but the loo at the pub didn't seem the right place. I know I should go back to

Suzanne's and do it properly, with Joel there on the phone, but when have I ever done anything properly? I can't wait any longer. So I throw some money in the donation box at the National Portrait Gallery and walk in.

A large painting of Princess Diana looks down at me. I give her a little wave. Wish me luck, Diana.

If I am pregnant, I'm going to be one of those morning-sickness women. I've been feeling queasy for days, although I've not told Joel. I want to be sure before I get his hopes up.

I go into the loo, and wonder if I'm the first person to use a pregnancy-testing kit in here. Probably not. I bet it happens all the time.

I look at the condom in my bag, which has been there since William decided to congratulate Joel and me on our engagement by kindly supplying us with two. As Suzanne said when she saw it, some things from the '80s deserve a comeback, but a condom date-stamped 1983 is not one of them. She is amazed that neither of us felt the first one break.

I flip the loo seat down, sit with my legs crossed and sort out all the bits and pieces in the kit. I am so nervous that I read the instructions eight times to make absolutely sure I have got it right. Then I do the weeing bit, and watch the little strip of paper like a hawk.

A bit of extra-purple-looking paper appears above the line. It's a boy! It's a girl! It's something! I have never been more excited by anything in my life. Except, perhaps, the thought of making the baby clothes.

I bolt out of the loo, find a quiet doorway to make a phone call, and ring Joel.

'Hello, Alice,' William Bastable says. 'I'm afraid he's not here. He's gone out for a walk.'

'I'm pregnant!' I shriek at him, like an idiot.

'What?'

'You had 1980s condoms! I just did the test. Tell Joel I'm pregnant. Tell Mum!'

'Oh, what marvellous news. Penny's seeing her friends in Brighton, I'm afraid, and she doesn't like mobile phones, as you know, otherwise I would have lent her mine. Goodness. Am I the first to know?'

'You are!'

'Many, many congratulations,' he says. 'I am so deeply sorry about my 1980s condom, but perhaps in time you will come to think of me as a living saint.'

Suddenly, Blossom Promise and all her strange predictions pop into my head.

'I wish you all the luck in the world,' William continues. 'And as soon as I can get hold of Penny and Joel, I will pass on the good news.'

I ring Suzanne and the call goes straight to message. Damn.

After that, I rush into a clothes shop near Charing Cross, where I immediately feel moved to tell the assistant I'm pregnant. 'I'm having a baby so I need some trousers with a really loose waistband. It's my stepfather's fault. He gave us a twenty-year-old condom from his disco days and it exploded.'

'Maternity's that way,' she points, trying to get rid of me.

I am too excited to try on clothes, so I take a tip from Princess Diana and walk in the direction of Kensington

Gardens, which my mother always calls The Park, as if there's only one in the entire world. My dad used to bring me here when I was little. It is the most amazing feeling to think I could bring my and Joel's children here too one day.

I have just seen one strip of paper turn purple in a loo and I am already planning an entire family. Joel would laugh at me. But why stop at one? I feel an incredible sense of achievement as I walk along the Serpentine. Being pregnant is like hearing you've got the best job in the world, even though you think you're the least likely applicant.

It's hard to believe that the last time I was here, Nash was having his weird flirtation with Lisa. It was summer, the week after Glastonbury finished, and there was some outdoor concert he wanted to see. We had a world-class argument here, because I was so miserable about Lisa. I never want to have any more of those. I think Joel and I can get through marriage without them. I hope so. Our kids should never have to listen to the kind of fighting that split his own parents up.

I also remember worrying about paying for the drinks, ice-creams and deckchairs at the concert. I never want to live like that again. I don't want to put my children through that either – Joel's right about hanging on to most of my money. The Tibetans need to put their own kids through school, and I can help with that, but it's time I grew up and went to talk to an accountant. No more jam jars.

I follow Princess Diana's trail of roses along the walk that bears her name. This is such a pretty little English park, even when the leaves have come off the trees. How did all those dainty English women cope when they settled in Australia centuries ago and found themselves confronted by bushfires and snakes?

As I walk back through Knightsbridge I suddenly get jelly legs, and realise I'm a pregnant lady now and I really should find somewhere to sit down.

When I get back to Suzanne's flat, her answering machine is crammed with messages from my mother – and one from Joel. Suzanne cries and cries, because she's remembered a drunken promise I made her years ago, at The Bell and Dragon, about being godmother to my kids.

'Did you mean it?' she sobs. 'I understand if you've changed your mind, but do you think you still want to?'

'Completely,' I say. 'Whooosh!' And I wave an imaginary fairy wand over her head. 'I hereby pronounce you godmother to this baby.'

Then my mother calls again. 'A grandmother and a bride!' she shrieks. 'I never thought. Here's Joel.'

We are on the phone for over three hours, which is a record even for us. Every time I mutter about going, he keeps me talking; and every time he says he really should hang up, I find another reason to stop him.

We spend a long time talking about his real dad. Now that he's going to be a parent himself, Joel says he wants to find him. 'He'll be a grandfather, wherever he is. He deserves to know.'

'Would Uncle Roland have any idea?'

'No. I'm going to have to ask Mum. She won't like it – but it's time.'

Joel says he can't believe how much has changed in his life. In India, the Tibetans were his extended family. Now he has a family of his own, which includes new faces, old faces and more surprises than he could ever have imagined.

'Bill's gone nuts,' he says. 'He already wants to put the baby down for Eton.'

'It could be a girl. He might have it all wrong.'

'It certainly could be a girl.'

We talk about all the names we've both secretly reserved all these years for future baby girls. None of them are the same. Some of his – in my opinion – would be better suited to the new hens we're going to buy. He says all mine are too English. I say all his are too silly.

'I'm going to fill our room with flowers when you come back,' he says. 'And if I can't find any flowers, I'm going to drag in tree branches.'

'It's early days yet,' I remind him.

'What are the rules on those things?' he asks. 'When can we tell everyone?'

'When did either of us ever follow the rules? We're going to tell everyone whenever we want to. At some stage, I might even ring Nash.'

Matty calls to arrange a meeting. He wants to talk about our business plan, he says, but things might be different now – because Jade has left him.

''Ere,' he says, when he sees me in The Bell and Dragon, 'this is my old mobile. It's on a proper network all over Australia. Stop living like a hippy and take it. If we're going to do business, you've got to sort yourself out.'

'That's exactly what Suzanne said,' I tell him. I've asked her to join us later, once she's finished a styling job.

Matty tells me that Jade's going to be a star. 'They were sort of hinting at it, but then it got serious,' he says. 'The other girl they had in mind wasn't up to it. So they gave Jade the lead and this other woman walked out.'

'Wow.'

'Jade's going to be on the side of buses in Australia.' Matty shrugs. 'She got a big head – you can't blame her. All these blokes were suddenly after her, and I was coming second.' He thinks about it. 'Nah, I was actually coming third. She got one of them toy dogs for her handbag.'

'Nightmare,' I say. 'I used to look after those kinds of dogs once.'

'I'm well out of it,' Matty says, then he sighs and pushes his beer mat around the table. 'Was this your local?' he asks.

'We used to play the pub quiz here,' I tell him. I picked The Bell and Dragon deliberately so I can exorcise the past. It's a great pub. There's no reason why my memories of Nash and Lisa should be allowed to spoil it.

'Your mate's late,' Matty says, checking his – much more impressive – new phone.

'Suzanne's hopeless. Do you want another drink?'

While I'm getting Matty's pint, Suzanne arrives. She introduces herself to Matty, and there's some confusion as he stands up at the same time that she's trying to sit down, and more flapping as he tries to kiss her on the cheek while she's offering him one of her business cards. There's a buzz there – a definite buzz. I'd never have imagined them being attracted to each other, but then stranger things have happened.

'I bought me laptop.' Matty gets it out of his bag and proceeds to show us his new website. It's a website called downthemarket.com and is based on a real street market, like Bondi or Camden.

'Be careful though,' Suzanne warns him. 'It might sound a little bit too much like "downmarket". You don't want that, darling.'

'No offence taken.' Matty suddenly gets sniffy and pretends to be interested in his computer keyboard. 'Anyway, it's a virtual shopping thing, yeah? You can pretend you're having a little bacon sandwich and cup of tea, then you can say 'ello to all your friends, then you can get out your credit card or your Paypal points and spend all your money.'

'Brilliant!' Suzanne gets it immediately, and moves closer to Matty so she can get a better look.

'So will our clothes be on there?' I ask.

'Yep,' Matty says. 'I was thinking about it on the plane. I've had it with Aussie-land. But if you keep things going at the Sydney end, I can keep everything ticking over here. I'll just need to come over every so often to make sure everything's alright.'

'Lovely tax-deductible holidays to Bondi Beach.' Suzanne's eyes widen. 'Now you're talking, Matty.'

'You ever been to Australia?' he asks her.

'I'm dying to go – when Alice has her wedding.'

Matty nudges me. 'Didn't tell me that bit.'

'It was a bit sudden,' I say, then kick Suzanne under the table in case she blurts out my other news too.

'Ooh, this website is so exciting!' she says, kicking me straight back. 'Did you design it yourself?'

'Mate of mine,' Matty replies. 'You girls have got to get off the streets and get on Web 2. The Americans are all over it like a rash.'

'God, I don't even know what Web 1 is,' Suzanne confides in me, when Matty's gone to the bar for more drinks. 'He's alright though, isn't he?'

'He's a good egg,' I confirm, thinking about my father again. For some reason, being with a bad egg like Nash seems to have helped me develop the egg-character-reading radar I have lacked all my life.

'What about his girlfriend?' she asks.

'They've broken up. The TV network wants to turn her into a star and it's gone to her head.'

'So he's coming back to London and you're staying in Oz.' Suzanne smirks. 'You're replacing each other.'

'Well, it keeps the population level.'

Matty returns with a tray of drinks and I try to see him as Suzanne might be seeing him. There are elements of her previous ageing Britpop lad boyfriend in him and I believe she may be weakening.

'It does require an investment,' Matty says, looking at each of us in turn.

Suzanne shrugs. 'Not a problem. Alice, are you in?'

'I'll need to see an accountant,' I reply.

Suzanne looks at me with a stunned expression. 'Glory be, Alice Templeton's getting herself an accountant,' she says, fanning herself with a beer mat.

'Right enough,' Matty agrees. 'If we're going to do this properly, then you need to get sorted.'

'I'm hopeless with money and I always have been,' I tell him. 'There's no point in hiding it. The last time I was in this pub, I was so desperate I was looking for change on the carpet. Honestly.'

'But now she's quids in,' Suzanne explains. 'I'm sure she can make a modest investment in –'

I jump in and remind her of the website name before she calls it downmarket.com and loses all the ground she's just won.

The conversation moves to local gossip and Suzanne and Matty realise they both know the same person in the Camden Market mafia. I drift off into my own world – and feel a sudden shot of panic about working and looking after a baby at the same time. Not to mention helping Joel to look after Henry, Chang, sheep, chickens, hens and a worm farm. I have a sudden vision of myself in a mud-brick house at some point in the future, working on my sewing machine while my children play with Chang and Joel builds a henhouse.

By that stage I may even have overcome my fear of spiders and snakes. Robyn asked me to take her to London Zoo the other day, and I didn't even flinch when she mentioned the Reptile House. Who knows – in ten years from now, I may even be able to look a goanna in the eye. Even if he's sitting in the front seat of a VW campervan.

When I drift back the conversation has moved on to Miss Great Britain. Matty thinks Suzanne looks a bit like last year's winner.

'That slapper!' Suzanne fakes indignation.

Suddenly I feel unbelievably tired and realise I have to leave. We all agree to meet again next week, and I'm about to put my coat on when Richard and Michael walk in. They immediately look the other way, but I'm not going to let them get away with that.

'Are you staying?' Suzanne asks me, as she waits for Matty to pack up his stuff. 'I think we'll go. We're going to split a cab. He's on my way. Well, actually he's not remotely on my way, but we've got a lot to talk about.'

I kiss her goodbye while Richard and Michael look on.

'Bye, honey. Oooh, hello, Richard and Michael. And goodbye, Richard and Michael!' She gives them a little wave and teeters off in her heels.

I sit down with the remains of our legendary quiz team, The Believers. They say they haven't been here for weeks and the team has gone to ground, but they're hoping to find some new members. I wonder if that means Nash has left them for good. I suppose it's a long way to travel from Oxford.

It's funny to think that the quiz night here was supposed to help save my relationship with Nash. In retrospect, nothing would have worked. He was always the kind of man who was capable of infidelity, and now I've found out he's also the kind of man who is capable of having a relationship with a schoolgirl. Nash always was lazy. He could never be bothered reaching very far for what he wanted – no matter if it was a new roll of loo paper or the light switch.

'Very convenient, Nash having an affair with one of his students,' I say to Richard.

'I think that might be over now,' he says, raising an eyebrow at Michael. 'Nash is leaving us to go to Wales,' he continues. 'The Oxford thing didn't work out. He's going to teach piano for a bit – part-time tutoring, that kind of stuff.'

I realise I will never see my money again and try not to feel upset. Maybe it's karma. That's what Joel would say. It all goes round in the wash, like some spiritual version of the Swiss Cottage laundrette.

I start telling Richard and Michael about Australia, and Joel, and the bushfire, but their eyes soon glaze over. Their world is this pub, and all the trivia they talk about, and the streets outside. What I'm saying might as well be about the planet Mars. For all their brilliance at the quiz and their knowledge of every piece of pop culture in the world, they don't really want to look beyond North London.

Perhaps I'm turning into a foreigner. They are certainly looking askance at me. I want to tell them I'm getting married as well, but then I remember I still haven't had the courage to tell Nash, so I make my goodbyes instead. I don't expect I'll ever see them again, unless I come back here one Tuesday night and find them still playing the quiz.

I go back to Suzanne's, pack my bag and go to Victoria, nearly missing my train because of the queue at the ticket machine but not really caring any more. All the effing, blinding and harumphing taking place in the queue is the funniest thing in the world. My children will love it, I think, when they are old enough to see it for themselves.

There are two little kids in my carriage on the way to Hove. They have colouring-in books and are both plugged into the same iPod – proper London children on their way to the seaside for the weekend.

Joel meets me at the station, with Mum and William. I tell them about Matty and the website idea, and they tell me that Robyn's trying to organise a farewell dinner before she flies back to Bondi and Mum and William set off on their honeymoon. In the car, Joel holds my hand in the back seat. I jokingly stick out my stomach as if I'm several months' pregnant and see if I can get my seatbelt around it. I've already practised with cushions, of course, and realised that Suzanne's beautiful red Dior coat will never fit me now.

Later on, Joel and I go for a walk along the seafront. I remember the first time I saw him – my Number Nine. My Australian cousin.

I tell him about Heidi and how she wanted to smuggle me the answers to the Australian citizenship test.

'What you forget is that Heidi is probably descended from a long line of smugglers,' Joel points out. 'It may even be how her ancestors got to Australia.'

'So dodginess is in the blood.'

Then I tell him about running into Richard and Michael at the pub.

'How was that?' he asks.

'It made my past seem very . . . *past*.'

We talk about the last few years of our lives, and how everything has happened at the right time. 'Even the things that went wrong helped make it right,' Joel says.

He agrees that it's sad that Jade and Matty have broken up, but right that Matty should have come back here.

'He emigrated back,' I say.

'Wrong way round, long way round. It usually works in the end.'